D1527807

THE DEATH SPEECH

A Connor Sloane Thriller

M.A. ROTHMAN

PRIMORDIAL
PRESS

Paperback ISBN: 979-8-5392122-5-4
Hardcover ISBN: 979-8-7775409-3-5

ALSO BY M.A. ROTHMAN

Technothrillers: (Thrillers with science / Hard-Science Fiction)

• Primordial Threat

• Freedom's Last Gasp

• Darwin's Cipher

Levi Yoder Thrillers:

• Perimeter

• The Inside Man

• Never Again

Connor Sloane Thrillers:

• Patriot

• The Death Speech

• Project Thor

Epic Fantasy / Dystopian:

• Agent of Prophecy

• Heirs of Prophecy

• Tools of Prophecy

• Lords of Prophecy

• Running From Destiny

CHAPTER ONE

He glanced at his watch, took in a deep breath, and let it out slowly. The air stirred as a cool nighttime breeze blew in from the Mediterranean, brushing away the heat of the day. He should have felt nervous, but as he looked across the growing crowd from his shadowy perch, he felt absolutely nothing. *Five minutes 'til go time.*

The mayor of Turin was in a pavilion at the far end of the Palazzo Reale, prepping for her annual speech, and for the first time in years, he was on sniper duty again. It felt great. Across the historic building's courtyard were several Italian flags, fluttering in seemingly random directions. Aside from the unpredictable gusts of wind coming across the buildings and into the plaza, it was a perfect setup.

As he sat back in the shadows of a rooftop five hundred yards from his shot, he imagined the trajectory of the bullet. The target location was a popular tourist destination, but with the heavily advertised speech from the mayor, the locals as well as the tourists packed the area. There had to be over a thousand people gathered for the late-evening event. There was going to be chaos when this went down.

Perfect.

At the gates of the palazzo, the organizers had erected a large platform with a podium in the middle, allowing a perfect view for the crowd. The platform was bathed in light, but the area around it was cloaked in the darkness of the Italian summer night. Bookending the platform were two statues of soldiers riding horseback, and at the base of each statue were armed guards.

The very idea of being shoved up against so many people nauseated him. It was hard for him to even imagine why people from all walks of life would willingly subject themselves to that… just to listen to one person speak. But the mayor was a popular figure in the city, and the growing crowd was excited to have a chance to see her in person. This made him feel like this job was worth it. It was a good beginning to his coming-out party.

Three minutes.

People began clapping. It was time to stop admiring the scenery and get to work.

Lying prone on the rooftop, he peered through his scope and spotted movement in the cordoned-off area. The mayor's two bodyguards, carrying what looked like H&K MP5s—basic nine-millimeter submachine guns—were escorting the mayor from the pavilion toward the platform. She left them behind as she stepped up onto the platform and walked leisurely to the podium, waving at the crowd. It seemed as though she was trying to wave at each individual person. Through the scope, he could almost see the smile on her face as the crowd responded to her presence with ever louder cheering.

He'd been concerned about the noise of his new MK13 sniper rifle, so he was not only using a suppressor, he'd also loaded the 190-grain rounds for a subsonic flight downrange. But he needn't have worried. With the noise the crowd was making, nobody was going to hear anything.

The mayor stopped at the podium and blew a few kisses to the crowd.

One minute.

She motioned for the crowd to settle down, but it took a little while for the crowd to comply. Clearly these people loved her. Still, the cheers slowly faded, and the mayor took a breath to speak.

He glanced at the flags, which now lay limply against their flagpoles.

Go time.

Peering through the scope, he placed the buttstock firmly against his shoulder and rested his finger on the trigger.

She began speaking into a microphone on the podium, and her voice carried across the plaza and into the darkness beyond. Her tone was dulcet, mature, but with a youthful energy.

He'd already adjusted the scope for the distance. Now he placed the crosshairs on the woman's forehead, and felt almost as if time slowed. Each beat of his heart pushed blood through his body, imparting the slightest wobble to his aim. To compensate, he waited. Waited for the pause between heartbeats, when his aim recovered from the almost imperceptible wobble and the crosshairs settled on the target.

He squeezed the trigger. The rifle bucked back against his shoulder.

It took less than two seconds for the bullet to travel through the barrel, over the heads of the crowd, and slam into the mayor.

She dropped as if she were a marionette and someone had cut her strings.

He paused, feeling disappointment. It was supposed to have been a much more graphic shot—one that would yield no uncertainty about what had just happened. He had missed his mark, that was obvious; it was supposed to have been a forehead shot. But instead... there must have been a slight downdraft. More than likely, he got her just below the jawline, severing her spine.

He rapidly disassembled his weapon and placed it back into its custom case, shaped like a guitar. Within fifteen seconds, he was on his feet and blowing a kiss to the crowd, which was now screaming with panic.

He turned toward the stairs. "Looks like I need more practice."

CHAPTER TWO

Connor Sloane's mouth burned from the mango habanero wings, but he chuckled at the sight of his two former CIA co-workers struggling with the heat as well.

"I'm glad to see you guys are enjoying it," he said.

Christina wiped her mouth and panted for effect. "I can't believe you talked us into trying these wings from hell. 'They're sweet, you'll like them,' he says. This is *stupid* hot." She grabbed the menu and fanned herself. "I think you've made me hate mango. Why do you eat these?"

"What can I say? I'm not that big into drinking, and this stuff gives me a buzz."

"I'm afraid I agree with Chris," said John. "If this is on the agenda next time, I'll have to pass."

It was a Friday night, and this time Connor had picked the spot for their monthly meetup. Of course he'd chosen his regular hangout, which had everything he ever wanted all in one place:

wings, a football game, and a happy hour that tended to bring in a fair number of single women.

He wiped his mouth with a napkin, his lips tingling from the spice. "How's Pennington these days? Have things gotten better or is he still the same old pain in the ass?"

The two of them gave him identical glares.

"Leopards don't change their spots," said Christina.

In other words, their boss, his former boss, was still a grade-A pain in the ass.

"I'll never stop being glad I got transferred out from under that guy's thumb," Connor said.

"Speaking of that," said John, "you've been on the new job, what… three months now? How's the SIO stuff working out for you?"

The personnel records all indicated that Connor now worked as a support integration officer—a plausible cover story. The truth was, he wasn't really working at the CIA at all anymore. But what John and Christina didn't know wouldn't hurt them.

"Why?" Connor asked. "You looking to transfer as well?"

"Nah, I just didn't figure you for the type. You were so gung ho, and now you're pushing papers?"

"John!" Christina smacked him on the shoulder.

"What?" John said. "Tell me I'm wrong. This guy was always *get there early, leave late, kick ass, shred the names.* Typical ex-Special Forces." He turned to Connor. "Sorry, but you know me: I have no filter."

Connor smiled. "I know. That's why you and I get along. I always know where I stand with you. But honestly, the SIO thing is underrated. I'll be doing lots of traveling, and who knows, maybe working some diplomatic angles. It's a nice change of pace."

He felt guilty lying to his friends about his new job. But nobody could know where he really worked—not even his closest friends with top security clearances.

Chris called their waitress over—a girl who looked like a college freshman, if not a high school student. "Can we get the check?" Chris asked.

"You can get whatever you want," the girl said with a wink before running off.

Connor had been watching the back-and-forth between the two women since they'd arrived. The waitress was clearly flirting with Christina, but Christina was either totally oblivious or she was determined to ignore it.

"It looks like the waitress has taken a shine to you," he said. "You're what, twenty-five? She's probably legal. Why don't you go for it?"

Christina muttered "asshole" under her breath.

When the waitress returned with the check, Christina focused on the bill and studiously ignored the waitress's friendly smile. But the waitress nervously twirled a strand of her hair and hovered.

Connor turned to her and said bluntly, "Could you give us some space?"

Looking embarrassed, the girl dashed away to another table.

John tossed a twenty toward Christina, but she slid it back to him. "You paid last time. It's my turn."

"Okay," said John, getting up. "Well, I have to get going. The wife's nursing and trapped at home. If I don't get home soon she'll kill me."

"New babies sound great for a relationship," Connor said with a grin.

John frowned. "What are you, thirty-five? Honestly, you ought to be thinking about settling down."

"I think step one is get a girlfriend, and so far, that hasn't been in the cards."

"That's because you're a curmudgeon and won't let me set you up," Christina said.

John leaned in and whispered dramatically in Connor's ear, but loud enough that Christina could hear. "Just don't bother making any moves on that cute waitress. Not only is she too young for you, clearly she's batting for the other side," he winked at Christina, "and has already taken an interest in someone else."

Connor laughed as his friend walked away, but Christina frowned.

"Connor, do me a favor and just follow my lead, okay?"

"Okay," Connor said, curious.

They both got up from the table, and Christina snaked an arm around Connor's waist and led him toward the waitress. Now Connor understood the game, and he had to press his lips together to prevent his smile from becoming too obvious.

The look of disappointment on the waitress's face was priceless when she saw Christina and Connor clinging to each other like a couple. Christina handed over the cash and the bill, said, "Keep the change," and she and Connor headed outside. She didn't let go of him until they were in the parking lot.

He chuckled. "You could have just left the money on the table. Or left me out of it and simply told her you're straight."

She canted her head to the side and smiled. "What makes you think I am?"

Connor felt heat rising up his neck. He'd never heard her talk about a boyfriend, but he just assumed...

"Sorry," he said. "I guess I have no clue."

"Well, I *am* straight, but I reserve the right to change my mind at any time."

"La la la," he said, making a show of sticking his fingers in his ears. "I don't need to hear this."

It was a late summer evening in Virginia, and some of the lights were out in the parking lot, so it took some time for Connor's eyes to adjust. A nice breeze carried the scent of pine, and the feel of the air told him they were near water. The shore of the Potomac was probably only a mile or so away.

They'd parked next to each other, and when they reached their cars, Christina leaned against her car and faced him.

"Something on your mind?" Connor asked.

She spoke in a low voice. "We've been getting a lot of chatter at work that's giving me some serious déjà vu from when you were still in our section." She paused. "I probably shouldn't be mentioning this."

Connor leaned against his own car and crossed his arms. "If you want to share, that's on you—I'm not asking. But it won't go any further if you want to get something off your chest."

She took in a deep breath and let it out slowly. "There's are a lot of strange threads of intelligence coming out of Nigeria."

"Didn't I see on the news something about threats of a civil war going on over there?"

"I'm not even talking about that. Now, realize this is only chatter, and we haven't put things together yet, but… it's got something to do with nukes."

"God, I hope not. I've had enough of that topic to last me a lifetime."

"Me too." Christina's frown deepened, and she stared silently at the asphalt for a good three seconds before giving Connor a quick hug. "Thanks for the assist back in the restaurant." She hopped into her car and rolled down her window. "Take care of yourself. I'll see you next month."

He gave her a smile and a wave as she drove off, but he was still thinking about what she'd said. Nukes. It couldn't be. Not again. It had only been a few months since he'd been involved in a mission that involved defusing a nuke—his first mission for his new employer, the Outfit.

He felt a sudden prickling sensation on his neck, and was instantly on alert. He always trusted his Spidey senses. Panning his gaze across the parking lot, he caught the silhouette of a man standing at the entrance to the restaurant. The man was wearing a black suit and sported a pair of shades, even though it was dark out.

The man started toward him, and Connor saw who it was. Thompson, the guy who'd recruited him into the Outfit.

If Thompson wanted to talk, he could have just called. There was only one reason he'd come to see him in person tonight.

There was a threat to national security.

Thompson pulled his black Lincoln to the curb a few blocks away from their destination. They were in Georgetown, one of the older sections of DC, and an area that Connor had become very familiar with since joining the Outfit.

Thompson had been silent the entire way, but as he shifted the gear into park, he turned to Connor. "I'll be introducing you to a man named Doug Mason. He's the director of OCID, the Organized Crime and Intelligence Division. He recruits members from the Mafia, Yakuza, Triad, all kinds of unsavory people. He also has a connection with the Area Boys in Nigeria."

Nigeria again? First Christina and now Thompson.

"I'm going to guess the Area Boys are some sort of gang," Connor said. "And now you're telling me the Outfit has people embedded in organized crime?"

The two got out of the Lincoln and began walking north on Main Street. The sidewalks were busy with locals in the midst of a pub crawl and couples walking briskly to make it on time for their restaurant reservations. Thompson kept his voice low as he spoke.

"We don't have people embedded in those organizations— not in the way you think. The folks Mason deals with, they're legit bad guys. Somehow he's simply found a few that we can trust."

"How many?"

Thompson shrugged. "Maybe a couple dozen. Ask Mason. If you think I've got eyes and ears everywhere, this guy makes me look like an amateur. He knows everyone, and that's including the crooks in our own government. You'd be surprised how big his Rolodex is."

They reached the Rooster and Bull, a seedy bar that looked worn with age. It was still hard to believe that this, of all places, was the entrance to one of the most secret spy organizations in the world.

They stepped inside and were greeted by the familiar scents of old wood, beer, and smoke from years past. Connor didn't usually come to work this late in the evening, so he didn't know what to expect. He was surprised to find the place was packed, and he and Thompson had to weave their way through a crowd to get to the bar. The bartender gave a nod to Thompson, then led them both down a back hallway to the men's bathroom.

Connor had done this a hundred times by now, but the strangeness of the process would never completely wear off.

Three closed stalls and two urinals lined one wall. On the last stall door was a wooden sign hanging from a nail, with the words "Out of Order" painted in white. The other side of the bathroom had two sinks and one long mirror. Connor looked for Harold, the old man who always sat on a stool next to a pile of hand towels, but a different elderly gentleman occupied that spot today. Different... but strikingly similar in appearance.

"I guess Harold is off shift?" Connor asked.

"Someone's got to keep an eye on things when he's a-sleepin'. I'm Gerald. Harold's my twin brother. Nice to meet you."

Connor took the towel Gerald handed him and entered the stall marked "Out of Order." It looked like an ordinary bathroom stall: toilet, toilet paper dispenser. The hand towel he'd been given looked ordinary too, except it was a bit heavier than it should be. He had no idea what was woven into the fibers, but he suspected there was some kind of RFID chip in the cloth... or some other form of electronic magic.

Thompson and Gerald began talking about something having to do with an old Ford Pinto, but Connor wasn't paying attention. With the towel in one hand, he reached for the toilet's flush control—and braced himself.

As he pressed down on the lever, the floor dropped. The brown walls of the toilet stall flew upward at an alarming rate, replaced by gray concrete walls with alternating yellow and black stripes. Before he knew it, the toilet and the small platform Connor was standing on had settled into a subterranean chamber. He stepped off the platform, and the toilet and its flooring shot back upward, returning to the restroom with a whoosh of hydraulics.

Connor walked down a concrete corridor to the second security perimeter for the Outfit's main offices. At the end of the corridor, two men were stationed on either side of a blast-proof bunker door straight out of the sixties. Both men wielded Heckler & Koch MP5 submachine guns, and as always, the four-position trigger group was set on burst mode. The Outfit didn't play when it came to security.

Connor wondered if they'd really drill him—not that he planned to test that. They didn't look like they were joking as they placed their fingers in the trigger wells.

"Good evening, Mr. Sloane," said the man on the right. "Bio-metric verification, please."

Connor pressed his hand on a metallic pad on the wall. A

blue line passed back and forth underneath his hand, a green LED flashed recognition, and a click echoed from inside the wall. He backed away from the door as the three massive locking bolts on the right side slid out of their retaining blocks.

"Stand clear," a digitized voice warned, and the four-foot-thick reinforced steel door began slowly opening outward.

As Connor waited, Thompson's footsteps approached from behind. He pressed his hand against the same scanner, and when the green LED lit up, he smiled at Connor and tilted his head toward the door.

"This entire place was dug out of the bedrock in the late nineteen fifties, and this door is supposed to be able to take a direct hit from a nuclear warhead. The thing weighs over eighteen tons. I know, because they had to replace the original door about ten years ago."

"How the hell did they even get it down here?" Connor asked.

Thompson shook his head. "It wasn't easy. If you really want to know, talk to Brice. Right now we need to meet up with Director Mason."

Passing through the door, they fast-walked down a series of corridors and eventually stopped before another door—this one ordinary, other than the fact that it had no knob or handle. They stared up into a camera, a green light beamed at them, and something within the door clicked. Thompson pushed it open, and they both stepped through.

They were in a vast rectangular chamber the size of a warehouse, carved directly out of the bedrock. The entry had placed them on top of a metal walkway about twenty feet above the floor, and below them dozens of individual cubicles were arranged in a grid. Men and women moved between work areas, handing off papers, exchanging words, pointing at computer screens. Connor had a cubicle down there in that maelstrom of activity, but he hadn't spent much time in it. He was a mission specialist, meaning he was rarely warming a seat before he was getting sent to some remote place nobody had ever heard of.

More offices were on elevated levels, positioned around the outer edge of the space, all with a view down into the area below. Four giant screens hung from the ceiling, displaying information, maps, photographs, time zones, satellite feeds, and news broadcasts.

Thompson's phone beeped, and he paused to answer it. After a few short words, he clicked off and turned to Connor.

"That was Mason. We're meeting in conference room A3."

As they went down the stairs and cut across the floor toward the bank of conference rooms on the far end, Connor asked, "What can you tell me about Mason? What kind of guy is he?"

"I've never actually worked with him. All I know is, he's the guy the higher-ups call in when the shit has hit the fan internationally."

International. Connor smiled. That likely meant travel. He liked travel.

They entered the conference room to find an array of weaponry laid out on the table. Connor gave Thompson a questioning look.

Thompson shrugged. "Mason said something about all the conference rooms being booked, so he had to kick someone else out of this room. I guess they must have left this random crap behind."

Connor walked the length of the table, smiling as he took in the display. "This is no random crap. Look at this. A SIG P229, a Beretta 84FS Cheetah, and a Makarov PM." His movie nerd came to the surface as he tapped one weapon at a time. "The SIG was used by FBI Director Carter Preston, played by Sydney Poitier. The Beretta is Bruce Willis's sidearm, but it's missing the silencer. And the Makarov was held by Major Valentina Koslova, who... I don't remember the actress's name."

Thompson stared at him like he'd grown a second head. "Are you saying those were all used in movies?"

"Yes. And not just those." Connor pointed to other weapons. "A Beretta 92FS. I think Richard Gere, who played Declan, had one of those for a period of time. And that one's a Heckler & Koch MP5A3 with an integral suppressor; the bad guy used one of those, although the prop master must not have had one on hand because technically they chopped up an HK94 and fitted it with a fake suppressor to make it look like one. And then there's the pièce de résistance... the ultimate weapon of the movie."

Connor walked over to a heavy machine gun set on a tripod and admired the workmanship. "The Polish ZSU-33 14.55mm heavy machine gun, which was a totally bullshit made-up gun, because this baby is actually a Browning M2HB mocked up to look like a KPV-style heavy in 14.55mm. This was the machine gun that Bruce Willis used in—"

"*The Jackal*," said a voice from the doorway. "A great movie."

CHAPTER THREE

Connor turned to the man who'd just entered the room. He wore a suit, an unusual thing to be wearing in the Outfit's US head-quarters. Most people wore regular street clothes here, which for Connor meant jeans, a pullover with a collar, and hiking boots. He wanted to blend in nicely with the folks on the streets, and this outfit worked in most of the world.

The new arrival patted Thompson on the shoulder. "Rick, you really should catch up on your action movies." Then he shook hands with Connor. "I'm Doug Mason. Glad to finally meet you, Connor." He motioned toward the table. "Grab a seat. I'll fill you in on what's happening."

As Connor sat, he studied this new guy, trying to get a read on him. He was short, not much more than five foot seven, and judging by the fine wrinkles around his eyes and the frown lines, he was in his fifties. Clean-shaven, light brown hair, with a slightly receding hairline, and very pale eyes that looked almost silver. He didn't look like an operator in the soldier's sense of the word, but with the way this guy focused on him, Connor could tell that he didn't miss a detail, ever.

"Connor," said Mason, "let me start by giving you a brief intro into what my part of the world looks like. In OCID—"

"OCID, sir?"

"Just call me Doug. Here in the Outfit we aren't too formal. OCID is our Organized Crime and Intelligence Division. We, or more to the point, I, am charged with finding resources in some very nasty places. In my Rolodex, I have folks in all of the major crime syndicates around the world, whether it's the various Italian mafia groups, the Russians, folks in many of the major Yakuza syndicates, or the various European gangs. They all act as resources to give us a real view of what's going on at the street level."

"Thompson hinted that we have friends in all those places. That's got to be a real undertaking."

"Not as hard as you might think, and certainly easier than the alternative. It would be nearly impossible to get our own people in there without them having their cover blown, and besides, even if we wanted to get our agents in, it would take too long. Years. So instead I just keep my eyes on likely candidates in the places where we need deeper penetration—and I turn them to our cause."

"How?" Connor asked, his opinion of this man rising.

"Trade secret," Mason replied with a dismissive gesture. "Anyway, that's not what we're here to talk about. We've got a mission cooking, and Thompson thought you'd be a good fit, and after looking over your file, I think he's right. We have reports that there was a crash landing of an airplane in the Yankari Game Reserve in Nigeria. POTUS's brother was evidently on the plane and is missing and possibly kidnapped."

He said this matter-of-factly, but Connor was stunned. This information was most definitely not in the news. He wondered if this was somehow related to the nukes Christina had talked about.

Mason passed Connor a manila envelope. "That's what we currently know about the president's brother. This information is not public knowledge—in fact, his very identity and relationship to the president are classified."

Connor opened the envelope and pulled out a series of photos, a map, and a single printed index card that read as follows:

Name: Ryan Crenshaw (Codename: Little Eagle)
   Age: 37
   Weight: 180 lbs
   Education: BS, MS, and PhD in Physics at Cal Tech
   Stationed: Los Alamos National Laboratory
   Current specialization: nuclear weapons research

Mason tapped his index finger on two of the photos. "Those two pictures are the last known images of him. They were taken at an airport in Peshawar, one of the tribal regions in the northern part of Pakistan, yet the State Department has no official record of him leaving our country. We have chatter that indicates that he was on a flight that ran into some kind of trouble, and landed in that game reserve in Nigeria. We're not sure how much of that is a smoke screen or what he's doing there. It might have to do with him helping them with their nuclear power plants, but that doesn't seem right for his skill set. Whatever his reason for being there, it wasn't on any of the normal high-side network traffic. What little we know was gleaned through alternate means."

The *high side* was what the intelligence community called the computer network that carried classified data. This made all sorts of alarms ring in Connor's head. If the Outfit couldn't find a trace of communications, was this guy on a rogue operation? Maybe even operating against the US for some reason?

"Let me get this straight," he said. "Somehow with all of our surveillance, passport tracking, video recordings of the comings and goings of everyone at every airport, we managed to lose track of a nuclear weapons expert that also is our president's brother?"

Mason shrugged. "I had that same reaction when I first heard about it. Anyway, that's where we stand—it doesn't do us much good looking backwards at this point. The goal of this mission is to help figure out where the hell our missing nuke expert is and bring him home alive. Along the way, we'll hopefully figure out how we got our asses into this situation.

"I believe you've already worked with Anastasia Brown. She'll be assisting you, as she's familiar with the area and has a working knowledge of the language and customs. Even though the official language of Nigeria is English, in the areas you'll be in they may speak a tribal language, so you may need to rely on her to communicate."

"Respectfully sir," said a voice, "Ms. Brown would hate it if you called her Anastasia."

Connor turned to see a slightly overweight middle-aged man with brown hair and glasses entering the conference room. Brice.

Brice placed a briefcase on the table and took the chair beside Connor. "She prefers her codename. Or Annie."

"If she doesn't like her real name, she should change it." Mason grumped and shook his head. "Okay, we're pulling in the Black Widow. She's already been briefed. You'll meet her midway to your destination."

"Is there a specific reason you picked me for this assignment?" Connor asked. "From my experience of her in the field, she seems to prefer being on her own."

Mason grinned. "First," he said, "we don't exactly have a base of operations in Africa, and the area is a total shithole. I don't like the idea of having any of our people out there solo. I read the report of the mission you two worked on together. You guys seemed to work well together, so if she ends up needing support, you'll be there to provide it, and vice versa.

"Second, you're a Special Forces–trained operator with experience in rescue ops. Annie is only there for her local language skills. She doesn't exactly have experience bringing folks back alive. She's more of a wet operations gal, if you know what I mean."

He did. The KGB used to refer to assassinations as wet operations, things that would turn bloody. That was Annie's stock in trade. A scary combination of deadly and attractive, with the mentality to handle what her job entailed. The latter was likely the most unusual. Most people couldn't stare death in the face over and over again and then live with it. It was as if she was born to do it.

Mason continued. "I'm counting on your hostage negotiation and retrieval skills. Our top priority is getting Little Eagle out of there. If the local warlords find out that POTUS's brother is in country, it won't be easy getting him out."

"You mentioned some criminal contacts," said Connor. "What exactly does that mean in this case?"

"I'm glad you asked." Mason unfolded the map from the envelope. It was a map of Nigeria, with one area circled in red marker. "My primary contact in the area is Ntabo Mutanga. He's solid, trustworthy, but he doesn't necessarily have the best judgment, so he may have some folks who work for him that *aren't* trustworthy. As always, watch your six." Mason leaned forward in his chair. "I cannot stress how important that is. Do not, under any circumstances, drop your guard around these people. They're still criminals, even Ntabo. His cohorts may consist primarily of children, but they're armed and trained to be soldiers and spies."

"Wait—children? I'm going to be working with kids?"

"There's a reason why Ntabo's gang is called the Area Boys. He has them everywhere around the major ports and cities in Nigeria, especially Lagos. They're tasked with gathering intelligence, stealing things, doing whatever else he wants. He sort of brings order to what for these kids might otherwise be a miserable existence on the streets. Still, some members of his flock are probably a bit feral. Annie has dealt with them before so she should be able to take the lead."

"What about the Nigerian government?" Connor asked. "How are they not getting involved in this?"

"The main government is in disarray. They're losing control due to the strength of the warlords. At this point about all they can manage is to somehow keep themselves together and try to keep the country from exploding into a civil war."

Before Connor could ask another question, Mason stood. "I'll let these two handle the operational logistics and finish the rest of the briefing while I go gather more intel stateside. We found out about all of this nonsense six hours ago, so we're playing catch-up. It pisses me off that this guy is supposed to be under Secret Service protection, yet they had no clue he'd left the country. I'm trying to get some intelligence on all of that and more. Good luck, Connor."

And with a nod to Thompson and Brice, he left the conference room.

"Okay then," said Brice. "Let's start with the fun stuff." The Outfit's head of technology and de facto quartermaster set a box on the table and opened it to reveal a set of filled syringes.

Connor groaned. "What are you sticking me with this time?"

Brice smiled and tapped the first syringe. "This is a vaccine for Lassa fever. It can cause vomiting, give you a hard time breathing, hearing loss, tremors, and can lead to organ failure and death." He tapped on the next syringe. "This one—"

"Sorry I asked," Connor said, making an impatient rolling motion with his hand. "Just poke me and get it over with."

Brice grinned. "I thought you'd like to know all about the exotic diseases you won't be getting."

Connor rolled up his sleeve. "It's not exactly my first rodeo. I've gotten the full med cocktail before."

"Oh, that's right. I keep forgetting you're ex-military."

Brice began injecting Connor with the syringes, one by one, and talked as he worked.

"Communication might be dicey in some of these locations, so I likely won't be able to see what you see through your glasses—not enough bandwidth. But I anticipate that GPS, distance tracking, and the built-in microphone will still work fine."

Connor touched the smart-glasses he'd been wearing ever since joining the Outfit. They were connected wirelessly to his phone, making him feel like he was always on ready-alert. He turned them on with a press of a tiny button on the right-hand hinge of the lens frame, and his current GPS coordinates appeared in the top right corner of his vision. In addition, when he looked at Brice, the man's name, age, and vitals appeared just beneath his face.

"You know," Connor said, "I still can't get over how cool these things are."

Brice waved dismissively. "Oh, that's just basic stuff—one of the first things I came up with when I started with the Outfit."

"So, my mission," Connor said. "Find the president's brother, and figure out why he was there. Is that about right?"

"That's a good summary. I'll give you a full mission plan and more details on this Ntabo guy in a minute. Annie has been given the same intel as you have, and you'll be meeting up with her in Paris. From there, you'll go on to Lagos. But all of this will be in your documentation."

Connor looked over at Thompson. "What's your role in this?"

Thompson pointed to the door. "I'm giving Mason support,

and interfacing between him and Brice. Brice is your go-to guy until you guys get back to the States."

"Alrighty then," Connor said, rubbing the sore spots on his arm where Brice had poked him. "Let's go figure out how Little Eagle got his ass into Nigeria."

Mason turned on a bank of displays, giving life to six separate video feeds, each displaying a different person's face. When the camera above the screens turned to aim itself in Mason's direction, he said, "Sorry I'm late, had some loose ends to tie up."

"Not at all," said the Outfit's Director of Intelligence for the Near East, his Persian accent clear. Like everyone on this call, he was in a room similar to Mason's—white, sterile, furnished only with a single large table. *"We just began reviewing some of what's transpired in the last week."*

Mason drummed his fingers on the table. "I assume everyone's up to speed on what happened with the US president's brother. If you have any insights or have heard anything unusual, I'm all ears."

The DI for Asia and Pacific answered first. *"I haven't heard anything from folks in my area, but I've got feelers out."*

Gregor Manheim, the DI for Europe and Eurasia, spoke next. *"We've had some unrest along the Mediterranean coast. The local authorities are looking into an assassination of the mayor of Turin."* An instant later, a copy of an article detailing the assassination popped up on the screen.

"When did this happen?" Mason asked

"About thirty-six hours ago."

"And the killer managed a clean escape, fascinating. I'm surprised that I didn't hear about this through any of my contacts."

"I'm guessing you mean your criminal contacts. Maybe the mayor just really upset the wrong voter and it wasn't a professional hit. Lots of crazies are out there."

"It's possible," Mason said.

Manheim continued. *"We've also had some riots in Belgrade that we think were initiated by anti-EU activists. We're digging into it to see what we can find out. Other than that, not much to add."*

Another voice spoke up. Sekou Cooper, the DI for Africa. *"We're having all sorts of strife, but none of it is unusual. Off the coast of Liberia, we're having pirate issues, and Nigeria, as most of you know, is in total chaos. My people think there'll be a civil war in the country before the year's out. My resources are spread thin. I'm sorry, but I just don't have the people to help with your president's brother."*

Mason nodded. "I understand, and I'm not asking for any additional boots on the ground. I just want intel." He turned to address the DI of the Americas, who was embedded in the Pentagon. "Adam, have you checked into your contacts stateside?"

Adam McCallister frowned. *"Trust me, I've been pulling on every string I know of, and can't even get a whisper of what's going on. Sorry, about that."*

"I know you're working your sources. And I need you to keep at it. You're closest to the president and his people, and if you have to twist arms, do it. We need to know what the hell is happening."

"I'll do what I can."

Mason nodded. "Okay, thank you everyone for coming together for this unscheduled meeting. Unless there's anything else to discuss, I suggest we leave it at that and sync back up during our normally scheduled meeting. I'm sure we all need to get back to work."

Everyone nodded in agreement, and as people began to sign off, Mason stood and stretched out his arms. His next step was to reach out to the man in charge of AFRICOM, the general leading all US military operations in Africa. There was no way the president's brother could have gotten out of the country, bypassing the standard customs areas, without the military knowing *something*.

It was ridiculously late, but when Mason popped his head into Brice's workshop, he heard the familiar tapping of keys. A lot of people around here worked long hours, and still they would have trouble keeping up with Marty Brice.

Instead of a normal office, the Outfit's head of technology had something more like a lab. The table that dominated the center of the room was covered with scraps of metal, wire, soldering tools, and random bits of electronics. Brice was in the corner, working on his laptop.

"Hey Marty, you busy?"

Brice swiveled his chair and looked up. "Just sifting through some data out of the Utah Data Center, looking for any hints on Little Eagle."

The Utah Data Center had been brought online in 2019 with little to no fanfare, but it acted as a conduit for almost all data traffic coming and going from the continental US.

"By the way," Brice said, "I caught some weird comms traffic coming out of the Pentagon to the folks in Stuttgart. What's up?"

Mason sat in the spare chair next to Brice's desk. "I don't know. But I'm about to reach out to the head of AFRICOM— they're headquartered out of Stuttgart—so maybe I'll find out soon. First, though, I need to make a message over JWICS look like it was sent yesterday. Can you do that?"

Brice scoffed. "You forget who you're talking to. Just tell me when you supposedly sent it and who it's being sent to. I'll intercept the message, modify the message's metadata, cryptographically re-sign the whole thing, and send it on its way."

"Great. Got a pen?"

"As a matter of fact, I stole a pen from the conference room, so yes."

"Seriously?" The Outfit was particularly conscious about supplies and property. The security protocols on such matters had been in place before even he'd started with the organization almost a quarter century ago. "You know somebody's going to have to file actual paperwork on where it went."

"Sorry. I've got sticky fingers I guess." Brice handed him the pen.

"Just get it back to Gene Kolifrath, please. That was his

conference room we poached earlier today. He'll have an aneurysm looking for it."

Mason jotted down the information regarding the message he wanted sent, then passed it and the pen back to Brice, who scanned the paper and nodded.

"I should have the filters ready by the time you get back to your office. Just call me when you're ready to hit send."

"Will do." Mason stood and gave Brice a fist-bump. "Thanks, you're the best."

"You're sure right about that, chief."

Mason went back to his office, which was practically right across the hall. It had everything a man might need who worked late nights: coffee machine, sink, small fridge, microwave. On many days his office felt more like home than his apartment ever had.

He sat down at his computer, went through the necessary security logins and a retinal scan confirmation, and logged into JWICS. It was a secure system on the high side, where classified data flowed across the network.

He tapped out a simple note to the head of AFRICOM.

TO: General Harry N. McCallister
SUBJECT: Missing asset in Nigeria

Harry, we've got some issues with a missing asset. Please try to be at your number at 9:00 your time.

Randy Holloway
Staff Operation Officer, DO
Central Intelligence Agency

Mason then dialed Brice. "You ready?"

"Filters are up. Fire away."

Mason hit send.

"Randy Holloway, eh?"

Mason leaned back in his chair. "One of my many personas. So I assume you've got it."

"Yup. Dating it at 1500 Zulu yesterday, as you requested—or about four in the afternoon German time. Even if he checked email later than that, this will just look like an unread email that he must have missed."

"Perfect. Thanks again for being awake and helping me out."

"No problem... Okay, it's sent. I'll probably clean up and head home in a bit. Call my cell if you need anything else."

Mason checked the clock. Almost two a.m. Which meant it was almost time for the general to arrive at his office. He drummed his fingers and waited.

When his cell phone vibrated, he answered without looking at who called. "Mason."

The Outfit's embedded agent at the German base reported in. *"General McCallister just cleared the main gate here at Kelley Barracks. Unless he takes a detour, he should be in his office in a few minutes."*

As Mason hung up his cell, he leaned forward in his chair and stared at his landline. That was the secure line he'd use to spoof a call coming from Langley. He needed to keep up appearances.

He waited a full minute before grabbing the receiver from its cradle and dialing the general's office number.

"General McCallister's office, this is Alice."

"Hi Alice, this is Randy Holloway, calling from Langley. I've got a nine a.m. with the general."

"Oh—I'm sorry, I didn't realize he had anything this morning. I'm not expecting him in until—oh, well speak of the devil, he just walked in the door. Hold for a second."

A couple of minutes later a gruff voice came on the line. *"Wow Randy, I'm surprised you called. I'm never in the office this early."*

"Didn't you get my email?"

"What email? Sorry, I just barely walked in the door. Hang on, I'll pull it up."

Mason's heart thudded loudly in his chest as he waited.

"That's from yesterday. Sorry, not sure how I missed it. Well, talk to me. What's this about a missing asset?"

"Evidently the president's brother has gone missing somewhere in Nigeria. As soon as I got notified, you were the first person I thought of. Would you happen to know anything about it?"

The phone went quiet.

"General? Did I lose you?"

"No, I'm just surprised by your question. I can't really help you with that."

"Can't because you don't know anything, or can't because you can't talk about it?"

The general chuckled. *"I'll let you figure it out. You're a smart guy."*

That non-answer was as good as an answer. The general did know something—but wasn't allowed to say. The good news was, that meant some kind of orders must have gone through to AFRICOM—and if so, Brice should be able to hunt them down.

" I understand," he said. "Thank you for your time, General McCallister."

"Not a problem. And if you're in-country at some point, look me up. We'll go light up the town again."

Mason hung up and leaned back in his chair. "Well, looks like it's time for plan B."

"We have now arrived at terminal 2F. For transport to other terminals we have the Charles de Gaulle Véhicule Automatique Léger that will take you to..."

Annie tuned out the pilot's announcement and listened instead to the people waiting to get off the plane. They were all speaking Russian, a language she was passably conversant in. But she'd spent the last month in Moscow, and would be happy to get away from Russians for a bit.

A few minutes later, she stepped from her gate into the terminal. She made a beeline for the flight directory, spotted the incoming flight number she'd been given, and noted it was arriving now at gate F41. By some miracle that gate was actually nearby.

Less convenient was that their flight to Lagos wouldn't leave for another three hours. She hated waiting around in airports.

She sent a text to her partner for this next mission.

I'm at the gate. Meet me at the bar right next to it.

Just as she hit send, a man's voice said, "Hey, pretty lady, don't I know you?"

She turned to find Connor walking up to her.

"Looks like we have some time to kill," he said. "Want to grab something…" He paused, pulled out his phone, looked at it, and laughed. "I guess you had the same idea."

It had been a few months since Annie had spoken to Connor. He wasn't completely awful to work with. He was a good shot, and not bad to look at. She was actually happy to see him, which was not something she'd say for most of the people she'd ever met.

They found a bar that was surprisingly upscale for an airport. The lights were low, with the rows of bottles behind the bar backlit by LEDs. Too bad she wasn't exactly the drinking type. An attractive thirty-something blonde woman behind the bar flashed a smile—more toward Connor than her—and slid two coasters in their direction. "English?" she asked with a thick Parisian accent.

They both nodded. "*Oui*," Connor said.

"What can I get you?"

"Do you have any Glenfiddich?" Connor asked.

"But of course. We have some twelve-year-old, an eighteen, and a twenty-five-year-old."

"I'm a simple guy. Twelve-year-old on the rocks would be great."

"And you, miss?"

"Just a Coke, please."

As the bartender turned away, Connor looked at Annie with his one eyebrow cocked. "Not a drinker?"

"Honest?"

He frowned. "I wouldn't ask if I didn't want to know."

"It makes me horny, and I figure now is not the time."

Connor coughed, and his cheeks reddened slightly. "You're something else."

"Don't worry, you're safe from my clutches for now."

Men were so easy to manipulate, and Connor for some reason brought it out in her. He wasn't handsome in the traditional sense —a slightly overlarge nose, and his jawline was a bit thicker, more brutish than her type—but he tolerated the teasing without ever taking the bait, and that fascinated her.

"I'm going to ignore your last comment," Connor said, "since the way you normally talk to me implies that's a constant state for you. Do you ever drink alcohol?"

Annie smiled. "Not really. It never did anything for me." She didn't want to just outright tell him she was a Buddhist—that'd be no fun. She decided to change the subject. "Did we get any more intel on why Little Eagle is where he is?"

Connor shook his head. "Afraid I know nothing—but then again I shipped out in quite a hurry. I'm not even sure what the deal is with supplies. Do you know?"

"We're being equipped once we land, or so I was told." She leaned in, her voice low. "CIA is already on site."

"CIA already knows about this?"

"Of course they do."

Connor looked confused. "I was told only a few people knew about the incident. Do you think Little Eagle might actually be some kind of rogue agent?"

Annie shrugged. "I supposed it's possible. But my money is on a black-market sale of some kind that needed Little Eagle's expertise, and something went wrong."

Before Connor could reply, the bartender arrived with their drinks. Annie lifted her glass, and the two clinked them together. "To Africa and Little Eagle," she said.

The bartender had started to turn away, but now she looked back. "You're going to Africa to study eagles?"

It was Connor who answered. "Absolutely. Have you heard of the African fish eagle?"

"No."

And with that, Connor began spewing a stream of nonsense about egg diseases, juvenile wing deformities, and conservation data. The bartender's eyes quickly glazed over and she raced away to help another customer.

Connor took a sip of his drink and turned back to Annie. "I hear you know a few of the African dialects."

Annie shrugged. "A few."

"I guess I wouldn't have expected lots of jobs demanding our folks go to the dark continent."

"Oh, there's plenty of things in Africa that need my attention," Annie said. "I look native, and I'm pretty good at getting close and flaunting my assets." Annie brazenly cupped her breasts, and Connor's cheeks predictably went beet red.

"Why do you keep doing that with me?" he said. "I thought you had a thing for Brice."

"What makes you say that?" It dawned on her that Connor was much more attentive than she'd given him credit for.

"Honestly? It's kind of obvious, no matter how odd of a match you two are."

He wasn't wrong, but Annie wondered who else might have noticed. She supposed it didn't matter. Whatever she did or didn't have with Marty wasn't something they'd even talked about, much less consummated.

"What about you?" Annie asked. She leaned in close, spreading her legs while putting her elbows on her knees. "You got anyone special at the moment?"

"No. But that's not to say I'm not open to the opportunity. When the time is right."

He had spunk. She liked that. She wouldn't mind having a little fun with Connor—but not on the mission. For now, she'd have to settle for just embarrassing him.

Connor drank the last bit of his whiskey and stood. "Well, I'm going to go find a bathroom. Doesn't hurt to get it out of my system before we get on a six-and-a-half-hour flight."

"Don't forget," Annie said with a wink, "there's a seventeen-hour car ride afterwards."

Connor groaned.

Mason stretched as he stepped through the metal detector, popping his neck and back as the green LED lit and the security guard waved him through. The chair he'd requisitioned for his office was extremely comfortable, but sleeping in a chair was still sleeping in a chair.

He walked through the winding hallways of the Pentagon to the cafeteria. It was just before ten in the morning, so the lunch crowd hadn't come in yet. Nor had his contact, Amanda Kovich. Kovich was a senior member of the Joint Chiefs of Staff, working for military intelligence. If she didn't know what was going on, nobody did.

He decided to get a coffee from the Starbucks while he waited. He approached the counter, where a barista was grinding coffee beans, filling the air with the scent of freshly roasted coffee.

"Slow morning, huh?" Mason said.

"Usually is around this time of day. What can I get you?"

"I'll take a venti, plain coffee. No cream, no sugar, no squirts of anything."

"Venti black, coming up."

"What kind of breakfasty stuff do you recommend?" Mason asked.

"Well, a lot of people ask for a plain toasted bagel. But the menu board shows what we've got today."

"That works," Mason said. "A plain bagel, toasted light."

When Mason received his coffee and breakfast, he still saw no sign of his contact. He pulled out his phone and sent off a quick text. *I'm here, where are you?*

The response was quick. *Sorry. I'm in an all-hands meeting that got called last minute. I can't make it.*

For a moment, Mason brooded. Then he smiled as he had an idea. He texted an Outfit agent stationed in the Pentagon.

Are you attending a meeting with Amanda Kovich?

Probably. There's like two hundred people in the room. Why, you need her?

As quick as possible.

I'll see what I can do.

He sipped his coffee and waited. Only a minute passed before his phone buzzed with another text. This one was from Kovich.

Something happened to the projector and we're taking a fifteen-minute break while it gets fixed. I can meet for a couple of minutes if you're still here.

Mason chuckled as he typed. *I'll be on the north side of the courtyard. Look for the dashingly handsome guy drinking an overpriced coffee.*

Then he stepped outside into the courtyard and parked himself on a bench along one of the walkways. A morning breeze blew through the trees and manicured lawn as he unwrapped his bagel and took a bite.

After a few minutes, a slim woman in a gray skirt and dark jacket walked toward him. Amanda Kovich.

"So, how's life?" she asked as she sat down, about as far on the other side of the bench as was possible. "We haven't met like this since we broke up."

Back then, she'd known him as a high-ranking member of the CIA, and on occasion they'd trade information. But that was then. Their breakup had been mutual. Neither of them had time for the other—simple as that.

"You're looking great, Amanda," he said. "I know you're busy, so I'll get right to it. I'm looking for the president's brother. Supposedly he's in Nigeria, and we've got people in-country looking for him. Why is he there?"

Amanda's back stiffened. "How do you know about that?"

"You're kidding, right? When a president's relative goes missing, that's gonna come out."

She pressed her lips into a thin line and shook her head. "I wish I could help you, Doug. But I can't say anything." She stood abruptly. "I'd better go. Please take care of yourself, and maybe call me about something outside of work next time?"

She gave him a strained smile, then walked away.

Mason scowled. Another dead end. He was getting nowhere, and he needed intel—fast. He didn't give two shits about the president's brother, but when a US nuclear weapons expert goes missing in a country with as much turmoil as Nigeria...

He shook his head.

That's the stuff of nightmares.

CHAPTER FOUR

Connor and Annie had been standing in line at customs at the Murtala Muhammed International airport for almost half an hour. The long circuitous line wound through several halls before spilling out into the large area where the officials went through everyone's paperwork. The place's air conditioning was struggling against the sea of humanity, and Connor felt sweat dripping down the back of his neck.

"Connor," said Annie, "I shouldn't have to say this, but just make sure you say you're a tourist on the exit paperwork. It'll make things much easier."

Connor gave her a wry smile. She definitely had a mothering instinct. Either that, or she thought he was an idiot.

He knew what he was doing. He had one carry-on, with basic backup clothes to replace what he was wearing—which was a black collared pullover and dark-gray cargo pants. He wasn't carrying any weapons—of course—and his only bit of nontouristy tech was his smart-glasses, which wouldn't activate unless the metal contacts in the stems were touching his scalp. They wouldn't work on anyone else's head.

Finally their turn came. Annie and Connor were waved to two different lines, and Connor stepped forward and handed the customs officer his passport.

"What is your business in Nigeria?" the officer asked. He spoke with an easy-to-understand accent that oddly reminded Connor of his time in the Bahamas.

"No business, just pleasure. I'm a tourist."

The customs officer frowned slightly. "How long are you planning to visit?"

"One week," Connor replied without hesitation. The visa for entry into the country already required an estimated entry and exit date.

The man gave Connor another once-over, then stamped his passport. "Welcome to Nigeria, Mr. Sloane."

Connor caught up with Annie just outside of customs. She beckoned for him to follow. "Come on. Let's go find our escorts."

They stepped outside the building, and Connor felt like he'd walked into a wall—a wall of oppressive humidity and heat. His glasses fogged up and he had to wipe them with his shirt. No wonder the airport's air conditioning had been struggling— this African heat was no joke. He was reminded of Afghanistan, which had probably been hotter, but without this extreme humidity, which added a whole new level of discomfort.

They were just above the arrivals terminal, and Connor had a clear view of the surrounding area. But beyond the airport, there wasn't a single building in sight. Just the vast expanse of Africa.

"We're not in Kansas anymore," he muttered under his breath.

Then he noticed a young kid, probably about ten years old, walking by himself but staying in the shadows of the terminal building, trying to remain inconspicuous. And the kid's gaze was locked on Connor.

"Annie, see the kid at three o'clock?"

"Which kid?"

"White T-shirt, cargo shorts, about ten years old." Connor now saw another kid watching him. This one was a bit older, wearing similar clothes. "I think we have some interested parties."

Annie frowned. "Maybe. They could be who we're looking for—or they could be pickpockets. Or both. Better stay on your guard—remember, our guy uses kids as his gophers."

The two pre-teen boys ended up meeting each other at the wall of the terminal about fifty feet away. One of them pulled out what looked like a walkie-talkie and began talking into it. And they continued to keep an eye on Connor.

"They sure have me pegged as something interesting," Connor said.

"Well, duh. You kind of stand out around here, my little white boy. They probably see you as an easy mark."

Connor looked at Annie, whose skin was about as dark as humanly possible. "Last I checked, I'm more a pale brown."

Annie laughed. "Around here, that makes you a white boy." She patted him on the back. "You're getting a glimpse of what it feels like to be a minority. Better get used to it, because where we're heading, they might never have even seen someone who wasn't a sub-Saharan African."

A green bus pulled up to the curb, its air brakes hissing as they engaged. At the same moment the two boys started toward them.

The bus's door opened and the driver, who looked to be no more than thirteen, shouted out to them. "Mr. Connor? Miss Annie? Security don't liking us be here. Come. Pigeon King is waiting."

"Pigeon King?" Connor asked.

"Aye. Ntabo be the boss man. He be the Pigeon King."

The two pre-teen boys had now arrived. But instead of making a move to pick anyone's pocket, they simply smiled and motioned toward the bus, as if to say, *After you.*

Connor looked over at Annie for guidance. She shrugged, grabbed his arm, and pulled him aboard.

The bus groaned and creaked on shock absorbers that had probably needed to be replaced years ago. Connor held on to the seat in front of him as he looked around. The bus was occupied by a half dozen raggedy kids ranging from about eight years old to early teens. At least all of them looked well-nourished; this Ntabo guy was keeping his people fed.

The bus picked up speed as it got onto the Apapa Oworon-shoki Expressway, and that's when it really started rattling— violently. Connor looked down and saw that the floorboards running the length of the bus had minor gaps between them, and he could see the asphalt racing past. He tightened his grip on the bench seat in front of him. This thing was a death trap.

Annie, who seemed unconcerned by all this, turned to the kids. "Where's Ntabo?" she asked, practically yelling to be heard over the bus's screaming protests. "We thought he'd be meeting us here."

Her question was met by a series of smiles. It was the driver who answered.

"Patience," he said. "Ntabo don't come out of base easily. No worry, you see him soon enough."

Annie grumbled, "Let's just hope this thing survives the trip."

After about twenty minutes, the empty countryside gave way to the capital city of Lagos. At first it looked modern and new, but as they moved into the heart of Lagos, that all changed. The side roads weren't paved, the power poles dipped crookedly, the sidewalks were mere dirt paths next to the street, dotted with the occasional red and brown pools of water. A couple stripped skeletons of cars along the side of the road were a clear indication that they weren't exactly in an upscale area of town.

The bus slowed due to traffic, and the smell of the exhaust gave Connor a headache—which he hoped wasn't an early sign of carbon monoxide poisoning. He leaned forward to talk to the driver. "Is traffic always this bad?"

"Today especially bad, but not usually good."

It wasn't just the traffic that was the problem. There were cars parked on the side of almost every road, leaving very little space to drive. Connor watched nervously as their teenage driver came perilously close to parked vehicles and maneuvered through what seemed to be organically forming lanes. At one moment there were two lanes, then a minute later there were four or even five, with barely a hair's-breadth between the cars. And Connor was convinced all the drivers were nuts. Motorbikes, of which there were a lot, often carried two or three people, and they would dart between the larger vehicles within inches of disaster.

"Those are Okada," Annie said, nodding to some motorbikes. "If you can believe it, they're the equivalent of taxis around here. The government doesn't like them too much, especially since many of the entrepreneurs grab more than one passenger to make more money, which can be dangerous."

"I'll say. And I thought this bus was bad." Connor shouted up to the driver. "Hey, did you have to get a license to drive?"

"Yes," said the boy, "but I didn't do test or anything, if that is what you ask. No one stop us, but Ntabo make fakes for the flock who look old enough, just in case."

Connor said a little prayer. It was a miracle that these people dealt with this on a daily basis and lived.

After cutting through the heart of Lagos, seeing both affluent and third-world conditions within blocks of each other, they turned onto a winding dirt road that ended at a metal gate. One of the kids jumped out of the rear of the bus to open the gate, and the driver made his way toward a literal mountain of garbage. It was a good fifty feet tall, and spanned the size of several football fields.

As the bus approached the dump, the reek of their surroundings grew strong enough to make Connor's eyes water. The driver weaved the bus between giant piles of refuse, stopped right in front of the central mountain of garbage, and opened the front door. The kid who had opened the gate raced ahead, somehow finding a meandering path that led deeper into the mountain of refuse.

The driver turned and smiled at Connor and Annie. "Go. Ntabo, he expecting you."

Connor reeled at the intense odor, which struck him as a combination of raw sewage and rotten eggs. But as they stepped off the bus, Annie put a hand on his shoulder and breathed deeply, as if enjoying a breath of fresh air. He wondered if she was just messing with him. The stench was *terrible*.

The kids led the way, winding through teetering piles of rusted appliances, unidentifiable mounds of rotting vegetation, and large tubs of horrifying brown goop that bubbled as if it were a carbonated hell broth. Connor reminded himself that he'd smelled worse in Saddam's killing fields, and he stiffened his resolve as he followed.

When they arrived at a shadow-filled entryway that led into a concrete building of sorts hidden underneath the mounds of garbage, one of the boys looked over his shoulder and grinned. "Good hiding place, yeah?"

It turned out that hidden under the mountain of garbage was a concrete bunker of sorts. Connor tried to keep track of their route through the labyrinth, but after the tenth intersection, or maybe it was the eleventh, he had to admit he was lost. He glanced over at

Annie's focused expression and hoped she was managing better than he was.

The route was strewn with crushed plastic bottles, broken toys, and shards of glass. Every now and then they would pass a circulating fan, stirring the rancid air. These were probably to prevent an explosion from pockets of methane or whatever else might be built up in this shithole.

Finally, the boys stopped, knelt, and pushed on a pallet of garbage. It slid easily on a well-oiled track, revealing a rusted trap door that looked much like a circular hatch at the top of a submarine. The hinges on the door shrieked as the kids pulled on it.

Connor was impressed. The metal door was easily three feet across and four inches thick—it had to weigh over a thousand pounds. Its smooth action belied the use of hydraulics. Here in the mountains of garbage was truly a well-maintained and secure entrance.

One of the kids ducked into the hole, while the other looked expectantly at Connor and Annie. "The boss man's waiting. You don't want to make him wait." With a flourish, he bowed and motioned toward the portal.

Annie didn't hesitate. She looked down the shaft, then used the handholds on one side to lower herself down. Connor came quickly after, delighted to leave the world of garbage behind.

At the bottom of the ladder was a surprisingly clean underground chamber. Its cinderblock walls were painted yellow, and dim fluorescent lights illuminated tunnels stretching in multiple directions. The portal above them shrieked as it closed, and their one remaining guide motioned for them to follow.

Even as Connor kept pace, he felt ill at ease. He didn't like not knowing what he was getting himself into. All he could do was trust that the Outfit wasn't going to toss him into a meat grinder without warning.

Much like the building above, this place too was a maze of corridors. After what seemed like a five-minute jog through endless turns, their guide stopped at an unmarked door and knocked softly three times followed by a heavy kick. After a moment, the door was opened by a huge, hulking man. He was at least half a foot taller than Connor and probably outweighed him by a hundred pounds of muscle.

The behemoth stepped aside and gestured for them to enter.

And as Connor did so, he at last met what the kids called the Pigeon King.

The man wore an odd assemblage of rags, yet he carried himself in a dignified manner. Connor immediately thought of the Bowery King played by Laurence Fishburne in the *John Wick* movies. The resemblance was so strong that for a moment he wondered if they'd cast the Bowery King off of this guy.

"You have arrived," the man said with a lopsided grin. He had a strong Nigerian accent but spoke clear, American English.

"We have," Annie responded.

"Do you have ID?"

Connor hesitated, surprised by the question, but when Annie dug out a silver coin from her pocket and extended it toward the man, he remembered and held out his own copy of the Outfit's only form of ID. The shiny coin had the symbol of a flying eagle on one side, a sword grasped in its talons, and a pyramid with the eye on top on the other.

The man briefly grasped Annie's coin and then did the same to Connor's. Connor felt the metal warm slightly, and the eye began to glow.

"I am Ntabo," the man said, releasing the coin and leaning on his cane. "And now we all know that we are who we say we are."

The man turned and said something to the behemoth who'd opened the door. Connor didn't understand his words—it might have been some form of pidgin English or Yoruba; he wasn't sure. But the guard opened another door, and Ntabo led them all down a winding tunnel that opened onto a brightly lit rotunda inside what looked like a decommissioned sewer system. Tunnels led in various directions, making this area the hub of a many-spoked wheel. A few teenagers were playing card games on the far side of the room, using bottle caps as bets. Some other kids, these younger, were talking in front of a large map that was duct-taped to one of the brick walls.

"Welcome to Nigeria, my friends," Ntabo said, opening his arms in a virtual embrace, "and welcome to my world. Your boss man didn't even need to tell me why you have come. It's about a kidnapping, no?"

"How do you know that?" Annie asked.

Ntabo smiled, and as he did, Connor got the distinct sense of a predator behind the friendly façade. "Come, I shall explain."

The mobster led them through the center of the hub and into one of the tunnels. Lights flickered on as they entered.

"Motion detectors in a sewer?" Connor said, gesturing to the lights. "Pretty high-tech."

"It's a matter of economics," Ntabo said with a smile, his pearly whites a stark contrast against his skin. "Electricity is a precious commodity down here; why should I pay for lighting things that don't need to be lit?"

Annie whispered to Connor, "At least we can walk along this tunnel without getting tetanus."

Ntabo gave Annie his ever-present toothy grin. "By the way, sound travels quite nicely in the tunnels; everyone can hear what you say down here. And yes, I admit the space above this sanctuary is not the most pleasant. But it keeps the curious away, and much of the garbage you saw produces the gas we use for the electricity down here. It's all very practical."

Ntabo turned into a narrow passage that led to a small room furnished with a wooden table, two metal folding chairs, and a beaten-up sofa. On the table were two AK47s, two Glocks, and two in-waistband holsters.

"These are yours," he said, indicating the weapons. "I thought you'd appreciate the gesture. The magazines are empty for now."

Connor gave the assault rifle a quick once-over. It looked like it hadn't been given a proper cleaning in years, and the iron sights had somehow been broken off. He wasn't going to be winning any shooting contests with this thing, but it was better than nothing.

The Glock, on the other hand, was in almost perfect condition, factory fresh. He dropped the empty magazine and pulled the slide back; it glided smoothly on its rails.

"You like my presents?" Ntabo said, plopping down on the sofa.

"Yeah, thank you."

"My men will have ammo in the jeep you'll take to the reserve. For now, I imagine you two have questions?"

"I do," said Connor. "For starters, why do the kids call you the Pigeon King?"

Ntabo leaned back and folded his arms behind his head. "Why not? You met some of my pigeons this morning. Like pigeons in New York or the rest of your country, they are every-where. They are my eyes and ears; nothing gets past me. Even the most powerful of the local warlords, Enitan and Sijuwade, come to me for information. Which I give to them—for a price of course. Their feud has fueled my little empire quite nicely." He laughed.

"Do these warlords know about Little Eagle?"

"I'm sorry? What's Little Eagle?"

"Our target," Annie said.

"Ah. Then your answer is no. The only ones who know about why you're here are me and my pigeons."

"And how do we know that you didn't kidnap him?" Annie asked. Despite her directness, she said this as nonchalantly as if she'd asked to borrow a cup of sugar.

Ntabo's grin gave him a distinctly menacing expression. "I may have plenty of resources, but my flock does not participate in kidnapping. Even if they did, I would not risk their lives for some American. There's little to no profit in such things. And the attention that could bring upon me would be most unwelcome. I prefer being in the shadows, if you know what I mean."

From his attitude, it seemed clear that Ntabo had no idea that their target was the president's brother.

"When can we talk to the flock at the reserve?" Connor asked.

Ntabo frowned. "You are making me think that you are already weary of my hospitality. We have barely even spoken together."

"No, that's not it," Annie said, giving Connor a look. "My friend is tired from a long trip and not thinking right. We all know why we're here. But it's proper that we relax a bit first before speaking of such things."

Ntabo nodded. "I suppose that is the American impatience. I must get used to it." He turned to Connor. "I will ensure you visit with my flock, because they have seen what you're looking for. Two of my best men will accompany you to their camp in the Yankari reserve. But my flock is precious to me. If you betray my trust, you will not go far. On that you have my word."

Annie patted Connor on the back. "I assure you, your flock have nothing to worry about from us."

Ntabo looked back and forth between Connor and Annie, his eyes narrowed. Then he pointed up at the ceiling. "It's late in the day, and soon the undesirables will be roaming around looking for the unwary. You will be my guests tonight."

Connor didn't like the idea of being here any longer than he had to, but Annie gave the gang leader a nod, and she had the lead here.

Ntabo stood and draped his arms over both of their shoulders. "You can leave early in the morning; I think about six would be good. My flock will behave, but I can't guarantee what may come, so you will have my presents with you so that you feel safer."

"Thank you," Annie said.

"Of course. You are my guests." Ntabo stood. "And since you're staying for the night, I'll have one of my flock cook a fine eba."

"Eba?" Connor asked.

"It's a staple of Nigerian cuisine." Ntabo smiled. "Come, we'll eat with my flock in the main area. You can leave the weapons here. Nobody will take them."

They went back the way they came, passing once again through the hub where the kids were playing cards. Ntabo yelled something at the boys, and they immediately raced in all directions, disappearing only to return moments later with tables and chairs and trays of food. Soon wonderful smells filled the subterranean chamber. It was controlled chaos, everyone seeming to know their role.

Ntabo took a seat at the head of one of the tables, and Connor and Annie sat beside him. The gang leader beckoned over a girl who looked to be about fourteen. In her arms she carried a large bowl of something that looked like stew.

"Ndidi has been learning to cook for about a year now," Ntabo said. "She's quite proud of her craft, and she should be. You'll see."

"Is she the only one cooking?" Annie asked.

"Oh, no. Any kids who are interested help her out when they have a chance—but she does most of the work."

"Boss man knows I don't be liking them to help too much," the girl said. "The boys are ruining more than they helping." She placed the bowl of stew on the table and then disappeared down one of the tunnels.

As they watched the setup continue, Connor turned to Ntabo. "I know only what has been in the news. What is really happening in Nigeria? Are things as bad as they seem?"

Ntabo sighed. "I'm afraid you two have come at a bad time for my beautiful country. There is war coming, I can smell it in the air. It's the government's fault. The money from oil has corrupted the politicians. Oil, oil, oil—but for the common man, it's the boot on their throat with taxes. The government man will take every single naira in a man's bank account before he even thinks about the welfare of the people. And the people know it. Social media, the television… it is a new world, and even here, you cannot hide the corruption from the common man. We can see it, and there will be a change."

"Are the other warlords what you hope would be the cure to this?" Annie asked.

Ntabo's eyes widened a bit. "Let's get something straight: I am not a warlord. I'm an information gatherer, that is all. A warlord has enough supplies to fund a war, which is what Sijuwade and Enitan are trying to do. I have only enough supplies to fund our daily lives and activities, and to share it with those who need it." He motioned to the kids, who were now beginning to take their places at the tables. "These children had no homes, no family. I pick them up and give them both."

A thin woman approached with two young kids following her. She was older than most here, probably early twenties, and a good six feet tall. She had her hair in a bandana that folded down to her shoulders, and balanced on top of her head was a large pot.

Ntabo followed Connor's gaze. "That is Chidi, the mother hen of my flock. She takes care of the younger kids, who are too fast for my old bones to chase. She was one of the first of my flock. It took a while for Chidi to train the kids, but she rules the flock with an iron fist, and they love her for it." As he spoke, his pride was evident.

Chidi set the pot on one of the tables and began helping the youngest ones dish something up. When she shouted something —with a surprisingly strong voice—Annie translated for Connor.

"She just yelled that dinner's ready."

Plates were passed around, and Connor noted that the older kids were taking care of the younger, who were served first. "You have a unique little family here," he said.

"Not so little this family of mine," Ntabo said with a smile, "but yes, I'm quite content."

In addition to a bowl of the stew, a plate was set before Connor, holding something that looked like a yellow lump of dough.

"Tonight, we eat eba with a vegetable stew," Ntabo said. He made a show of pulling off a piece from his own lump of dough, rolling it into a ball, pressing it flat, and then dipping it into the soup. "Eba is casaba flour and water, a very tasty and hearty staple of my people. Like your bread in America." He used the eba to scoop up some broth and vegetables, then popped it into his mouth.

Although the eba looked to Connor like Play-Doh, he did the same. As he chewed, unfamiliar but delicious flavors filled his mouth. He immediately went for another bite, and Ntabo laughed.

"I see you are liking it." He then turned to Annie, who was

merely nibbling at the eba and not touching the stew. "No stew?" he asked.

Annie looked almost embarrassed. "I'm Buddhist. I don't eat meat of any kind."

Connor turned to Annie and tried to keep the look of surprise off his face. He knew very little about Buddhism other than they didn't drink alcohol and he thought they were pacifists. A Buddhist assassin?

"Pfft!" Ntabo said dismissively. "I promise there is no meat used in the stew. No bones, no meat flavoring. I will show you."

He waved at Chidi, and she came running over. "Is something wrong with the food?" she asked.

"Not at all, I just want you to tell our guests if there is any meat in the stew."

The woman shook her head. "No. Just fresh vegetables and spices are from the market. Is that a problem?"

"No, that's good. Thank you, princess."

Chidi replied with a relieved smile that lit up the room. "I'll bring you some zobo—it should be cool by now. Our guests should like that."

As the girl dashed into one of the tunnels, Connor asked, "Zobo?"

"It's a drink," Annie said. "A very tasty one, if I remember correctly."

Ntabo grinned. "It is… but an American might find the taste a bit strange. It's made using a native plant also called zobo. Zobo leaves, some kanafuru…"

"Cloves," Annie remarked. "It's the same flavor you sometimes get in pumpkin pie."

"Ah, I learn something every day. It also is mixed with ginger, pineapple, and water. And don't worry, Chidi always uses filtered water. I don't like the bugs in our water system. It upsets my stomach too."

Chidi returned with a plastic pitcher and three cups, and poured the dark-red drink. "I hope you enjoy it."

Ntabo took a big swig and made a smacking noise with his lips. Annie also took a drink, and nodded with appreciation. But when Connor tried it, he found it anything but sweet. It reminded him of unsweetened cranberry juice, except it was definitely not cranberries he was tasting.

"Oh wow, that's puckery," he said.

"Yes, we don't put sugar in ours. All that sugar slows you down. Zobo is a good refreshing drink as is. It wakes you up."

Connor took another big sip. It tasted better now that he knew what to expect—though he didn't know how to even describe the flavor. "It's good," he said.

"Everything my Chidi makes is delicious," Ntabo said. "She is a wonder." He leaned forward and lowered his voice. "Chidi's parents died before she was old enough to even remember them. I was there when it happened. Sijuwade's men slaughtered almost an entire village who'd committed themselves to Enitan."

"Does she know what happened?" Annie asked.

"Oh yes, I told her when she was old enough. And this kind of thing is not entirely uncommon. I love my country, but the politics of Nigeria have made it a bad place to be for almost twenty years. Sijuwade and Enitan are fighting to gain control, and the government is fighting to stop them. It's a struggle for power between three bad groups. All I can hope for is that, whoever stands in the end, they can help my country regain its former glory."

Connor raised his glass. "Well, here's to the day when Nigeria is at peace."

As the meal continued, Connor found that, between Ntabo's hospitality and Chidi's bright smile, he could almost forget that they were under a garbage dump and dealing with a notorious gang leader who was responsible for innumerable crimes. *They're still criminals,* he reminded himself. Mason had stressed that repeatedly, warning him of the dangers of letting his guard down.

When Ntabo at last leaned back in his chair, patted a full belly, and let out a satisfied burp, Chidi and the kids swooped in, cleared their table, and vanished from sight. Dinner was clearly over.

Ntabo stood. "You two have an early morning start, so I presume you would like to get some sleep."

Annie and Connor both stood. "Yes, if you wouldn't mind," Annie said.

"Of course. You'll stay in the same room we visited earlier. I had some of my flock clean it up for you."

"Thank you for your hospitality," Annie said as the three began heading back down the tunnel once more.

When they got back to the room where they had left their weapons, they found the table and chairs gone, and the sofa as well. There was now no furniture at all, and their weapons lay on the stone floor.

Ntabo chuckled and placed a hand on Connor's shoulder. "I guess we got here a little too soon. My flock will be here any minute with mats and blankets. And feel free to ask them for anything else you need. What's ours is yours during your stay in Nigeria."

With a smile to Annie, he walked back down the hallway, leaving the two alone.

Connor looked forlornly at where the sofa had been. He wouldn't have minded sleeping on that. Then he turned to the door. "There's no way to lock this thing."

Annie draped her arm over his shoulder. "Oh honey, you don't have to worry. I'll be here to protect you."

Before he could come up with an appropriate retort, two pre-teen kids raced into the room with rolled-up straw mats and woolen blankets. Within the span of a few heartbeats, they dropped their loads and raced off.

"Well, I guess that was our turndown service," Annie said dryly. "You want the first or second shift?"

"I'm pretty much awake, so I'll take first."

Annie nodded. "That works, but no funny business while I sleep. I want to be awake if there's any funny business, you get me?"

Connor rolled his eyes. He wondered how much of Annie's bluster was real versus an act.

"Don't you roll your eyes," she said. "Don't think I haven't caught you staring at my breasts every now and then." She traced her fingertips along the back of his arm, then unrolled her mat and plopped down. "It's ten p.m. now, so wake me at two."

Her moods seem to change like someone flipping a switch. From playful to serious in milliseconds. Connor preferred serious. Even if he was interested, which he wasn't, a romp in the sack with Annie was the last thing he needed while on the job. When he was on a mission, he liked to keep his head clear.

He sat against one wall, and after a few minutes, the light turned off. It too must have been on a motion sensor. Connor listened quietly to the occasional banging of pipes in the distance, and settled in for first watch.

CHAPTER FIVE

The wind buffeted them as their jeep raced down the Sagamu Benin Expressway, providing some small relief from the oppressive African heat. Connor and Annie sat in the rear, and Ntabo's guards—two behemoths—sat up front. One was very tall, closer to seven feet than six, the other was short and had a body builder's physique.

Achoja, the taller of the two, veered onto a connecting road and raised his voice over the sound of the wind. "I am turning off to the A122. Must be getting fuel up for the car and fill up our extra fuel canisters."

Connor saw the makings of what looked like a reasonably sized town up ahead, the first one they'd seen in a long while. They turned into a gas station with the letters REC in bolded white on red, and a man with a beret and a green uniform put up his hand, motioning for the driver to stop.

Even though many people in the country spoke English,

Connor often had trouble understanding them even when they did, thanks to the accents and the use of colloquial terms he simply didn't know. But this man's message was clear.

"License and registration please."

Achoja handed the man some paperwork, but it was ignored as the official leaned in and stared at Connor.

"Who are you?"

"My name's Connor."

The man stared silently at him for a few seconds, then barked, "Why are you here?"

"I'm studying for a book I'm writing." It was the canned answer they'd come up with before they'd even left the Outfit's headquarters. Their weapons were hidden under a removable floor panel in the jeep's back-passenger compartment, but if need be, Connor could have his Glock in his hands within seconds.

The officer sniffed, looking unsatisfied, but glanced at the paperwork in his hands and handed it all back to Achoja. "Go ahead."

Achoja pulled forward to the nearest pump, and the officer returned to a shaded spot beside the station building.

"What was that all about?" Connor asked.

"That's one of Sijuwade's men," Achoja said matter-of-factly. "They tend to be more friendly to white people." He hopped out of the car and jogged over to the attendant.

"Wait—*more* friendly?" Connor said to Annie. "He looked at me as if I'd just insulted his family."

The other guard, a man named Debare, turned back and gave him a gap-toothed smile. "You need to understand, everyone has heard of people like you, but out here, in the middle of small village areas, not many people have actually seen a white man in real life."

"I think he'd make a good trophy for some village woman," Annie said.

"What's that supposed to mean?"

Her only response was a subdued smile and an intense stare. Then she turned to Debare. "Is it mostly Sijuwade's men between here and our destination?"

"Yes, mostly. But don't think that Sijuwade's people are any better or worse than Enitan's. There's trouble in Nigeria no matter where you go. But I know the areas to avoid. Don't you worry."

When Achoja was done filling up the tank, he returned to the jeep with a scowl. "These people are thieves. Twice the price of gas because we carrying a tourist, they say."

Connor had seen that kind of game played plenty of times in the Middle East and Asia. Prices were "flexible"; there were local prices, and then there were tourist prices. Unfortunately, there was little to be done about it, and he couldn't exactly pass himself off as a native.

Achoja started the car and pulled out. Only when they had left the station did he say, "I noticed Sijuwade's man talking on a satellite phone while staring at you." He hitched his thumb at Connor.

"Is this a problem?" Annie asked.

Debare answered. "I don't think so. But just in case, I know some better routes." He lightly smacked the driver's shoulder. "Go left on A122. I show you a better way."

Connor and Annie shared a tense expression. It felt to Connor like there was something they weren't being told. One way or another, he was sure there was trouble ahead.

After half a day in the cramped back of the jeep, Connor's legs ached—and the midday African sun beating down on them was intense.

"When's our next stop?" he asked. "I'd really like to stretch my legs."

"The village of Keffi is just ahead," Debare said. He turned to Achoja. "Turn right on the next dirt road. Keffi is nice and should have beverages and some good street foods."

Annie whispered to Connor, "Be ready for Montezuma's revenge."

"Duly noted," Connor whispered back.

In his time with the military, he'd traveled to plenty of places that had questionable food. He knew all about the gastrointestinal parasites teeming in tap water that could cause diarrhea, also known as Montezuma's revenge.

After a few minutes of the bumpy dirt road, they entered a decent-sized town—a bit bigger than most villages he'd visited in Afghanistan, but definitely not what he'd call a city.

"Welcome to Keffi," Debare announced.

Achoja parked in front of an open-air market with a large wooden sign announcing it as *Keffi Central Market*. As soon as he turned off the engine, Debare grabbed the car keys from him and hopped out.

"I need to go find a bathroom," he said. "Meet back here in thirty minutes."

"Hold on," Achoja said. "You're the one who suggested we come here!"

But Debare was already walking briskly away through the crowded market.

Achoja growled something unintelligible, then turned to face the Americans with a pasted-on smile. "Well, let's go explore what this place has to offer! I help you two experience Nigeria during a moment of peace, you know?"

They stepped out of the car, and Connor was met by a mixture of contrasting aromas. The scent of spices hung in the air, along with the smell of roasted meat... and the unmistakable stink of dung. No matter where in the world he went, whether it was the Middle East, Asia, San Francisco, or evidently here in Africa, he couldn't escape the smell of crap.

"You've been here before?" Annie asked Achoja.

"Only once, a long time ago," he said. "I found a place that had some fresh fruit you wouldn't find anywhere else but in Africa. You want to try?" Achoja smiled. "Believe me, no getting sick with the fruit."

"Fruit sounds great," Connor said, returning the smile.

"Alrighty then, follow me."

Achoja led them through the marketplace. The place was crowded, and they passed all variety of stalls—cheap pots and pans, clothes, cleaning supplies. Each vendor was shouting over the others to catch the attention of any would-be shopper. Large bags of produce were tossed from one stall to the next, and Connor had to duck as a fishmonger threw a catfish over his head to another hawker, who lifted the still-wriggling animal and yelled, "Fresh *tarwada*! Only supplier in Keffi!"

Connor chuckled. Showmanship was universal in markets like this. In Pike Place Market in Seattle he'd seen the exact same thing, but with a salmon instead of a squirming catfish.

Achoja stopped in front of a fruit stand featuring an array of fruits in baskets, few of which Connor could identify. Clear plastic bags were filled with colored liquids, and a refrigerator held various bottled sodas.

"Here we are!" Achoja said. "With some food and drink you'll feel better, no?"

Behind the table, an older man smiled at Connor. "We don't see many *oyinbo* around here. Can I help you?"

Connor looked over at Achoja, who merely motioned for him to go on.

"Uh, yeah," Connor said. "We're looking for something to eat and drink, but I'm not sure what's good."

"I have many delicious things, as long as you got some naira to part with." Naira was the name of the Nigerian currency. "It's early in the season, but I just got some *agbalumo*, and—"

At that moment a small monkey crept up to the fruit stand, its eyes on a basket filled with red star-shaped pods. The old man grabbed a large stick and smacked it loudly on the ground, startling the monkey and sending it scurrying away.

He turned his attention back to Connor. "As you can see, the monkeys know when I have a shipment of *obi edun*, also called monkey kola."

Annie picked up one of the pods, checking its weight. "I haven't had one of these in a long time. I'll take this one."

Achoja clapped his hands together. "Good. We get two of the monkey kola pods, and a kilo of the *agbalumo* for my *oyinbo* friend."

"Fine choices," the old man said.

Achoja pointed at the bags of colored liquid. "Is that zobo?"

"Yes, and *kunu* too. Both freshly made. Very good for health and stomach problems."

Annie nudged Connor. "Feeling adventurous?"

Connor shrugged. "I'm game if you are. There's no way it can be worse than the *casu marzu* I had in Sicily."

Annie's face brightened. "Oh, I love that stuff! Italian maggot cheese. I just wish the maggots were a little bigger so you could appreciate the little pops when you bite down on them."

Connor shook his head. "You're twisted."

"Aw, you know how to make a girl blush." She turned to the shopkeeper and pointed to the bags filled with a creamy-white liquid. "Two *kunus*, please."

This wasn't the first time Connor had seen drinks dispensed in plastic bags. In some parts of the world canning operations were expensive, whereas it was very easy to fill plastic bags and heat-seal them.

"Do you have Orange Fanta?" Achoja asked.

"Sure do." The farmer bent down and came back up with an actual bottle this time.

The cost for everything came to a thousand naira—or about three US dollars. Pretty cheap considering the amount they'd bought.

Once more they pushed through the crowds of the market. Achoja led them to a thick-trunked baobab tree. "Here, some nice shade to enjoy your good food. Not a bad way to spend time off the road."

The three sat with their backs against the tree. Connor grabbed one of the *agbalumos*—round orange fruits with some sort of sticky white sap on it—and studied it curiously.

"I promise you will like it," said Achoja. "It's an *agbalumo* in my native tongue, but I think it is called an African Star Apple. It's a very precious fruit to our people. Only available short time during the year. Now is about the only time you can get the star apple and the monkey kola at the same time. It's still early in the season, so maybe more bitter than sweet, but sometimes both." He grabbed one of the fruits, split it open, and showed them both its cross-section. "See the star shape? Now just pluck the seeds out, eat the pulp from around the seed, and spit the seed back out."

The man puckered as he swished a pulp-covered seed in his mouth and spit it out.

"Sour?" Connor asked.

"Sometimes yes, sometimes no. This one was a bit bitter, but is good and refreshing."

Connor managed to break his fruit into two. He squeezed the half of the fruit without the seeds and tasted the orange pulp. It was sweet, with a slight tannic quality; it reminded him of an almost-ripe persimmon. As he dove into the rest of the fruit, Achoja laughed.

"Ah, I can see you got a sweet one."

Achoja pointed to the bags of milky-white liquid. "Now you need to try the *kunu*. It's very good for you. Recipes can change, but almost always *kunu* is made from ground millet, ginger, and corn. Often sugar is added too, but not always."

"In my experience, when someone says is good for you," said Connor, "that usually means it tastes terrible. But the ingredients don't sound too bad. Well, here goes nothing…"

Connor bit the top of the bag's pouring strip and took a swig. The concoction was surprisingly thick, and wasn't sweet—but it was good. It had a musky, almost vegetal taste. He nodded approvingly. "Not bad. I can taste a bit of the corn and ginger too."

"And Miss Annie… what you think?" Achoja asked.

Annie had finished almost half of the bag in one swallow. "Creamy, thick, and warm. It seems quite familiar." She gave Connor a lascivious grin. "Yummy."

He shook his head, and they snacked in silence for a while. Connor was just trying to figure out how best to clean the stickiness off his hands when a strange animal approached, its tail up high in the air. It looked like a mix between a cat and a small bear. Before Connor could react, the animal snatched their shopping bag and scurried toward a man and boy nearby.

"Hey!" Annie shouted, chasing after the animal.

"Titi!" scolded the boy. He grabbed the shopping bag from the animal, which made a grumbling noise in protest. "Don't steal food from people! That's bad."

The man took the bag and handed it to Annie. "I am sorry. My brother came back from China with this binturong for my boy to have as a pet. Unfortunately, the pet likes to steal."

"No, Da," said the boy, "he's just very curious."

Connor sniffed the air. "Am I imagining things, or does Titi smell like popcorn?"

The man nodded. "Yes, I have often thought the same thing. A very unusual scent for an animal."

Annie sniffed a few times. "I've heard of an animal that smells like that, but I never figured I'd be near one."

The kid gave the binturong a hug. "I like his smell."

Achoja tapped Connor on the shoulder. "It's almost time to meet up with Debare. We should get going."

They waved to the man and his son as they headed off, retracing their steps to the jeep, where Debare was already waiting. The burly guide tossed Achoja the keys, and within minutes they were back on the highway.

All the while, Connor's Spidey senses were tingling. Why had Debare taken the keys and disappeared for so long? And the way these two men interacted didn't seem natural. It was almost as if they didn't trust each other.

Not everything was as it seemed.

The sun had already dropped well below the horizon when they pulled off the highway toward a farming village. "We are a few hours from Yankari," Achoja said, "so we are stopping at this place where Ntabo has good friend. She will keep us safe."

Connor looked around. They were literally in the middle of nowhere.

They pulled up to one of the outermost homes, little much more than a ramshackle hut with plywood walls and a tin roof. A woman came outside, gesticulating wildly and uttering a rapid-fire string of words that meant nothing to Connor.

"She's yelling at us for being late and ruining her family's supper," Annie explained.

Connor held up the bag of fruit. "Achoja, will this help?"

The driver nodded, his eyes widening. "Oh yes. But... you give it to her. She's less likely to be mad at the *oyinbo* offering gifts."

Connor found it amusing that a woman in her forties had cowed a jeep's worth of operators solely with the power of her anger.

He stepped out of the car, holding the bag up with one hand, one of the orange fruits in the other. The woman beckoned him forward, barking more words he didn't understand. He walked cautiously over to her and offered the bag.

She peered into it, then sniffed with annoyance. But as she looked up at Connor, her demeanor suddenly changed, and she smiled.

The others got out of the jeep then, and she shot all three of them a venomous glance before smiling once again at Connor. She spoke to him in a soft voice, grabbed him gently by the upper arm, and led him inside.

They'd clearly been expected. Four brand-new sleeping bags —literally still in the plastic bags from the factory—were piled up on the dirt floor. The others entered behind them, but the woman still paid attention only to Connor. She patted him on the face, said something else that included the word "oyinbo"— white guy—then departed, leaving them alone.

He turned to find Annie was grinning at him. "What?" he

said.

Annie chuckled. "Oh, nothing. It's just that that woman said she's never lain with a white guy before. I'm pretty sure she wouldn't mind putting you up as a notch on her bedpost."

Connor just shook his head.

As they all began unrolling their sleeping bags, claiming different corners of the hut, Debare said, "We will leave at six in the morning. The Yankari Game Reserve opens at eight."

They settled in, and it wasn't long before Debare's eyes were closed and Achoja was snoring. Yet Connor still felt uneasy about this arrangement. He had no specific reason not to trust these guys, but he couldn't shake the feeling.

He rolled over to face Annie, flashed four fingers, then pointed at her before pointing at himself.

She nodded in understanding. She was taking the first four-hour shift.

Before the break of dawn, they were back on the highway, on their final leg to their destination. Somewhere in the Yankari Game Reserve was a disabled plane—and that was where their mission would truly begin.

"Do you know these people at the reserve? The ones who reported a plane landing." Connor asked.

"Aye, they're Ntabo's boys," said Debare. "His pigeons are everywhere. Even here in this far-off place. They have a presence within the reserve. We'll go to main entrance of the reserve first, then to the camp."

"We're entering Alkaleri government border area now," Achoja announced as he turned off onto a better-maintained road. "There may be guards from the warlords. If so, hopefully it's Sijuwade's men."

Sure enough, they soon encountered a road block with an armed soldier waving them to take a detour, which led them to a village just off the main road. Another soldier motioned for them to stop and he approached the vehicle. The soldier's uniform was almost identical to the one being worn by the man back at the gas station, except this one had some red striping along the collar, and his beret was gray. And this man was enormous, north of six and a half feet, with muscles to match. Slung on his shoulder was an AK-47, and it looked like a toy on him.

He looked into the vehicle, gave Connor a look of contempt, then motioned for Achoja to roll down the window.

Connor didn't understand the guard's words, but the anger in his voice was unmistakable.

Annie nudged Connor. "Give him your passport."

Connor handed his passport forward.

The man flipped it open and began yelling.

"Hold on," Annie said, and abruptly she hopped out of the car and began yelling back at the soldier in the same language.

Achoja muttered, "Miss Annie is not happy at all."

Annie and the giant guard yelled back and forth for at least a minute. Annie occasionally gestured back toward the jeep, and more than once the guard raised the muzzle of his AK-47.

And then Annie slapped the man in the face with a resounding smack.

CHAPTER SIX

Connor drew his weapon from under the jeep's floorboard. It suddenly looked like he would need it.

Achoja seemed to feel the same. "Oh no, Miss Annie," he muttered. "That is one of Enitan's soldiers. They don't care women or no women."

But for a long moment the musclebound soldier merely stared at Annie, clearly stunned at having someone half his size slap him in the face.

Annie took the initiative. She withdrew an envelope from her pocket and pushed it into the man's chest. He grabbed the envelope with his free hand and lowered the barrel of his rifle.

Connor, his gun in his lap, watched all this closely. Sweat dribbled down the back of his neck, as he ran through the options at his disposal if things went sideways. He didn't see any other men backing this one up, and with the man's barrel lowered

Connor could probably double-tap him in the chest before he could raise it again.

Connor glanced at the buildings ahead of them, some of which were multi-story. For all he knew, there were others in overwatch positions.

The soldier ripped open the envelope and looked inside. Cash, Connor presumed. Annie leaned in, said something more to the man, and grabbed Connor's passport from the man's front shirt pocket. Then she spun on her heel and got back in the jeep.

"Go," she said.

As Achoja put the car into gear, Annie gave Connor his passport. "You can put the gun away," she said.

Connor glanced back at the guard counting his money. "So a bribe is all it took?"

"A bribe wouldn't have worked," Annie said. "But a 'bonus' from one of Enitan's captains, on the other hand…" She smiled. "I made it clear that it was to ensure safe passage of an *oyinbo* scientist studying animals in the wildlife preserve. Worked like a charm."

Connor was impressed. "You came up with that on the spur of the moment?"

Annie almost looked embarrassed. "Well, heated appeal to reason wasn't working with the big idiot, so I *sort of* lost my temper."

"Ya, I *sort of* noticed." He turned to Achoja. "Do you think we'll be encountering more of our warlord's buddies?"

"I don't think, not in Yankari," Achoja responded. "It is tourist area and should be okay."

Debare made a snorting sound.

Connor wasn't used to being someone else's second fiddle, but in this country, with Annie, that's what he was. He was literally a stranger in a strange land. And he figured that if he'd played it just like Annie had, he'd probably have been drilled full of holes. Sometimes life was messed up.

"How far until we get to the reserve?" he asked.

"About thirty minutes," said Achoja.

Connor tried to relax. Somewhere in that wildlife reserve were clues to why he'd traipsed halfway around the world. What was the president's brother doing out here? Was he dead? Injured? Kidnapped? Working for the bad guys, whoever they may be. A mystery wrapped in an enigma.

Finally... something that he'd be able to sink his teeth into that was useful since having arrived in-country.

The guest area just inside the Yankari Game Reserve was a modern oasis of pavement and well-constructed bungalows. They parked under some shady trees at a place called Wikki Warm Springs, and while Achoja and Debare wandered off, both of them with satellite phones to their ears, Connor stretched his limbs. On the far side of the parking lot, groups of tourists walked in and out of a large single-story building, many of them wearing bathing suits and carrying lawn chairs. Connor heard the splashing of people in the nearby stream.

"Keep your eyes open for the damned baboons," Annie said.

Even as she said it, a baboon jumped down from a nearby tree, snatched up a hat that had just blown off a woman's head, and race back up into the tree with it. The woman yelled up at the baboon in French, shaking her fist helplessly.

There were, in fact, a lot of baboons here. Many seemed to be hanging out near the pathways, chittering at tourists with their hands outstretched like tiny, hairy beggars. There were signs everywhere warning people to not wear dangling jewelry and to keep their possessions close at hand. Connor patted at his gun to make sure it was firmly seated in his in-waistband holster.

After a few minutes, the two guides returned. "None of Ntabo's local pigeons are answering," Achoja said. "But I think they must be near, at least during the day. The tourists is what they like. Easy to pick a pocket or two."

"Why do we need the kids anyway?" Connor said. "If a plane crashed in the park, I'd imagine someone around here knows where it is."

"I know of the plane you're speaking of," said a voice.

Connor turned to see a teenage girl crouched in the shadows of a minivan.

"It came down four or five days ago in a big crash," the girl continued. "I can help you find it… if it's worth my time."

Achoja spoke to the girl in a dialect that Connor couldn't make out, but the girl merely snorted at him and turned back to Connor. "You make it worth my time?"

Annie crouched in front of the girl. "That depends. Can you take us there?" she asked.

"No. But I can take you to those who can."

Debare sucked air through his teeth and frowned. "Ntabo's boys will get us there. We don't need this girl's help."

The girl grinned, her white teeth a bright contrast to her skin.

"Good luck with that, boss man. All of Ntabo's boys have been chased out by the special police. They bang them good and took their things."

Achoja groused, "So that's why the boys don't answer."

Connor pulled a ten-dollar bill and held it up in front of him. "How about this. A ten-dollar bill will be yours if you can take us there."

The girl laughed. "You think that's a lot of money to a poor girl like me? One hundred dollars."

"Twenty dollars, not a penny more," Connor said.

The girl's eyes narrowed. "Fifty, and not a penny less." She held out her empty palm. "American money."

Connor was about to haggle further when Annie slapped a fifty-dollar bill into the girl's hand.

The girl tucked the money into her pocket. "Where is your car? It is some ten kilometers from here."

Achoja pointed at the jeep. "Come. You sit in the front and show us the way."

The girl glanced at Debare, who had worked his way behind her, as if worried she would take the money and run. She laughed. "You no need to worry about me. We made a good deal and I won't be cheating you. And besides, you too fat to catch me."

———

Connor held onto the seat in front of him as the jeep dove headlong into a dry riverbed. Achoja drove like a man possessed, gunning the engine, and the car launched itself up the embankment on the opposite side and crossed over onto the grassland.

The girl pointed. "See there? Near the large tree, next to the termite mound."

Connor could only barely make out the tree on the horizon. There had to be a few miles of grassland between here and there —no way would they have found the place without a guide.

After several minutes of bouncing around in the jeep, the details of the tree began to be clear. "The dogoyaro tree?" Achoja asked the girl. "Are you sure?"

The girl nodded. "It makes for a good shelter, and the boys use the leaves for their girlfriends."

"How is that?" Annie asked.

The girl turned in her seat. "You don't know? You can use it with your *oyinbo* friend to have fun. The leaf of the dogoyaro tree, it helps keep babies away." She tilted her head toward Connor with a smile.

Annie snorted and patted his thigh. "That's okay, I don't need it. I have other medicine for that." She whispered into Connor's ear: "I'm on the pill, just so you know."

Connor arched an eyebrow at her, giving his best Spock impression. "I think it's Brice that needs to know about that."

As they came close and their vehicle slowed, a child's head popped out from behind the termite mound, and within seconds a swarm of pre-teen kids were surrounding the car. Debare yelled something at them in Yoruba.

"It's Ntabo's pigeons," Annie said. "Guess they're not all gone after all."

As they all got out of the jeep, one of the older kids said

something to Debare. Connor heard the mention of Ntabo, but didn't understand the rest.

Achoja explained. "The pigeon says some of Enitan's people came through the area, took their equipment, and stole the safari bus for the tourists."

One of the little girls walked right up to Connor and said in perfect English, "The plane crashed and scared the police people. Enitan's men said we cannot go near that area anymore. It's not safe."

Connor crouched and gave the girl a warm smile. "Did you see the plane crash?"

The girl nodded emphatically. Then she took a step closer and asked, "Can I touch your hair?"

Connor was moved by the girl's innocence. He leaned forward, and she gingerly touched the top of his head.

"It's very soft," she said with a giggle.

"Is the plane nearby?" Annie asked.

The girl pointed to the northeast. "It's that way." Then to Connor she said, "I took pictures of the other *oyinbos*. Do you want to see?"

"Yes," Connor and Annie both responded.

While Achoja and Debare continued to speak with the other pigeons, the girl grabbed Connor's hand and led him toward the termite mound. It was huge—a good fifty feet in diameter at its base—made of what looked like sunbaked clay.

Annie patted Connor on the shoulder. She leaned into him and whispered, "The kids back there are saying there's been a lot of soldiers in the area recently. Like a *lot* more. Both the government and private warlord types."

Connor was going to reply, but the little girl yanked him forward. "Come, mister. I show pictures."

On the other side of the termite mound, a tunnel, complete with steps, had been hollowed out, leading underground. Right here in the middle of this grassy plain, in an animal refuge next to a lone tree, the kids had created their own little shelter.

Except it was not so little. As they walked down the steps, Connor felt like he was stepping into a cavern—one created by the insects that had long ago abandoned the nest. Cots and boxes were strewn throughout. There was room for a lot of kids here.

The girl led them to a cot, then pulled a box out from underneath her bed. Inside were her treasures, which included a collection of poor-quality Polaroids.

She began laying them out on the bed. "See here, this is the plane that crashed."

Connor recognized the turboprop's wreckage. "Looks like a C-130," he said to Annie

"Lockheed L-100," she replied. "The civilian version... CIA all the way."

Connor's mind raced as he considered the ramifications. What would the president's brother be doing on a CIA operation? Their intel was that nobody knew how or why the president's brother was out here. What was the CIA pulling?

"Here are some of the *oyinbos* from the plane," the girl said, laying out another picture. "They're mostly like you."

Connor examined the image. It had been taken from a distance, but it clearly showed a twelve-man protective escort formed around an asset.

"That looks like Little Eagle being escorted by an ODA."

Annie frowned. "Speak English, soldier boy."

"ODA stands for Operational Detachment Alpha. A Special Forces A-team."

"Are you sure? Looks like everyone is in their civies."

"Civilian clothing or not, I recognize an SF team when I see one. Someone in the Pentagon has to know why Third Group has folks out here."

Annie pulled out her phone and snapped a picture of the Polaroid. "I'll send this over to Brice. See what he can tell us."

Connor turned back to the little girl and pointed to the picture of the plane. "Can you show us where this is?"

The girl smiled. "I can take you there."

"We are arriving at Berlin Ostbahnhof, please make sure all personal belongings aren't left in the overhead compartment or under your seat. Thank you for riding the ÖBB Nightjet, and have a good rest of your evening."

His gloved thumb repeatedly pressed the button at the top of his pen as the train pulled into the station. Things were falling into place, and it was time to make sure that his target was reminded that he'd been thinking about him.

The doors opened, and he gathered up his guitar case and stepped onto the platform. The station was clean, with lots of lights, shopping, and bustling crowds, yet the cool evening air brought with it the burning scent of urine. About fifty feet away, two German uniformed cops were talking to a disheveled man, probably the source of the stench. All big cities had problems with the homeless nowadays. It would only get worse as the weather got cooler.

After a few minutes of hunting for an exit from the mall-like station, he stepped out onto a street called Erich-Steinfurth-Straße. Hanging a left, he found Koppenstraße, the street he was looking for in the first place, crossed under a bridge to the other side of the train tracks, and reached his destination. It had neon signs for a Subway, various local German businesses, and, importantly, the Deutsche Post.

It was exactly where Google Maps had said it would be.

He climbed the stairs and found the small office that passed as a post office in this part of the world. An attendant behind the counter greeted him in German.

He pulled out the crumpled sheet of paper he'd written notes in and said, in horribly pronounced German, "Can I get a small pre-paid shipping envelope?"

"Ah, an American." The clerk smiled and spoke in English. "How small do you need it to be? And how heavy will its contents be?"

"About the size of my fist, and it's very light."

"Less than a kilogram?"

"Yes."

"Is this for domestic or international shipment?"

"International, and there's no declared value."

"That makes things simpler." The attendant reached down behind the counter and came back with a stamp and a self-sealing shipping envelope. "That will be three euro seventy, please."

He set down his guitar case and paid the man.

"If you have the item on you, we can take the package and ship it for you."

"No, I'll take care of that. Thank you."

"Not a problem." The clerk pointed at the guitar case and smiled. "Good luck with your music."

He smiled back, then turned and left.

As he walked along the Am Ostbahnhof, he was drawn to one of the food trucks parked alongside the road. Its fare reminded him of carnivals when he was a kid: everything was fried and dusted with sugar. He pointed at a tray of pretzel-shaped pastries. "Pretzel donut," he said.

The cook used a sheet of wax paper to hand him the treat, which was like a pretzel-flavored funnel cake covered with sugar. He paid the man, then crossed the street into a park, where he settled under a shade tree. He took a moment to consume the pastry before wiping his gloved hands on the grass, retrieving the envelope from the bag, and dropping a shell casing into it—the one he'd saved from Italy.

Down the street was a yellow mailbox. Could he send something internationally through those, or was it only good for domestic mail? He wasn't sure.

He waved to two gangly teenagers who were laughing and kicking a soccer ball. "Hey!" he said. "Do you guys speak English?"

The two boys jogged over. "Do you need help finding something?" one of the boys said in accented English.

You had to hand it to the Germans, they were an educated people. He didn't know of anyone back home who spoke more than just English, other than the folks he knew in the service.

He pulled out two ten-euro notes. "Can I ask you to mail something for me at your post office?" He shifted his gaze to the other boy. "And for you to follow him and make sure it gets done?"

The first boy waved off the cash. "There's no need to pay, I can tell you where it is."

His friend smacked him on the arm. He wanted the money.

But the first boy ignored his friend and pointed down the road. "The post office is in that building just over there."

"Actually, I'm supposed to meet someone at this park, and they could show up at any minute. It would be a favor to me if you did this."

The first boy looked at his friend, then nodded. "You really don't have to pay, but if you insist." He took the two notes. "Where's the package?"

"One second." He pulled the pen out of his pocket and wrote in block letters the address on the envelope: *The President. 1600 Pennsylvania Ave NW, Washington, DC.*

As the jeep bounced across the uneven terrain, the little girl sitting in Connor's lap yelled over the wind noise. "See there! Next to the river. The crash, it be there. I tolded you I know where it is."

Annie would never admit to it in a million years, but she was miffed that the girl had shied away from sitting on *her* lap and instead had felt more comfortable being with the only *oyinbo* in the vehicle. She'd long ago scratched motherhood off of her lists of things to do, her job was incompatible with it, but she was nevertheless bothered by the idea that she might actually *repel* kids.

Connor looked in the direction the girl had pointed and couldn't make out any details. "The plane crashed?" He pantomimed an explosion for the girl.

The girl shook her head. "No, not like that. But the plane is broken."

As they drove closer, Connor reached forward and tapped Achoja on the shoulder. "Stop about a hundred yards from the plane. Annie and I will check things out to make sure there aren't any problems."

"Aye, no problem."

As the vehicle came to a stop, Annie frowned at the foul odor of death in the air. She glanced at Connor and could see he'd detected the scent of something off-putting. He was a soldier and would know what it was. That odor alone was enough to confirm that wreckage was very recent. Certainly within the last week.

The plane was still mostly intact, but a good half-mile stretch of the African plains behind it were badly scarred. "Looks like they tried landing it," Annie said.

Connor nodded. "Yup. But they didn't quite make it."

They lifted the jeep's hidden floor panel, retrieved their Soviet-era assault rifles, and hopped out. The little girl hopped out too, but Annie picked her up and plopped her back down in the seat. "You need to wait here—it could be dangerous. I promise that we'll be back in a short while."

The girl frowned—she clearly wanted to stay with her *oyinbo* —but stayed where she was put.

As Annie and Connor approached the wreckage, Annie pulled a pair of glasses from her backpack, slid them on, and pressed the nearly invisible button on the corner of the right lens. A translucent holographic display flickered into existence on both lenses. She put in a pair of earbuds as the glasses ran through a set of diagnostics and began syncing with her sat phone and home base.

"We've got visitors," Connor said. He motioned with the barrel of his AK47 at a pair of wolves scrambling out of a gaping hole in the exposed front section of the plane.

Brice's voice spoke through Annie's earbuds. *"Those would be a breeding pair of Canis lupaster, the African golden wolf. Nothing to worry about—unless of course they're rabid, In which case I suggest shooting them."*

"Brice!" said Connor, who also had his earbuds in and synced up. "Good to hear a voice from home." He tapped at one of his ears. "And by the way, one of my earbuds is producing nothing but static."

"Brice, honey," said Annie, "you know I'm rough with the toys you give me, and evidently Connor is as well."

"Sorry about that. You know everything I sign out to you two has been put through the shake and bake. But there's ruggedizing and then there's abuse."

"One girl's abuse is another girl's fun."

"Anyway..." Brice said, wisely changing the subject, *"it looks like you guys are coming up on a Lockheed L-100—the civilian version of the C-130. From the GPS coordinates I'm getting off you two, you're on target for where Little Eagle was said to have landed. From what I'm seeing through your glasses,*

it was more a controlled crash than a landing. Can one of you pan your glasses to the registration markings? They'll either be on the tail or between the trailing edge of the wing and the leading edge of the horizontal stabilizer."

Annie turned to face the spot.

"There," said Brice. *"Interesting. The N designator means it's a US registry, and X marks the—"*

"Spot?" said Connor.

"No, marks the plane as experimental. Which means we're probably dealing with spook central. Those CIA types are always doing unsupervised mods. While I run the registration now, can you give me a good look across the wreckage? Are those holes what I think they are?"

Annie focused on the nearest wing, which was peppered with holes.

"Looks like someone had fun with a .50 caliber all over this thing," said Connor, studying the mud beneath the wing. "This thing definitely didn't go down because it was out of gas; there's jet fuel leaking from the wings. I'm surprised they didn't turn into a fireball when they crash-landed."

"With the warlords in the area, it wouldn't surprise me if those guys had old Soviet 12.7-millimeter heavies on the back of pickups."

"You've got to be kidding me," Connor said. "That's the same weaponry the Syrians were shooting at us back during their civil war."

Annie had moved to the front of the plane, which had buried its nose upon impact. The airframe had twisted, breaking into two pieces just in front of the wings

"Syria, eh?" she said. "I didn't know we were that deeply involved with—"

"Annie, let's stick to the current mission. You two can violate OPSEC some other time. I just got confirmation that the plane is a CIA asset."

"Not surprising at this point," Annie said. "Hey, did you get the images I sent?"

"I did, and we confirmed that it's Little Eagle. We're working on getting some facial recognition on his escorts, but the image is total crap, so I'm not optimistic."

Connor climbed up into the front half of the plane and whistled. "It's a miracle anyone made it," he said, his voice coming through Annie's earbuds. "There's bullet holes everywhere."

Annie ducked under a low-hanging section of the ripped fuselage and climbed in after him. The smell in here was intense. There were large jagged rips all along the bottom of the aircraft, and part of the landing gear was sticking up through the holes.

"Looks like they tried to land but the landing gear failed," she said. "The nose dug into the ground, and I guess the stresses split the plane in half."

"Well, they got it down, but the pilots didn't make it out alive," Connor said from the entrance to the cockpit. "They're still strapped into their seats. It looks like the *Canis whatever* have been sampling them."

"Annie, I need you to search through the cargo hold. Connor, check the outside for tracks. And try to be quick. I don't like you guys being there any longer than necessary."

"Copy that, Brice." Connor looked back at Annie. "You good here?"

There was something about the question that brought a smile to Annie's face. As an assassin, she was used to working alone—and usually she preferred it that way. But it was nice, just for a moment, to have a partner who treated her like part of his team.

"I'm good. Don't get eaten by a hippo while you're out there."

He smiled. "No promises." And he hopped out of the plane.

Annie reached into her backpack and pulled out her Geiger counter. She extended its arm and pressed the power button, and it clicked as she slowly swung it back and forth and walked through the rear section of the plane. Her glasses automatically highlighted the streaks of blood on the floor. There had been bodies in here, and they had been removed—though whether by people or wildlife, she couldn't be sure.

"It looks like a bloodbath," Brice said.

"I'll tell you what, it doesn't smell very pretty, either."

At the back of the passenger cabin, the door to the cargo bay was lying on the floor.

"That's not good. Someone pried that door open and snapped the hinges right off the frame."

"Maybe the SF guys did it."

"Maybe."

Although the passenger cabin was well-lit—thanks to all the bullet holes in the exterior—the cargo bay was inky blackness. Annie waited for her glasses to automatically activate their rudimentary night-vision, and the details of the room appeared in a greenish hue. Dozens of boxes were strewn across the hold, partially opened, and mechanic's tools were strewn across the floor.

"Whoever was here wasn't particularly worried about keeping things neat. This looks like someone's garage got torn apart. Not like a smuggling operation."

"Did you notice there's no bullet holes? I'm guessing there was extra armor put into the cargo hold."

"You thinking Little Eagle was back here when they were fired upon?"

"Exactly."

Annie's Geiger counter clicked rapidly as she swung it over a mound of rags and scattered pieces of angle iron.

"What the hell is that thing detecting? It looks like a disassembled loading rack."

Annie moved the detector slowly over the pile of junk. The clicks slowed as she passed it over the iron bars and spiked as she moved past the rags. With the toe of her boot, she moved the rags to the side, revealing a fist-sized hexagonal tile. As she waved the Geiger counter over it, the clicking went berserk.

"Brice, please tell me that isn't what I think it is."

"Can you turn it over?"

Using one of the pieces of angle iron, Annie flipped the tile over. On the back, a snipped wire protruded from its center. Her mind instantly jumped back to a time not so long ago when she'd been faced with a sphere the size of a soccer ball, covered in similar hexagonal tiles.

"Oh, crap. It's happening all over again, isn't it? That's a piece of high explosive, and it's freaking the Geiger counter out because—"

"Shit!" Brice exclaimed. *"It looks like our guy was busy disarming something that shouldn't have been in that plane."*

Annie's chest tightened. "Brice, it's one thing trying to rescue a nuke expert, but I didn't sign up for playing with another bomb. This isn't cool, not by a long shot. You hear me? Tell Mason I'm not happy about this."

"Annie, I'm sorry. But nobody's asking you to deal with a nuke. By the looks of that segment, it looks like our guy removed it from the core, effectively disarming it. Your mission is about him, nothing more. The nuke isn't your concern. You hear me?"

Annie focused on taking deep breaths. "I hear you. My mission is Little Eagle."

"Exactly. You let me worry about the nuke."

Connor crouched low in the tall grass about a half mile east of the crash site. As he scanned the horizon, his glasses flickered with various distances—and then highlighted a herd of about thirty antelopes migrating across his path. As far as he could tell, the president's brother had been escorted in this direction. And directly ahead of him, past the antelopes, a village lay on the horizon.

"Connor, are you there?"

It took a second for him to recognize Thompson's baritone through his one working earbud.

"Hey, Thompson. I'm a little busy at the moment."

"Well I'm gonna need you to get busy with something else. Mason is calling in transport for you. I need you in Switzerland ASAP. Brice is pulling in some other resources to assist Annie."

"Whoa, hold up. You do realize that we've just now caught the trail of Little Eagle? And you're wanting to pull me?"

"I know, but there are things going on that you don't yet know about, and you're the right person for this job. I'll fill you in when you're on site."

Suddenly the herd of antelopes began scattering, a large portion of them racing in his direction. Connor raised the barrel of his AK-47 and jumped up from his crouching position as he saw what had spooked them.

A cheetah.

It had singled out one antelope in particular, and just Connor's luck, that antelope was running straight at him. The panicked animal barely zigged around him, and the cheetah came just as close, its giant cat's tail whipping him across the knees as it ran past.

Connor stared after the receding predator, his heart racing a mile a minute. "Holy crap," he breathed. "Did that just happen?"

"You okay?" Thompson asked.

"I'm fine. Just got reminded that I'm in Africa."

"Maybe Africa's telling you it's time to go. Get back to Annie and give her whatever recon you have on the target. We've got your transport already on the way."

Connor squeezed on the frame of his glasses, taking snapshots of his orientation and GPS coordinates, then began jogging back to the wrecked plane. "Are you going to even give me a clue about this other job that's so important?"

"Not now. We'll talk at the safehouse in Switzerland."

CHAPTER SEVEN

As Annie's jeep bounced across the terrain, she muttered a tiny prayer for Connor's safe travels to wherever the Outfit was sending him. The truth was, she felt some relief at not having him around anymore. He was a good partner, a professional who could hold his own—and he was fun to mess with—but through no fault of his own, he stuck out like a sore thumb in Nigeria. She'd told Mason right from the jump that having a light-skinned guy on a sub-Saharan mission was a mistake.

She surveilled the ground ahead of the vehicle, and her smart-lenses highlighted some otherwise invisible tire tracks. She shifted her gaze upward, to the village ahead—the one that Connor had directed them to.

"What do you know about this village?" she asked her guides.

Achoja and Debare both shrugged. "Probably doesn't even have a name," Debare said.

Annie thought he might be right. It was a stretch to even call it a village. The place had no more than two dozen buildings, mostly tin-roofed homes of mud, clay, and straw.

Achoja slowed as they approached. "Miss Annie," he said, "do you want us to come? You know. For in case of trouble?"

Annie had to use serious restraint not to laugh. She knew the man was making a sincere gesture. Instead she reached forward and flicked her wrist, and a dagger with a gleaming six-inch blade appeared in her hand. Just as quickly, it vanished again within her long-sleeved shirt.

"I think I can manage," she said. "I'll call out if I need help."

They stopped about fifty yards from the first building, and Annie walked from there.

The village smelled of manure and burning peat—a sour, earthy smell that reminded her of the last time she'd travelled to rural Ireland. A few women sat on stools in front of their homes, tending clay pots resting on small dung fires. Nearby a teen boy was pumping furiously on a long metal pole attached to the head of a well; water trickled from the spigot into a bucket.

Annie walked right up to the nearest woman. She looked older, late fifties, and tended her fire by adding what looked like dried cow patties to the embers. Annie now knew where the peat-like smell was coming from. Honestly, it wasn't nearly as bad as she'd have expected.

Before Annie could say a word, a little girl, maybe four years old, skipped excitedly out of the doorway. "Bibi!" she shouted, staring at Annie with wide eyes.

"Hello, do you speak Yoruba?" Annie asked in Yoruba, one of the dominant local languages that she had a passable fluency with. She couldn't speak it like a native, but then again many native Nigerians couldn't either.

The girl ducked her head and crawled onto the older woman's lap.

"Yoruba?" Annie tried again, now facing the woman.

The woman shook her head.

"Hausa?" Annie only knew a few words in that language.

The old woman clucked her tongue and stirred the contents of her pot with a wooden stick. After a few vigorous stirs, she looked up at Annie and said with a mild British accent, "Young woman, do you speak English?"

Annie laughed. "English. Yes, English is perfect. I'm sorry, I didn't—"

"No you didn't. Just because I live in a rural home, I can't be educated? Is that what you thought? I will have you know that I was educated at Oxford. I came back home to help my ailing mother, and have been here ever since. But *you* sound American." She said that as if being American was a distasteful thing. "What are you doing here?"

Annie sat on her heels and did her best to put on a friendly smile. She liked this woman; she was taking no crap from anyone. "I'm looking for some people who passed through here recently."

"*Oyinbos* or the army men?"

A chill raced up Annie's back. "You've seen both?"

The woman nudged the girl off her lap. "Chinara, go inside. I'll call you when the fufu is ready."

The shy girl avoided eye contact with Annie as she went inside, closing the sheet metal door behind her.

Only then did the woman continue. "Listen bloody well to me when I say this. This small place doesn't need trouble. First there's a plane crash." She pointed up at the sky. "The thing flew past us, its engines choking and sounding like a wheezing old buzzard. And then a dozen or more *oyinbos* come driving through here, nearly running over my granddaughter in the process. And then the real trouble came. I don't need *more* trouble from some American with questions."

Annie pulled a fifty-dollar bill from her pocket and held it out. "I understand your reluctance. This is for anything you can tell me about what you saw. You won't see me again, I promise."

The woman stared at the offered bill for nearly ten seconds before taking it. "What do you want to know?"

"Tell me about the people who came. What kind of trucks they had, the direction they went. And you mentioned trouble… what kind of trouble? From the army?"

The woman tucked the money inside her colorful blouse, then leaned forward and spoke in a hushed whisper. "The *oyinbos* came in two vehicles. One vehicle was smaller, like what you came in." She pointed at the jeep in the distance. "The other was a covered lorry, a truck to you Americans. There were more *oyinbos* in the back." She pointed to the east. "They were heading that way."

"Was there anything else in the truck?"

The woman shrugged. "Maybe some boxes. Maybe not. I can't be sure. That was a few days ago. Then the army men came."

"How soon after?"

"A few hours, maybe."

97

"Nigerian army? Or warlord?"

"Is there a difference? None wore a uniform or gave ID, if that's what you're asking. They asked about the *oyinbos* and were gone."

"Anything else?"

"No. This is a quiet place." The woman pointed to the northeast. "Most of mine are tending the cattle and farms. We're a simple people. We don't need others intruding."

"I completely understand. Thank you for speaking to me. I'm sorry to have taken your time." Giving the woman a respectful nod, Annie turned and walked back toward the jeep. But she paused while still out of earshot, and dialed up home base.

"Annie, what's up?" It was Thompson on the line.

"Where's Brice?"

"He's running down the intel on the plane, as well as the A-team that nobody wants to admit was sent to retrieve Little Eagle. What have you got?"

"I've tracked the A-team to my position. I got some intel from a local. Sounds like the crew had two vehicles stashed somewhere, one of them was a covered transport of some kind. They were heading east, but hot on their trail were some folks who were looking for them. Could be Nigerian regulars or one of the warlords' men."

"You still have Ntabo's resources with you?"

"I do."

"Good. For now, keep on the trail, but don't do anything stupid like get yourself dead, you hear me?"

"I hear you loud and clear."

"And Annie, I know it's not normally your gig, this whole

saving lives thing. But I have a feeling that before this is over, the Black Widow is going to get a chance to do what she does best."

Annie flicked her wrist, producing the dagger, then made it vanish just as quickly. "Roger that," she said. "We can only hope."

"Cabin crew, please take your seats for landing."

The airplane banked as it descended, and Connor's ears popped. He always hated this part of the flight.

The Outfit had been remarkably efficient about getting him out of the African bush and onto a plane. After being flown into Lagos on a puddle jumper, he flew directly to Ankara. From Turkey's capital he caught this connecting flight, and had somehow managed to sleep most of the way here. Now he looked out the window as the lights of the runway loomed closer. Soon he was gripping both of his armrests tightly as they landed a bit too heavily on the wet runway. For a second he could have sworn the plane had bounced and begun skidding sideways, but the aircraft quickly settled, and a woman's voice spoke calmly over the speaker. At first it was all in German, but then she repeated her message in English.

"Ladies and gentlemen, welcome to Zurich Airport. The local time is seven fifteen p.m., and the temperature is nine degrees. For your safety and comfort, please remain seated with your seat belt fastened until the captain turns off the Fasten Seat Belt sign. This will indicate that we have parked at the gate and that it is safe for you to move about."

Connor let out the breath that he'd been holding, and waited patiently until he and the others were allowed to disembark.

When at last he set foot on Swiss soil, he found the airport to be bright, air-conditioned, and immaculate—a far cry from what he'd experienced in Africa. Connor breezed through customs—the Swiss were known for their efficiency—and walked outside to see a man holding a sign with his name on it. The man was built like a linebacker and had the cauliflower ears of a wrestler.

"Are you Luca?" Connor asked.

In response, the man held out a silver coin between his thumb and forefinger. One of the Outfit's identification coins.

Connor squeezed the exposed end of the coin between his own thumb and forefinger, and the LED on the coin lit up.

Luca tilted his head toward the exit. "Follow me."

Luca insisted that Connor sit in the back of the big Mercedes sedan, and the moment he felt the comfort of the plush leather seats, he was overwhelmed with the desire to take a nap. He had slept on the plane, but this here was real comfort.

Unlike the craziness in Lagos, the traffic here was fairly relaxed. Luca weaved leisurely down a street called Butzenbüel-ring, then turned onto a highway called A51.

"How long will it take to get to Mason?" Connor asked.

"Maybe thirty minutes," Luca said. His German accent was strong.

Night was falling as they entered a part of town that looked a bit rough around the edges. Along a street called Langstrasse the sidewalks were occupied by homeless people, prostitutes, the occasional roaming gang of street toughs… This was not the kind of place Connor would have expected to meet his boss.

And then it began to rain, sending many but not all of the sidewalk-dwellers scurrying.

"We're getting close to the night club," Luca said.

"A night club?"

The driver cracked a smile, the first sign of any emotion from the guy, but said nothing.

They stopped in front of a plain-looking building where two men stood on either side of a set of double doors, protected from the elements by a red awning. Techno music hummed from somewhere inside.

Luca didn't say a word, so Connor grabbed his duffel and stepped out of the car. The minute he closed the door behind him, Luca pulled out into traffic and vanished.

Connor stepped up to the two bouncers. "I'm supposed to meet someone here," he said.

"I'll need to see some ID, Mr. Sloane," said one. His voice was so gravelly it sounded like rocks rubbing against each other.

Connor wondered how the man knew his name, but he pulled out his passport and flipped it open to the page with his picture.

The man shook his head. "Not that kind of ID, sir."

It took only a second before it clicked in Connor's head. He dug the coin out of his pocket and held it out. The bouncer grabbed the other side of the coin, and the LED lit up.

The two men stepped aside and motioned for Connor to enter.

As Connor opened the door, he braced himself for an auditory onslaught. But despite the sound of techno music coming through the door, the inside of the building was utterly silent. And when he shut the door behind him, he heard only the muted sound of the music—coming from *outside*.

Or, apparently, from the door itself.

The whole thing was a ruse.

He stood inside a wood-paneled lobby, fresh with the scent of wood polish and pipe tobacco. A reception desk stood across the room, manned by a tall, thin, white-haired gentleman.

"Mr. Sloane, I was told to expect you tonight." The man spoke with a light German accent. "ID, please."

This time Connor knew what to do. He held out the coin, and when the attendant grabbed the other side, the coin began glowing.

"Very well, sir. It's very good to meet you. I'm Mr. Gruber, the proprietor of this establishment."

Connor looked around. "I'm sorry, Mr. Gruber, but what is this place?"

"That's a simple question with a complicated answer. This establishment meets the needs of those who seek its assistance. And I believe you are here with such a need."

"Actually, I'm here to meet with Mr. Mason."

Gruber motioned toward a hall on Connor's left. "Ah, yes. Director Mason left me with some instructions to exercise on his behalf. Please, follow me."

The hallway was lit by old-fashioned sconces with lightbulbs that flickered as if they were aflame. At the end of the hall a door stood slightly ajar.

"Sir, this is our quartermaster's section," Gruber said. "When you arrived, it was this wing that was unlocked." He stopped before the door, stepped to one side, and motioned grandly. "After you."

Connor pushed the door open, and was surprised by how slowly it moved. It was six inches thick and must have weighed many hundreds of pounds, but its hinges were well-oiled, as it moved soundlessly. He stepped through, and lights flickered on, revealing a room filled with largely unmarked lockers. But he didn't see any way of opening them.

Mr. Gruber motioned to a pole in the center of the room. At about eye level was a visor, like one might see on a submarine's periscope. "If you will, Mr. Sloane, please peer into the biometric scanner."

Connor put his eyes against the visor. A green light flickered, and a series of clicks followed. He stepped back and looked around. Several of the lockers had popped open.

"Let's start with this side of the room, shall we, sir?" said Gruber, gesturing.

He paused, looked at the well-dressed man and then panned his gaze across the rest of the room. This all felt like he was in some secret lair in a James Bond film. Between the headquarters and this place, the Outfit certainly had a flair for the dramatic.

Connor's curiosity was undeniable as he looked into the first open locker. Inside was a change of clothes, including a suit jacket and tie, and beneath was a black diplomatic US passport. He opened the passport and saw his face smiling back. "Interesting."

"It's a standard precaution for our agents in the European theater," said Gruber. "You can leave behind your old passport. It isn't needed. Also, please change into these clothes. They should fit you properly."

Connor turned to face the man. With his almost-white hair and the wrinkles around his eyes, he had to be in his late sixties at least—but his voice was strong, he had perfect posture, and he gave off a youthful energy.

"How long have you been doing this?" Connor asked.

"This, sir? What do you mean?"

"Walking people through whatever it is I'm doing."

"You mean prepping for a mission?"

"Is that what this is?"

"Of course. And as to how long I've been doing this..." Gruber pressed his lips tightly together and hummed. "I suppose this would be my fourth decade. Yes, just about forty years."

Connor's eyes widened. "I guess I'm in good hands."

"Most certainly, sir."

"You can call me Connor."

"That's very kind of you, sir, but I think after forty years, I'd be more likely to spontaneously combust than to fall out of protocol."

Connor laughed. "Should I change right now?"

"I think that would be for the best." Gruber motioned toward a table next to the biometric scanner. "Please keep your assigned glasses and your Outfit-assigned ID, since they are keyed to your biometric signature. The rest you can leave behind."

As Connor changed outfits, he noticed that there was a label on the inside of each article of new clothing, featuring the all-seeing-eye logo and his name. When he was done, Gruber motioned toward the next locker.

"Shall we continue, sir?"

Inside this locker was a thinly padded vest. Connor removed his suit jacket and shrugged into the vest. "Kevlar?"

"It serves the same purpose as what you wore in the military, I am sure. However," said Gruber, smiling, "I think you'll find the vest to be much more effective and concealable."

Connor adjusted the straps and put his suit jacket back on. "I don't know how effective it would be in comparison. Back in the day, I wore a battle vest with SAPIs and ESBIs—small-arms protective inserts and enhanced side ballistic inserts—and I certainly wouldn't think about wearing a suit over them."

"Yes, well... the Outfit provides its agents with the best of what's available. The military has different priorities on some things."

The third and last open locker held a Glock 19 with a shoulder holster. It was a nine-millimeter pistol with a fifteen-round magazine, and it already had a round in the chamber. The locker also contained a wallet, already stocked with some euros and an American Express card.

"Mr. Sloane, I should inform you that the gun laws are different in the EU. I'd recommend that you keep your weapon concealed. I'm not privy to your mission's parameters, but if at any point you have trouble, you're instructed to use your diplomatic credentials as a way of ensuring that any actions against you are delayed. You are not officially a diplomat, but we can work out any complications if they arise."

"Roger that, don't wave the gun around," Connor said. "Okay. What's next?"

"Follow me, sir."

Gruber led him back down the same hall through which they'd entered, but instead of leading to the lobby, it took them to a set of stairs going down. Connor was certain that the lobby had been here. It was a straight hall—no way could he have gotten turned around.

"Hold up. Where's the lobby?" Connor asked.

Mr. Gruber simply motioned toward the stairs. "Sir, the train is waiting for you."

"Train?"

As Connor spoke, he heard a click behind him and turned back—only to find himself facing a blank wall.

"Wait a cotton-picking minute," he said. "Where the hell's the hallway? Where's the locker room?" He spun around. "Where's Gruber?"

The white-haired man was gone.

"What the hell is going on?"

Connor's mind raced as he pushed against a seemingly solid wood panel. Were the hallways on some kind of casters and moved silently while his back was turned? This entire building had suddenly taken on a haunted house vibe.

Whatever was going on, at this point Connor had nowhere to go but down.

He descended the stairs. They led to a tiny train platform, no more than ten feet wide, where a sleek railway car was already waiting, its doors open. Once again, Connor had no choice but to board.

The doors slid closed behind him, and a disembodied voice announced, *"The train will be departing in ten seconds. Please hold on to a rail or you will likely be thrown backward. This is your only warning."*

"Lovely." Connor took a seat and gripped one of the poles.

"Five seconds. Four. Three. Two. One."

Connor slid backward as the train accelerated at a rate rivaling that of a race car. Within seconds, wind was keening loudly outside as the train flew through the darkness.

Given the train's obvious speed, Connor expected to arrive at his destination quickly. And yet the minutes passed, and all he saw was darkness. He checked his watch repeatedly. Thirty minutes. Forty. An hour.

How long is this tunnel?

Just over two hours passed before the sounds indicated the train was decelerating, and the disembodied voice returned. *"We will be arriving at the Dresden Safe House in approximately five minutes. Please disembark only after the train has come to a complete stop."*

Dresden? That was deep into Germany, just on the border of Czechoslovakia. *Four hundred miles* from where he'd started.

He did the math in his head and supposed it could be possible —*if* the Outfit had an underground train, straight across Europe, dedicated to its own personal use, that rivaled the speed of Japan's bullet train.

Evidently, they did.

When the doors opened, Connor stepped out. An elderly man waited on the platform, and greeted Connor with a salute.

"Mr. Sloane," he said with a thick German accent, "can I please see your ID?"

After Connor went through the process of mutual identification using the coin, the old man gestured to the stairs behind him.

"Welcome to Dresden, Mr. Sloane. Herr Director Mason is waiting for you."

"Good to see you, Connor," Mason said as he shook Connor's hand. "I hope the reroute didn't spook you—things came up while you were en route and I had to switch some stuff around."

"Not so much spooked as impressed," Connor said. "You've got your own private bullet train."

"Actually these tracks, which the Outfit had recently upgraded, are the oldest underground train tracks in the world." Mason shrugged. "Getting from place to place quickly and in an unseen manner is particularly useful in some parts of the world. Anyway, we have a lot to cover, so let's get down to business."

He led Connor to an ordinary conference room, and once they were both seated, he launched right into it.

"We ran the tail number from the crashed plane that you and Miss Brown provided. It's attached to a CIA asset that, eight days ago, was sent to take control of some critical items that had been smuggled out of Pakistan. Are you familiar with the PNCA?"

Connor shook his head.

"The Pakistan National Command Authority. They have command and control over Pakistan's nuclear arsenal. And last month, a dozen of their members were arrested and then executed—in a very hush-hush operation."

"But not so hush-hush that we didn't find out."

Mason nodded. "We may have been caught flat-footed with this Little Eagle debacle, but we have our ears to the ground in most places where it counts. These twelve members had been radicalized by a local jihadist tribal leader, and they cooperated in breaching the security for one of the depots that contain nuclear assets. Pakistani security forces didn't discover the breach until two thirty-five-kiloton nuclear weapons turned up unaccounted for."

Connor groaned. He'd had enough of missing nukes.

Mason continued. "Our friends in the CIA identified the cargo plane that was supposed to take the nukes out of the country, and they quickly set up an interagency strike team to take control of that plane. Embedded with them was the president's brother, who we presume was there to help with the weapons if required. Thankfully, they succeeded in their mission. They transferred the nukes to their own plane, and filed a flight plan that would have taken them to Lagos and then to the US. That was when things didn't quite work out the way they'd planned."

Connor frowned. "Obviously. And who were the people in those pictures I saw?"

"Once the shit hit the fan about the crash, the Pentagon dispatched a Delta unit on a rescue mission to bring back Little Eagle. We haven't heard anything since those guys hit the ground. But that's currently Miss Brown's problem. I've got something else for you."

Mason took out his phone, put his thumb on the fingerprint scanner, tapped a few times, then turned the screen so Connor could see it. "This was mailed to the White House and addressed to the president of the United States."

His phone showed a scanned image of a printed letter.

This is for you, mon ami.
Don't start giving speeches; you may live to regret it.

Lewis Payne

"Okay," Connor said slowly. "And why are you dealing with this? This is an election year—you can expect crazy people to be coming out of the woodwork. Shouldn't the Secret Service handle this?"

"Normally, yes," said Mason. "And in fact they are. But this is not just some crazy. Included with the letter was a shell casing. Forensics showed that it's a match for the bullet that killed a mayor in Italy. We assume that the sender is the person who killed that mayor."

"And since they've already proven they're capable of killing…"

"Exactly. We view this as a serious threat. I need you to help track down the identity of the sender. Brice is already doing research on the name, though we suspect that's a fake. There were no prints on the casing or the letter, and the only prints on the envelope belong to a postal worker and some high school kid in Germany. What we want is visual identification, and we think the German police can help with that. They have extensive video surveillance on the streets. Unfortunately, Brice hasn't been able to hack in. That's where you come in."

He slid a billfold across the table. "These are FBI credentials in your name, and a business card for a chief inspector in Berlin who's expecting your arrival. You'll need to convince him to give you access to their video footage—and then try to find an image of the sender."

Connor pulled open his suit jacket, exposing his holstered weapon. "Does the FBI have clearance to carry here?"

Mason shook his head. "The Germans are real bastards about folks carrying, even foreign law enforcement. I'll arrange for one of our guys to drive you, so when you go into the police department, just leave your weapon with the driver."

"Roger that. When do I start?"

"I'd say immediately, but the chief inspector won't be in his office until the morning. So for now I'll take you to one of the guest rooms where you can rest up. You've got a long day tomorrow."

CHAPTER EIGHT

Connor focused on the road as Karl, one of Mason's local agents, chatted non-stop about everything from food to politics and the damned traffic. From the moment Connor had climbed into the passenger seat, the man hadn't stopped talking. After a while, he caught the pattern sufficiently to be able to respond with a "yup" or "nice" and turned the driver's voice into a droning backdrop of white noise as they crossed into Berlin.

Berlin was a modern city that didn't look at all like the Bavarian city he'd imagined. For the most part it felt like he was in any big city from the Midwest, complete with plenty of neon and high-rises, but every once in a while he'd catch sight of something that reminded him he was definitely in a foreign country.

Karl eventually slowed as they approached a glass-covered building, big enough to be an airplane hangar, that spanned the roadway. "This is our destination," he said. "The Berlin Central Station." He reached a hand back. "This would be a good time to leave anything behind you don't want to be seen with."

Connor had already removed the Glock from the shoulder holster. With his palm covering the bulk of the gun, he dropped it into Karl's hand.

Karl pocketed it. "You have my number. I'll be waiting nearby."

He pulled up against the curb inside the building, and Connor hopped out. He couldn't help but feel a bit lost in this strange cross between an airport, a train station, and a mall.

He turned to a woman passing by. *"Bundespolizei?"* he asked.

She pointed and continued walking.

With his contact's business card in hand, Connor followed the direction she'd indicated. He got lost again—there wasn't much in the way of English signage—but eventually found his destination, and walked through the glass doors.

The station's reception area featured a large transparent pane that separated him from the attractive policewoman at the front desk. She gave him a bright smile and greeted him in German.

"Sprechen sie English?" Connor asked. He could converse very little in German, other than to order a beer and ask where the bathroom was.

"Yes, can I help you?"

Connor pulled out the business card Mason had given him and showed it to her. "I'm supposed to meet Deputy Director Becker. I'm here on an official assignment from my headquarters." He flipped open his recently-acquired FBI credentials and showed them through the clear barrier.

The woman scribbled something on a piece of paper. "Herr Sloane, I'm afraid that *Leitender Polizeidirector* Becker hasn't arrived yet this morning." She motioned to some chairs in the waiting area. "Can you please—"

Another voice spoke. "Special Agent in Charge Sloane?"

Connor turned to see that a tall uniformed officer had entered the reception area. "Yes, I'm Agent Sloane."

The man shook Connor's hand. "I'm *Polizeidirector* Becker. My division chief informed me that I'm to give you access to our video logs and a patrolman."

Mason had given Connor the impression that getting this access would require some convincing, but he certainly wasn't disappointed to have it offered up straight off the bat, and with a quick nod, he followed the officer into the back of the police station.

"Unfortunately I have some security details I need to oversee today, so I'll be leaving you with Inspector Elias Schmidt," Becker said as they walked. "He's the head of the local gathering unit and will help you to get any information you need." He handed Connor a business card. "On the back of that is my cell phone number. If there's anything else you need, call me and I'll make sure it gets taken care of."

They stopped in front of a door with the word *Videoaufzeich-nungslabor* stenciled on it, and Becker knocked. A long beep sounded, and the door opened to reveal an officer wearing coke-bottle glasses. His eyes widened at the sight of the deputy director, and the two men exchanged a few words in German. Finally Becker gave Connor another quick handshake and departed without further explanation.

Inspector Schmidt looked at Connor. *"Du sprichst nicht Deutsch?"*

Connor knew just enough to know he was being asked if he spoke German. *"Nein. Mein Deutsch ist very bad. Not gut."*

Schmidt grinned. *"Mein English ist not gut entweder."*

The man beckoned Connor into a room filled with monitors, cycling through hundreds of different video feeds. "Viele videos. Lots," Schmidt said. "Was needing you?"

Connor was beginning to wonder if Becker hadn't intended to be very helpful after all. Without a translator, it would be nearly impossible to communicate what he needed to see. But then he spied a terminal sitting at the Google search screen, and he got an idea.

Between Google Translate and text-to-voice, he had all the translation he needed.

Before long, Schmidt had shown Connor how to use the controls to review recorded footage. The man was extremely helpful, and even apologized for the lack of an English-speaking officer. *"We are short-staffed today,"* he explained through Google Translate. *"The chancellor is giving a speech nearby and extra security has been called for."*

When he had Connor set up with the video surveillance of the post office from which the assassination threat had been sent, he went back to doing his own work at another terminal in the next room over, leaving Connor to do his own video search.

Connor twisted a knob, and the surveillance footage moved quickly through the minutes and hours of the day that the letter was postmarked. There was no doubt this was the right place. Brice had provided Connor with the faces of the two people whose fingerprints were found on the envelope—one was a blond-haired fifteen-year-old, and the other was the thirty-year-old postal clerk—and the clerk in question was indeed behind the counter at this post office.

Now he just had to look for the teenager.

Connor moved through the video at 5x speed. When a customer came in, he slowed it down. Unfortunately, some of the customers that came in were wearing hoodies, making it almost impossible to tell what their faces looked like due to the camera angle and the shadows. And the faces he could make out weren't his teenager. When he reached the end of the day with no ID, he rewound to the beginning and paid more attention to the customers whose faces were covered.

The first customer with a hoodie was mailing a large box. Connor knew his suspect mailed an envelope, not a package, but he wrote down the timecode anyway before continuing his search, scrolling through the video more slowly now to be sure he didn't miss anything.

The next hoodie guy had an envelope in his hand. He was tall and lanky, but that was about all Connor could make out. The customer dropped off the envelope, filled out some paperwork, and exchanged money with the clerk, then walked out the door.

Connor froze the video and switched to the next camera feed that Schmidt had shown him. This camera was mounted just outside the post office, with a full view of the building's entrance. He turned the knob to advance to the same timecode, and sure enough, there was his guy, coming out the door. Connor watched at normal speed as the suspect walked past.

Connor had to rotate through a few more street-level cameras to track the suspect as he walked to a parked Volkswagen, got in on the driver's side, and drove away.

Connor called to Schmidt, who was still in the next room over, monitoring traffic feeds. "How old do you need to be to drive in Germany?"

"*Achtzehn.* Eighteen."

Connor scratched this suspect off the list. The kid he was looking for was fifteen. This wasn't his suspect.

Again he returned to the first feed, moving carefully through the day. But the process was taking forever, and as he stared at the screen, getting a headache, an idea popped into his head.

He tapped on his smart-lens and muttered, "Brice."

It took a few seconds before he heard the first ring, and then Brice came on the line. *"What's up?"*

"I'm going through video footage of the German post office where that letter was sent, and it's kind of a slog. Do you by chance have a specific time for me when the letter got logged into their system?"

"Hold on—let me see if that's something I can get access to."

Connor continued to watch the video as he waited, and had marked down the timecode for Hoodie Guy #3 before Brice came back on the line.

"You're in luck, I managed to get in pretty easily. The payment was logged just before six."

"Thanks. That's a big help."

Connor disconnected, fast-forwarded to five o'clock just to be sure he didn't pass anything, and started watching from there. Sure enough, at about five minutes to six, two customers walked in, both wearing hoodies. The taller of the two was holding an envelope. He dropped off the letter, paid, and got a receipt. Then both guys left.

Again swapping between feeds as needed, Connor followed them out of the building and down the street. They didn't go to a car; instead they crossed the street into a grassy park and stopped beneath a tree. Connor zoomed in, and saw the taller of the two hand a slip of paper to someone who must have been waiting on the other side of the trunk.

His heart racing, Connor looked for a video feed that could give him a different angle. He found nothing. Somehow this guy had picked one of the few spots in the area that was completely without direct video coverage.

Resuming the earlier video, he watched the two teens walk away. Connor didn't track them; he just kept watching the same feed, staring at the tree.

"Come on, you bastard. Walk somewhere so I can see who you are."

As he watched, people came and went, but no one stepped out from behind the tree. The sun was going down, and soon it was too dark for him to see a thing.

Cursing under his breath, he again used his smart-lens to call

Brice. "Brice, I need more of that technology magic of yours."
He explained the situation, then gave Brice the GPS coordinates
of the tree and the local time. "Clearly the guy knew exactly
where the cameras were located, and chose the end of the day to
do the exchange so that he wouldn't have to wait long before he
could escape under cover of darkness."

*"Well, my grandfather always told me to assume everyone is
at least as smart as you,"* Brice said. *"Even criminals, unfortunately. I'll see what I can come up with, but this might take a
while."*

"Roger that."

Connor rose from his seat and walked to the doorway of the
adjacent lab where Schmidt was working. He almost ran into the
officer, who was apparently coming to see him.

Using his smartphone, Connor pulled up Google Translate
and tapped out a message. "Can I get your help with something?"
The phone spoke his message in German.

Schmidt typed into his own phone, and after a moment the
phone spoke: *"I've just been called out onto the street while the
chancellor is giving her speech. Come with me and get some
fresh air? Then I can help."*

Connor nodded, and followed Schmidt down the hall. His
muscles were sore from being hunched over a terminal for hours,
but it was worth it—he was now just a tree's width from identi-
fying a would-be assassin.

All he needed now was some caffeine.

Nobody questioned him as he got off the bus with the union members, crossed Daimlerstrasse, the road named after the company, and walked through the security gates. He'd done his research, and he'd insinuated himself into a group of German metalworkers being bused into one of the Daimler assembly locations for a rally. Political rallies were full of distractions. Exactly what he needed.

Today would be a bit more complicated than the Italian job. More moving parts. But as he looked across the street and spotted his handiwork, he smiled.

This was going to work just fine.

A long string of buses continued offloading union members in front of building 25 of the Daimler plant, but he was already walking away from the crowd, his guitar case slung over his shoulder.

The speeches would start in thirty minutes. Plenty of time.

From his overwatch position, he panned his gaze across the crowd gathered in the open area outside of building 25. The organizers for the event were very efficient, like most Germans. In just the last thirty minutes, they'd managed to assemble a platform for the chancellor to speak from, cordoned off zones for the various groups of attendees, which had to number nearly a thousand, and had camera crews stationed strategically to capture the rally from various angles.

None of those cameras were pointed in his direction.

A long Mercedes sedan pulled through the gate and drove up to the speaker's platform. The crowd began applauding. The federal police, who were everywhere, mixed in with the crowd, watched over the German chancellor as he stepped out of his vehicle.

The chancellor waved as he energetically hopped up the stairs to the dais. He put both of his hands on the top of the podium, and the screens behind him displayed the larger-than-life image of the German leader in all his smiling glory. Like all politicians, he spent a few long seconds preening in front of the crowd, allowing the cameras and raised cell phones to capture this moment.

Lying prone on the rooftop of the building just opposite, and peering through a scope, he paid careful attention to the plain-clothed men who were standing on the corners of the dais, out of view of the cameras. Their gazes panned across the crowd, looking for threats... looking for anything out of the ordinary. One of them had the barrel of what looked like a submachine gun peeking out from the bottom of his suit coat. Definitely not cops. Likely this country's version of the Secret Service.

"You guys suck," he muttered under his breath.

He dug into his pocket and pulled out a small metal box that he'd assembled himself. It was a simple thing with a digital readout and a toggle switch. He'd used just such remote arming mechanisms in previous jobs and when he was in the military. The army sometimes didn't approve of his tactics, but he was effective. That's all that mattered.

He flipped the switch. A cell phone symbol blinked several

times on the LED display, and was then replaced by a checkmark.

Everything was a go.

He glanced at the tree across the street and then back to his device. It was already counting down from thirty. Peering once again through the scope, he placed the buttstock firmly against his shoulder and rested his finger on the trigger.

Down below, the chancellor had begun speaking into the microphone, the loudspeakers broadcasting his words with enough volume that the politician would be heard well past the gates of the plant.

He took a deep breath and began measuring his heartbeats. This time, things would be a little different. He needed to time the landing of his shot with the unveiling of his little surprise outside the plant.

Ten seconds.

Up on the flagpole, the German flag flapped in the breeze. It hadn't been there when he'd scouted the site earlier, but it helped confirm the wind direction near the podium. He placed the crosshairs on the chancellor's forehead and shifted ever so slightly to the right, compensating for the wind.

Three seconds.

Feeling the pulse of his heartbeat, he felt almost as if time had slowed.

Two seconds.

Each beat of his heart pushed blood through his body, imparting a slight wobble to his aim. His focus was so acute, the sound of his blood rushing through his system was almost deafening, even with the loudspeakers blaring.

He waited for the pause between heartbeats, when his aim would recover from the momentary wobble.

One second.

A blindingly bright explosion erupted just outside the plant. The chancellor's head swiveled in that direction—

Damn it! It went off too early!

He squeezed the trigger.

The rifle bucked against his shoulder.

Chaos erupted as fragments of the tree rained over the crowd and the dais was cleared, except for one body.

One of the guards.

The chancellor was now surrounded by a wall of clear ballistic shields and was being rushed to his car.

With a blur of practiced movement, he disassembled his weapon, packed it, and raced down the stairs and into the building's empty assembly lines. Everyone else was out front, in a panic. As he jogged across the building, his mind raced. It was a faulty timer. No doubt about it. In this business, tenths of a second meant everything.

It would have worked if it wasn't for that split-second screw-up.

He slammed his booted foot on the exit door's push bar, exited the building, and fast-walked to the perimeter fence.

What a total screw-up that was.

His face burned with anger as he stepped through the flap of pre-cut security fencing, wedged a note into one of the cut seams, and walked away from the chaos.

Next time, he wouldn't let budget electronics get in the way of a job done right.

Connor stood at the corner of Titlisweg and Daimlerstrasse, munching on a bagel as Schmidt and the other officers routed traffic away from the factory where the German chancellor was giving his speech. There had to be at least two dozen uniformed police lining the street, expecting the unexpected. He'd never been on a security detail for a VIP, but this level of security seemed excessive considering it was the middle of the day, the traffic was light, and the chancellor was giving a speech from within the fenced perimeter of the Mercedes factory.

Connor was a few hundred feet from the entrance of the factory, but he could easily hear the chancellor's voice over the sound system. Of course, he couldn't understand a word the guy was saying, as it was in rapidly-spoken German, but the man's voice was warm and inviting. No matter the country or language, most politicians shared the gene for skill at public speaking.

Suddenly, a brilliant light flashed near the factory entrance, followed by the short, sharp, concise—and familiar—sound of high explosives.

He ducked low and yelled, "A bomb!"

The nearby uniformed officers stared slack-jawed for a moment. And then chaos erupted up and down the Daimler-strasse.

Mason sifted through the cabinets in the Outfit's break room, looking for something to eat. He hadn't left the office in thirty-six hours, and of course they had no food delivery service. The pickings were sparse, but ultimately he settled for a bag of chips.

"Fiery nacho cheese is a flavor?" he muttered. He opened the bag, tried one—and then threw the rest of the bag in the trash. What he needed wasn't artificially flavored snacks, but real food.

Thompson poked his head in. "Oh good, you're here."

"I'm here. What's up?" Mason said.

Thompson handed him a manila folder. "Hot off the press. Looks like someone tried to take out the German chancellor. I think we have a hitter loose out there."

"A professional?" Mason scanned the printouts, half of which were in German, and cursed himself for letting his German get rusty.

"Sure looks like it, though they screwed up all the same. The shooter set up a distraction—about a kilo of C4 with a remote detonator. Brice thinks the bomb didn't go off at the right time, which messed up the shot. The chancellor got lucky. But one of his guards was taken out."

"Or maybe the hitter is just a terrible shot, and not so professional after all," Mason said. "Why are you bringing this to me? Sure, they're a NATO ally, but…"

Thompson had just opened his mouth to speak when Mason's phone buzzed, and he held up a hand.

"One second." He put the phone to his ear. "Mason."

"It's Connor. I've got some data for you out of Germany."

"You don't say." Mason stared in Thompson's direction. "Okay, but Brice is coordinating—"

"Brice told me to call you directly with this."

"Hold on a second." Mason motioned for Thompson to

follow him, and they went to the nearest conference room, where Mason put the call on speaker. "Okay, Connor. Shoot."

"Someone tried to take out the German chancellor."

Mason glanced at Thompson. "So we've heard."

"Well, I happened to be there when it happened, and I tracked the shooter to where he or she escaped through a previously cut section of security fencing. I found something there that Brice thought you should know about right away. On the cut security fencing was a note."

"What did it say?"

"It was written in English, and to me it sounds American. I took a photo, and this is verbatim what it said: 'Dear Chancellor, I'm sorry I missed you today. Your support for the union cause totally pissed me off. You and I know that you're full of it, just like all political leaders. Speak the truth or the truth will extract its revenge.' And then a signature: George Azterodt.

"It looks like the hitter added the 'I'm sorry I missed you today.' part after he'd written the rest because it's squeezed in with tinier letters."

"That last name, can you spell it for me."

"A-z-t-e-r-o-d-t. Does that name ring a bell?"

Mason leaned back in his chair and rubbed his temples. "As a matter of fact, yes. It came up during our research on the sender of the note you're tracking. That one, as you know, was signed 'Lewis Payne.' Turns out Lewis Payne and George Azterodt were friends of John Wilkes Booth."

"The guy who assassinated Lincoln?"

"The very same. Wilkes assassinated Lincoln. Lewis Payne tried to assassinate the Secretary of State. And George Azterodt was recruited by Booth to assassinate the vice president. There was a lot more going on than just offing one man; they were looking to overthrow the entire government. Hold on one second." Mason pressed mute on his phone and turned to Thompson. "What do you think?"

Thompson's dour expression didn't give up much. "If the German hitter is the same hitter from Italy, then we need someone who can track human prey. I'd pick the Black Widow for that."

Mason shook his head. "She's busy, and besides… my Spidey senses are tingling about this guy. I'm thinking he's ex-military, probably a sniper, and I think he's got a hard-on for the president."

"Then why go after the chancellor? You're thinking that was a warmup?"

"Yes. And a professional hitter wouldn't be doing warmups. But it's likely he does have sniper training, and he obviously had access to a block of C4, which makes him current or former military. And that means Connor's the right guy for this."

Thompson's phone buzzed in his pocket, and he held up a finger. "Sorry, it's Brice." He answered. "Hey, I'm with the director right now."

He paused.

"Are you sure?"

A few more seconds passed, and he pocketed his phone.

"Brice wants me to relay to you that he retrieved the preliminary report out of the German forensics team's computer. The rifling marks on the bullet that hit the guard pointed to only a couple of possible rifles it could have come from. One of them is an MK13 sniper rifle."

"The same rifle used on the mayor in Italy."

Thompson nodded. "Yep."

Mason took the phone off of mute. "Connor, go back to the safe house and take the first flight back to the States. I want to see you here ASAP."

"Now? But I'm close to getting an ID on the sender."

"I'll have one of our guys debrief you at the safe house, and they'll continue the search. I need you here."

"May I ask what the assignment's going to be?" He sounded annoyed.

"The situation is evolving, but I think the hitter you're after is using political targets in Europe as practice for a bigger target. A domestic one. We think you're the best equipped to track this guy."

"Are you thinking the target is the president?"

"It's possible. That's why I need you to connect the dots quickly."

Connor blew out a breath. *"Roger that. I'll be wheels up as soon as I do the debrief and get a flight."*

As Mason hung up, Thompson spoke.

"Let me guess: you want me to arrange the flights and work with Brice on getting an ID on our shooter."

Mason nodded. "You read my mind. Also check up on the Black Widow. There's two nukes in play on that continent, and if the wrong things happen over there, a presidential assassination may seem insignificant in comparison."

Annie looked through the windshield at the emptiness of the African plains. Her smart-lenses highlighted the vehicle tracks on the dirt road, and she hoped they were catching up to their quarry. Since leaving the first village, they'd been on the road for nearly half a day, only stopping at the occasional collection of simple homes to ask about the vehicles they were following.

The people's stories didn't waver. One group of vehicles, manned by foreigners, had passed through, and some time later, another group of vehicles had raced through, manned by Enitan's men. From all indications, the warlord's soldiers were catching up to the foreigners.

"Slow down," Annie yelled over the road noise. The highlighted paths in her glasses had shifted direction.

She grabbed hold of the jeep's roll bar and stood to get a better view. Fifty yards ahead one set of tracks veered to the right. Another set continued forward for another fifty yards before also turning right. She pictured the lead vehicles taking evasive action and Enitan's men matching their moves.

"The tracks are going off to the right," she told Achoja. "Let's move slowly."

The tall driver squinted through the windshield as he turned the wheel. "You have very good eyes, Miss Annie."

Debare frowned. "Be careful—there's a dried-out riverbank somewhere ahead with a steep slope. I grew up near here," he explained.

It was obvious there had been a high-speed chase going on.

No smart-lenses were required to see the kicked-out mounds of dirt from a four-wheel drive losing traction.

After about ten minutes of slowly following the tracks, Achoja pointed. "There's trouble."

About a quarter mile away, vultures had gathered.

Annie grimaced. "Let's go see what we have."

As they approached, the winds shifted, and the smell of death wafted over the jeep.

"Achoja, stop. Let me go alone and take a look."

The driver stopped. "Miss Annie, you sure you no want—"

Annie shook her head, hopped out of the vehicle, and jogged to what looked like the scene of a crime. Most of the vultures fled as she approached, but a few merely hopped away and stared, unwilling to abandon their meal so easily.

Eight metal spikes had been set into the ground. And atop each spike was a head. Six were obviously Anglo, and the other two looked to be of African descent.

The corpses, half-eaten, were piled up nearby.

Annie kept her breath shallow, not because of the smell, which didn't particularly bother her, but because of the flies. She wasn't eager to breathe those things in.

She tapped on her glasses. "Brice."

It took about thirty seconds for the satellite link to complete, then his voice came over the line as he saw the gruesome scene through her glasses. *"Oh, damn. Have you ID'd them yet?"*

"No, just got on the scene." Annie walked closer to one of the heads and brushed away the flies. The eyes had sunken in, dried by the African sun, and the leathery lips had begun pulling back to reveal drying gums and teeth. A piece of metal was stuck inside the gaping mouth, and she reached out to retrieve it. It was a set of military-issue dog tags.

"Staff Sergeant Brandon Castillo," she read aloud.

"Damn it. He was one of the guys on the rescue mission."

Annie moved quickly to the other heads. She wasn't surprised to find a set of dog tags in each. She was immune to the emotions that other people normally felt about death and violence—she believed that things worked out for people according to their destiny—but she did have a sense of pride in a job well done. Her job today was rescue, and this wasn't looking good.

After showing the last set of dog tags to Brice through her glasses, she stepped back. "Doesn't seem like any of these are our guy."

"No."

Annie moved over to the headless corpses, all of which had been stripped naked. The vultures gathered here were more reluctant to depart. Annie kicked at one, and when it only barely hopped away, she pulled her handgun from its holster and shot the thing. The noise sent the other scavengers fleeing.

"Brice, I've got eight headless corpses. If you're saying none of them are our guy, then…"

"He's probably still out there. There were twelve people sent to rescue him."

"If you're going to kill eight, why not just kill the rest?"

"I don't know. Maybe use the others as leverage to squeeze information out of them. Anyway, taking out an A-team isn't something a couple villagers is going to do. Do you have any data on who it might be?"

"Yes. The villagers we've spoken to saw a group of Enitan's men going after our target."

"Damn, that's going to be a problem. Enitan is likely to eventually turn that entire country into a slaughterhouse. I hate the idea of you having to—"

"Brice, if you think I need to be protected from this shit, then I'm going to knock you on your ass when I get back."

"No, no, nothing like that. It's just, given this guy's reputation, I wouldn't expect him to take a hostage. I hate the idea of you risking your butt for a lost cause."

Annie turned and began jogging back to the jeep. "You can worry about my butt when I'm back home. In the meantime, I'll see what I can find out and get back to you."

"Annie…" Brice breathed deeply. "Be careful."

As she ended the call, Annie couldn't help but smile at the emotion she'd heard in his voice.

———

The outside of the building on H Street was dingy, not what anyone would expect of the headquarters for the Secret Service, but they had always been a low-profile organization. Mason sat across the table from Jim Murray, the head of the five-thousand-person agency, and he too exuded a sense of normality. Flashy wasn't in the man's DNA.

Jim, the head of the Secret Service, leaned forward and shook his head. "Doug, you're telling me there's an unidentified sniper killing European politicians, and he's coming to DC? And why is this coming from you, of all people?"

"Don't forget the shell casing," said Mason. "I know you guys probably have indigestion over that one."

"I don't know how you know about that shell casing, but what do you seriously think I can do? This is an election season. I just got a message not more than fifteen minutes ago that we're rounding up a travel team and warming up Marine One to take our guy to a previously unscheduled event. I had to throw an absolute fit just to get enough time for an advance team to do a quick once over of the location. It would take a whole hell of a lot more solid intel for me to get in the way of the president's political machine, and you know that."

Mason sighed. "I know. I'm working on getting more action-able intel, but I figured you need to know. There's a lot of crap being hidden from the wrong people, and I want to make sure that you're in the loop."

"And I appreciate it. I'll double up on the CS teams at the president's speaking venues; it's the only thing I can do." Jim scribbled something on a notepad, then paused and focused on Mason. "Our counter-sniper teams are the best there are, but you realize they've never once had to take that shot. We're really good at defusing a situation before it becomes one. I'd feel a lot better if we had an ID on our suspect. Any idea when you'll have that?"

"No ETA yet. But I'll let you know as soon as I do."

"Doug, level with me. I did some digging when you called me. Your ID still says CIA, and you're still on the roster. You're not *really* with them anymore, are you? I'd like to know the truth."

"The truth will set me free." Doug smiled at the second half of the unofficial motto of the CIA. "In the end, we're all on the same team."

He rose, shook Jim's hand, then turned and walked out of the office. There was another friend he needed to visit. If there was anyone in the world who could put together an ID from the disparate pieces of data they had, it would be Kevin Dowers.

CHAPTER NINE

Mason stood in the visitor's lobby of the J. Edgar Hoover Building in DC, his eyes darting back and forth impatiently between the turnstiles and the metal detectors. Had it been anyone else making him wait like this, he'd be annoyed, but Mason had known Kevin Dower for almost thirty years, since freshman year of college. Kevin had studied psychology and ultimately joined the FBI, while Mason pursued work in the intelligence field, but they'd always stayed in touch. Two very different personality types, but still close friends.

More importantly, Kevin was the best profiler the FBI had. He'd received just about every award there was for his lifetime's work in cracking cold cases that nobody thought were solvable. Right now, that was what Mason needed. He needed his Sherlock Holmes to tell him what he might be missing.

He was checking his watch for the umpteenth time when

Kevin walked in—a bald, thin man with thick-framed black glasses. Kevin spotted him and came right over.

Mason shook his hand. "Thanks for meeting with me on such short notice."

"Not a problem." Kevin hitched his thumb toward the entrance. "Let's go to Central and talk there. Post-pandemic they have some nice outside seating where we can talk with a bit of privacy."

They stepped outside and turned right on Pennsylvania Avenue. The café known as Central was only a block away. As they approached, one of the waiters recognized Kevin and called out to him with what sounded like an authentic French accent. "Monsieur Dower, I have your table."

Kevin pointed at the empty tables outside. "Can we get a table out here today, Francois? My friend and I need a bit of space."

"But of course."

The waiter walked them to the table farthest from the entrance, and in less than a minute they had ice water and had ordered some appetizers.

Mason nodded with approval. "Pretty efficient."

Kevin shrugged. "So what's this about?"

Mason scooted his chair closer to Kevin's and spoke in a low voice. "The details of this conversation cannot go beyond the two of us. We on the same page?"

Kevin frowned. "Don't make me regret this, Doug. But okay."

Mason quickly summarized everything he knew about the

assassination attempts that had occurred in Europe, the clues
pointing to DC, and the messages left by the would-be assassin.
As the tale unfolded, Kevin's brow furrowed. He was just about
to say something when the waiter arrived and set a plate full of
greenery in front of Kevin.

"For Monsieur Dower, a salad of frisée, crispy lardons of
bacon, and a poached egg."

The waiter then placed in front of Mason a plate of food that
was beautifully arranged.

"And for you, monsieur, we have a tuna carpaccio, with
cubed avocado and mango, accompanied by sourdough toast
points."

He held out a large pepper grinder. "Would either of you like
freshly ground pepper?"

They both declined, and the waiter wished them *bon appetit*
and left the table.

Kevin ignored his food and focused on Mason. "These
messages from the assassin. What did they say?"

Mason pulled out his phone and pulled up two images. First
was the note left for the chancellor:

Dear Chancellor,

*I'm sorry I missed you today. Your support for the union
cause totally pissed me off. You and I know that you're full of it,
just like all political leaders. Speak the truth or the truth will
extract its revenge.*

George Azterodt

. . .

Second was the letter to the president. "This is the one that came with the shell casing," Mason said.

This is for you, mon ami.
  Don't start giving speeches; you may live to regret it.
  Lewis Payne

"The word choices in the messages sound American," Kevin said. He tapped a finger on his chin, deep in thought. "Well, first let's dispense with the obvious. Our perp is almost certainly a male. I'd say mid-thirties to fifty."

"How would you know that?"

"Planning out a place to shoot someone from a distance—I assume the shot for the German chancellor was also at distance?"

"It was."

"Then you need to be prepared to have a location that has a visual advantage, meaning it's up high. To get up and down quickly isn't an old man's game. You need to be fairly spry and confident in your physical ability."

"And why do you think the perp is male?"

Kevin shrugged. "I'm not trying to be a chauvinist or anything, but nearly eighty percent of all homicides are committed by men. That's a worldwide figure, but the US doesn't stray much from that statistic."

Mason thought of the Black Widow. He had to suppress a grin.

"Also, this feels personal," Kevin added. "No hired contract killer would give you clues like this guy has. Why send a letter? And it being handwritten is just the height of stupidity—or it's sending a message. Hell, he's even telegraphing the punch with those names he used. If I'm not mistaken, both names were associated with the Lincoln assassination, right?"

"As always, your memory is like a steel trap."

Kevin shook his head. "He's doing everything other than putting up a billboard outside the White House gates saying, 'I want to kill the president.' And he's sent you proof that he's serious, via the shell casing. He wants his threat to be taken seriously. Again, there's something personal about that."

Mason made notes in his smartphone as Kevin's analysis rolled on.

"Hell, the more I think about it, the more I'm convinced. This guy knows the president. Why show your cards? Why not just take the president out? He's on the campaign trail, or will be, right?"

Mason nodded. "The Secret Service doesn't have enough to warrant putting his campaigning on hold, so yes, he's out there."

"This guy *wants* the president to know he's in danger. He wants the people around the president to know it as well. He's playing a game, and there's no advantage to playing this kind of game unless his goal is to get in his intended victim's head. I'll bet you that once you figure out who this guy is, it'll turn out that the president knows him as well. He's someone from our president's past."

"How can you say that with such certainty? Could just be some wacko. All presidents attract them."

Kevin shook his head. "Our guy took out two people in

Europe and telegraphed that he's coming for the president. A wacko doesn't do that. That's some serious commitment, and too organized for the mind of someone who's truly deranged. So he's not a wacko. Psychotic? Oh, most definitely. And with sniper training."

Mason nodded and continued taking notes. What Kevin was saying made sense, and wasn't too far from where his head was at.

"Sniper training can come from several places. The military, obviously, or the variety of private companies that train people for that sort of thing. Hell, there's probably quite a few long-range game hunters that could likely give our best snipers a run for their money. And with dry runs on another continent? That's a sense of planning and organization. I'll bet you our guy has a military background. If not military, maybe SWAT training. A former or maybe even current member of law enforcement."

Mason stayed silent, letting Kevin think out loud.

"So, what does that leave us with?" Kevin said. "A former soldier, he's done his twenty or left before that, so probably now in his forties. He's not active duty, because otherwise scheduling his cross-continent training might be a little problematic. Maybe he's in the reserves."

"Or a cop," Mason said.

"It's possible, but I'm still leaning military. At least seventy-thirty. And since I don't think he's crazy, that means he's got a motive—a deep-seated one that's almost certainly personal. Remember, he's telegraphing what he's doing. This guy is confident. Doesn't think he's going to get caught. And he's testing himself... that's what Europe was all about."

Mason nodded. Confidence was either foolish or well-earned. He prayed it wasn't the latter.

"The president is a former attorney," Kevin said. "I'd start with people in his law firm. People maybe even in college. I'd screen all of the people around him. And despite our assassin saying 'Don't start giving speeches,' he doesn't mean it. He knows the president is a sitting duck, and he's taunting him. He's pointing out the one thing the president can't really stop doing during a campaign season. Are you sure the Secret Service can't stop the president from campaigning? Maybe have him do it via a live feed or something?"

Mason shook his head. "He's a politician, Kevin. He's not going to voluntarily step away from the campaign trail. Even with a lunatic stalking him."

"No," Kevin said emphatically. "He's not a lunatic. This is a cold, rational, and serious killer. He's biding his time for the perfect shot. You need to get him before he can take that shot, Doug. Because if he pulls the trigger... he won't miss."

The computer brought up a feed of what had to be the one-hundredth suspect Connor had taken a look at over the past hour. But this man was no legitimate suspect. He was in his seventies, and wore thick corrective lenses. The only reason he'd come up on the search was because his name, Ed Booth, had matched one of the dozens of names Brice had come up with as possible aliases for the inbound assassin. Edwin Booth was the name of John Wilkes Booth's brother.

"Too old and he's got bad eyes," Mason said to Brice. "Per our teenage informants in Germany, our hitter is mid-thirties to fifties."

Brice tapped at his keyboard. "Let me narrow down the search a bit for age parameters."

After a moment, a new video feed popped up.

"Okay. Next," Brice said, "is Dave Herold. From Miami International."

Connor leaned in closer. He was the only person who'd seen the security camera footage of their suspect, and though that had provided only glimpses, with no clear facial features, it was enough to give him an impression of general body shape. Which ruled out Dave Herold.

"This guy's practically a string bean," Connor said. "I don't think so."

Brice again began typing, but before he could bring up another candidate, the door beeped and Mason walked in.

"Connor, I need you for something." He snapped his fingers at Brice. "And Marty, I'll need your help on this as well."

Brice looked up from his monitor. "I thought the top priority was tracking down Connor's assassin."

"It is," Mason said. "I've talked with some folks in the BPOL, the German Federal Police. They're going to spool some of their security tapes to a server that you'll be able to access to help with the search. But in the meantime, I want you and Connor to take a slightly different tack." He handed each of them a printed sheet. "That's the profile of our guy. Brice, I need you to work your magic and come up with a list of the president's past associates. Anyone who might hold a grudge and would fit the profile. Past enemies, people he's crossed, former clients, anyone who'd have a reason to be particularly annoyed with the president and meets the criteria."

Brice nodded. "On it."

Mason turned to Connor. "When Brice gets you that list, I need you to follow up on the targets. Our hitter is likely ex-military or law enforcement—your kind of people. Between the two of you, hopefully we can get our crosshairs on our guy quickly."

Brice was scanning the sheet of paper. "I don't know about that, sir. The president's a politician, and word on the street is that he can be a real ass if you get on his wrong side. The enemies list could be pretty long."

Connor looked at his own copy of the profile. "True, but we need someone who, and I quote, 'is holding a personal grudge that's significant enough for him to want to kill.' Politicians' enemies don't typically go nearly that far. That should help us narrow things down."

Mason eyed them both. "You two straight on this change of direction?"

Connor and Brice both nodded. "Yes, sir."

"Good. Stuff's gonna get ugly soon. Let's try to get ahead of it."

As Mason left the lab, Connor turned to Brice. "How long do you think it'll take to come up with a list?"

Brice looked up at the wall clock and groaned. It was approaching seven in the evening. "Long enough that you should go home and get some sleep. I'll have something for you by morning."

Connor hopped up from his chair and gave Brice a fist bump. "Good luck."

Brice sighed. "Go on. I've got digging to do."

CHAPTER TEN

Annie held tight to the jeep's roll bar, the wind rushing through her hair. They were about a dozen miles east of Biu, approaching yet another village that the convoy of trucks had passed through, another unnamed dot on the map in the middle of sub-Saharan Africa. But even places like this occasionally yielded unexpected treasures. In the last village they'd actually found a working gas pump with a full reservoir tank.

This village consisted of no more than a dozen ramshackle buildings, and probably didn't even warrant a dot on the map. The buildings seemed unoccupied, and there were no signs of activity, but the eerie silence made Annie feel a tickle at the base of her neck.

They drove slowly through the buildings, and her lenses highlighted not only the vehicle tracks, but also foot traffic. These mostly led to and from a central well with a manual pump.

The ground around it was still damp, and the footprints in the mud looked fresh. Which raised an obvious question.

"Where is everyone?"

Debare shrugged and pointed east "Maybe at the farms over there?"

Annie followed his finger, but saw only flat, desiccated land.

"It could be there was a sickness," Achoja volunteered. "Cholera. It happens sometimes." He sounded uncertain.

They continued eastward, following the vehicle tracks, and Annie patted Achoja's shoulder. "There's nothing here. Let's speed it up a bit. We need to catch up to them."

Debare turned in his seat, a deep furrow between his brows. "If we catch them, then what? We can't fight these people."

Annie smiled. "I have a plan."

Achoja stopped the vehicle next to two older men who were standing outside a small home. He shouted to them in Yoruba, "Hey, did a bunch of trucks go through here not long ago?"

The men looked at each other, then shrugged and said they'd seen nothing. By the looks on their faces, Annie didn't buy it for one second.

"Let me talk to them in private," she said.

Debare shifted his muscular bulk to turn and look at her. "Are you sure, Miss Annie?"

"I'm sure."

Annie hopped out of the jeep and motioned for Achoja to

drive forward a bit, which he did. Then she smiled at the two men.

"I'm looking for a friend," she said.

"You're an American?" said one of the men, switching from Yoruba to English.

"Yes, and my friend is also American. Are you sure no one has driven through?"

The men looked at each other, and the second man nodded, as if in telepathic agreement.

"It's hard to know who to trust these days," said the first man. "But I suppose an American is unlikely to be working for Enitan."

"Who?" Annie said, feigning cluelessness.

The man chuckled. "It's not important. Yes, many men drove through not long before you arrived. They had a white man with them. Would that be your friend?"

Annie nodded. "It could be."

"Then I am sorry. A bad man has your friend."

The other man spoke for the first time, in Yoruba. "Please don't go after him. Your friend is gone. If he lives, maybe you see him again. But someone as young as you... pretty girl. It would be bad." He nodded toward the jeep. "Your friends will not be able to help either. Too many bad men nowadays."

The first man nodded in agreement. "If you interfere, they will rape you, or worse. And your friends will be killed."

Annie smiled. "Elders, I appreciate your concern. But the white man is a brother to me. I must do what I can. Do you have any idea where they might have taken him?"

The two men shook their heads sadly, and the second man

spoke, again in Yoruba. "I urge you again not to go. It will end badly."

"I am going whether you help me or not," Annie said. "But it may go better if you tell me what to expect."

The man sighed. "Enitan has a camp about fifteen kilometers east. There are many men there. More than many. Too many."

The first man nodded and spoke in English. "Maybe one hundred. Maybe two hundred. They are not good people. They ignore our traditions and just care for their power." He spit on the ground. "I wish they were gone."

"Thank you, elders. I will be careful."

Annie gave the men a small bow, then walked out of earshot before tapping her glasses and calling for support.

"Annie, are you okay?"

"I'm fine, Brice, but grab my GPS coordinates and tell me what you see about fifteen kilometers east of my position. Supposedly there's an encampment."

"Hold on, I'll pull up the latest satellite flyover data."

Annie paced back and forth, ignoring her guides, who were watching her from a distance. They couldn't hear her, but they could surely see her talking to thin air.

"Okay, I see what looks like a town about fourteen klicks east of you. It's hard to tell exactly, but from the shadows being cast, I'd say there's a couple of multi-story towers that may be watch towers. Lots of vehicles, and there's something that looks like a grain silo or maybe a water tower."

"Are there any land features or anything obvious with regard to my approach?"

"No, it's right in the middle of lots of featureless African

scrub. What are you planning to do?"

"What I do best," Annie said. "Sow chaos."

After hiding the jeep in a ravine, Annie and her two escorts trekked for half a mile of thick brush and what passed for a forest in this part of the world, paralleling the dirt road that led to Enitan's encampment. The scrub didn't provide much cover, but the growing shadows of sunset helped conceal their position. The sky turned a dark red and the sound of crickets chirping grew ever louder. Nighttime in Africa was quickly approaching.

Annie looked through her high-end infrared binoculars at the walled encampment. It reminded her of what Connor had described as an FOB—a forward operating base. About half a mile across, and though the wall wasn't particularly high, maybe six feet, the entrance was guarded by a twenty-foot-tall watchtower. Even from this distance she could smell the smoke of cooking fires, and hoped that the camp was settling in for the night.

Lowering her binoculars, she turned to her two African companions. Achoja seemed like a decent enough person, just trying to do what he'd been asked to do by his boss, but there was something about Debare that didn't sit right with her. And both of them were Ntabo's men—which meant she wouldn't trust either one to watch her back. She wished Connor was here. He was a standoffish prude, but he was good people, and more importantly, he was someone she could count on.

She made a quick decision. "It's easier if I do this myself," she said. "You two go back and wait with the jeep. I'll meet you there before sunup."

"And what if you don't come back?" Achoja whispered.

Annie grinned in the darkness. "Then go back to Ntabo and tell him you did what you needed to do."

For the next two hours, Annie studied the encampment, waiting as darkness fell over the land. The moon was new, so the darkness was almost complete—and the damned crickets were so loud that she was sure nobody would hear her approach. Through the night vision built into her smart-glasses, the nearby world took on a pale greenish hue, allowing her to navigate the uneven ground and study the defenses.

She was crouched low behind cover, a mere fifty feet from the front gate. There was nobody up on the watchtower, but two guards were sitting on either side of the entrance, handguns strapped to shoulder holsters. Both men's heads were slumped to their chests. They were probably asleep. Annie was almost certain she could take them without anyone being alerted, but the risk was too great. For all she knew, there were more guards just on the other side of the wall, and the moment she walked in the entire camp would be alerted.

So instead she circled around to the western side and studied the cinderblock wall. It was a bit higher than she'd initially thought, around seven feet tall, and had loops of razor wire running along its top. She pulled on a pair of gloves with sharpened metal hooks at the end of each finger. This was something she'd come up with ages ago, and was very helpful in these types of situations.

She tilted her head, stretching her neck's muscles until she heard and felt a comforting crack, then repeated the stretch on the other side. She was ready.

At the base of the wall she crouched like a cat, gathering tension in her legs. Then she leaped up and grasped the topmost part of the stone. The hooks in her left hand dug into the concrete and held her up without her needing to strain with her finger grips. With her right hand, she pulled a pair of wire cutters from her pocket, reached up, snipped away wide lengths of the razor wire, and discarded them behind her.

Then she pulled herself up just enough to look over the wall. The coast was clear. She was directly behind a low building, with no one around. Quietly, she heaved herself up and over, and softly touched the ground on the other side. She stowed her pack in a nearby thicket of native bushes, peered around the corner of the building, and scanned the layout of the camp.

At the center of the camp was a large open area where a large number of vehicles were parked. Some of them could easily have been the ones she'd been following; there was no way to be sure. But she had to proceed on the assumption that the president's brother had been brought here. Him, and whatever else had been taken from that cargo plane.

A single guard was patrolling, with what looked like a Russian-made AK-47 assault rifle slung over his shoulder. Annie shook her head. These people were amateurs. The sleeping guards in the front, the patrol guard who didn't even have his rifle at the ready. This was going to be easy.

But as soon that thought ran through her head, she admonished herself for such lazy thinking. Nothing is ever easy until it's done.

She pulled a hand towel from one of her pockets, unwrapped the small bottle it concealed, and waited.

When the guard came nearer, she saw that he was no more than five-foot-six. That was a lucky break. She'd once had to do this to someone who was nearly seven feet tall, and that had been one of the few times she'd had to fight for her life.

With adrenaline pumping through her system, she poured some of the contents of the bottle onto the towel and waited for the guard to pass within striking distance.

Ten feet…

Five feet…

When the man walked past the corner she was hiding behind, she leaped onto him like a savage. He didn't get a chance to shout before she'd pressed the noxious towel against his face and pinned one of his arms to his side. With his free hand he flailed for his weapon, but it took only seconds before the chemical did its job and he collapsed silently to the ground. Annie kept the towel pressed firmly against his face for several seconds longer before rising. Then she dragged his limp body behind the building.

She'd done this move more times than she could remember. But for the first time ever, she wasn't claiming him for a kill. He would be useless to her dead.

She smiled as she began unbuttoning the guard's shirt. She had very special things in store for her unconscious friend.

CHAPTER ELEVEN

Connor rubbed his tired eyes and renewed his focus on the large flat-screen monitor in Brice's workshop. He was reading FBI dossiers on the president's known associates, then enhancing that with information on these same people from the Outfit's private database. The FBI dossiers had all variety of classification markers, making it clear that this material was not for public consumption, and yet somehow the Outfit had managed to get these writeups without any text blacked out or redacted. Even when Connor was in the CIA, that was almost unheard of.

He was currently reviewing the file for a Robert Edward Tanner. The man was an attorney at Smith, Beecham, and Cline, a high-priced boutique law firm that specialized in defending white-collar crimes. Their biggest clients were the Minnelli family out of Chicago, a known criminal syndicate who by some miracle had managed to avoid serious jail time for most of their members, despite countless racketeering and money laundering charges.

The president had gone to the same law school as Robert Tanner, and the FBI profile included several pictures of the two of them at some bar, along with one picture of them at the beach accompanied by two ladies in possession of fantastic figures. Both ladies were staring at the future president, who was undeniably a good-looking guy.

But while the president dove headlong into politics right out of law school, Robert Tanner entered private practice for a year, then signed up with the army after 9/11. And the man proved to be a legit operator—Connor was impressed. Tanner had wanted to join the Navy SEALs, but after failing the colorblindness test he'd instead gone through the Ranger pipeline and got selected for the Army's 75th Regiment. He was assigned to 3rd Battalion, where he landed a slot at sniper school and served one tour in Afghanistan followed by another in Iraq. Thirteen confirmed kills on the first tour, nineteen on the second.

Connor finished up with the FBI dossier and moved on to the Outfit's additional information. Tanner had an active passport, and the Outfit's records contained a list of his known departures and arrivals. But there was nothing in the last six months.

Connor turned in his chair to face Brice, who was wearing a pair of magnifying spectacles and held a soldering iron in one hand and a small circuit board in the other.

"Hey, Inspector Gadget. If one of these guys traveled under a fake or borrowed passport, is there a way for you to dig up that information?"

Brice looked up from whatever project he was working on,

and his eyes looked huge through the magnifying lenses. "If you have someone you think might be our guy, I could run a facial analysis across international flights."

"Let's do that then. I'd like to search for Robert Edward Tanner."

Brice removed the glasses, rolled his chair away from the lab bench, and began typing at his computer. "I have all that video footage cached already, so it's just a matter of getting the pattern match algorithm to scan through the video feeds. At transfer rates of nearly a terabyte per second, with over eighty streaming multi-processors and over five thousand CUDA cores, this won't take long."

Connor shook his head. "I don't speak computer genius, my friend. How long is 'not long'?"

Brice's screen flickered, and he tapped on it. "Not long is right now. No matches, sorry. Not in the last three weeks, anyway, which is the video traffic I have. It doesn't mean he didn't take a private flight, but that will be tougher to get. Not all private aircraft terminals have video feeds."

Connor frowned and turned back to his computer. "Thanks. Guess I'll keep looking."

He'd reached the end of the FBI dossier list, but the Outfit's database search had produced a few additional names that the FBI didn't have. Connor looked through a few, finding nothing of interest. The closest he came to even a potential possibility, just based on age and gender, was Joshua Cleary, a childhood neighbor of the president. But the two men hadn't interacted since their youth, and Cleary was now a store manager at a Home Depot, married with two kids, with no criminal record. The only risk factor was that he had bought a variety of guns in the last dozen years, but these were mostly hunting calibers like the .308, .30-06, and .270 Winchester, none of which could ever be confused with the .300 Win Mag that was used in the European incidents.

Cleary did have one interesting factoid in his medical records. At the age of nineteen, a doctor had noted that he had one leg significantly shorter than the other:

The nineteen-year-old male patient presents with an LLD (leg length discrepancy) measuring two inches. X-rays show that the growth plates have closed. Surgical options were discussed, but declined. Continued use of orthotics is prescribed and a referral has been filed.

Still, nothing about him made any sense as a would-be assassin.

Connor moved quickly through the Outfit's other acquaintances of the president, then waded through a few more pages on the president himself. His parents were farmers in Montana—a fact he often brought up when campaigning—growing apples and canola. Connor had no idea what a canola even looked like. The president did exceptionally well in school, getting a national merit scholarship along with other academic kudos. Before going to Harvard for undergrad and law school—par for the course for the political set—he had attended a high school called Mount Ellis Academy.

Connor looked over at Brice, who was again staring bug-eyed at items on his workbench. "How the hell did you get a copy of the president's high school yearbook?"

"Not exactly rocket science," Brice said without even looking up. "The man's already putting together data for his presidential library. Like most politicians, he thinks everyone wants to know everything about him. He even dumped copies of Valentine's cards he received in second grade on the presidential archivist."

Connor shook his head and flipped through the scanned yearbook pages. Not surprisingly, the president was pretty popular, and almost every page was signed by someone or other. One signature stood out: Kathy Strauss. That name rung a bell and it took him all of a few seconds to do a quick search and realize that it was the current First Lady's maiden name. She'd written a short note in French:

Mon chéri, j'attends l'avenir avec impatience.

According to Google Translate, this meant, *"My darling, I am looking forward to the future."*

Connor scrolled through the yearbook and didn't see a picture of a French class, but he did find a page titled "Future French Chefs," which showed a bunch of students rolling dough. One of the pictures showed the future president and First Lady holding up a set of misshapen croissants, both smiling widely for the camera.

Connor leaned back in his chair, staring at the screen, the wheels turning in his head. Finally he dialed up Mason.

"Did you find anything?"

"Nothing specific yet. I'm guessing talking to the president is out?"

Mason chuckled. *"I tried already, and no dice. Let's just say that he's aware of what's going on and is pretty dismissive of it all."*

"What about the First Lady? Any chance I could talk to her?"

"It's possible." Mason paused for a long second. *"Why?"*

"A small thing. In the president's high school yearbook, the First Lady wrote him a note in French."

"Ah, I see where you're going. The assassin's reference to 'mon ami' in his letter. That's good."

"Does she know about the threat?"

There was silence on the line for a few seconds before Mason responded. *"I'm not sure. And if I help arrange this, you can't be the one letting her know. I don't know the woman, and it might cause a shit storm that won't do us any good in the future."*

"I promise to be discreet."

"Then come to my office. Let's see if I can arrange for you to stumble into her without getting shot by the Secret Service."

Annie heard another muffled scream in the distance—the sound of someone being tortured. The sound had no emotional effect on her, but she did analyze it. When a prisoner is beaten, it's rare that such treatment yields ragged screams like that. This screamer was likely being whipped, or maybe even flayed alive. Screams were a human's natural reaction to a jolt of pain, and there was only so much pain a person could take before shock and even death would follow. She could only hope it wasn't the president's brother being tortured. She needed him alive, and the clock was ticking.

Turning her attention to the trussed-up guard she'd rendered unconscious, she broke open an ammonia-filled capsule and shoved it under the man's nose. The guard grimaced and squirmed, turning his face left and right, but Annie kept the volatile chemicals directly under his nose.

When the man lurched into a sitting position, eyes wide, Annie put a finger to her lips and whispered in Yoruba, "Remain silent and I won't kill you."

The man didn't have much choice in the matter. She'd bound his legs and arms, shoved a cloth into his mouth, and bound his jaw shut with so many rolls of muslin that he looked like a mummy.

The man blinked rapidly as awareness of his predicament registered.

Annie grabbed him roughly by the neck to hold him upright, then squeezed lightly on the carotid arteries supplying blood to the brain. With her free hand, she held up a pen and pressed her thumb on the cap. A red LED glowed. She showed it to the guard, then slid the pen back into her black fatigues.

"You're wearing a suicide vest," she said. "You make one move that I don't approve of... and you're dead. Do you understand?"

Despite the relatively cool evening, beads of sweat rolled down the man's panic-stricken face. He nodded vigorously.

Annie leaned closer and tightened her grip on the man's neck, and only when his eyes began to go out of focus did she ease her grip. She spoke with a menacing tone. "I called my people and told them about Mohammad, Jabril, Arwa, Dhakiyah, and Iman. If my people don't receive a daily call from me, your sons and daughters are all dead. Now remain silent while I loosen your restraints."

She removed the ropes and cloth binding him and pulled him up onto his feet by his scraggly beard. The man swayed a bit, and his eyes grew wider when he looked down at his unbuttoned shirt and saw the tubes and wires wrapped around his chest. Then his gaze shifted back to Annie, his chin quivering with fear.

"Get dressed," she said. "Look presentable."

The man buttoned his shirt, then opened his mouth as if to ask a question. But he snapped his jaws shut and instead meekly raised a finger.

With a flick of her wrist, Annie had a gleaming blade of obsidian black pressed against the man's throat. "If you have a question, you may whisper it now."

The man gulped nervously. "What is it you want me to do?"

Another scream of pain pierced the night. Annie pointed her chin in that direction. "Who's screaming?"

"An *oyinbo*. I don't know who it is. He came earlier today."

Oyinbo... white man. That was all she needed to know.

She removed the blade from the man's neck, retrieved his AK-47, and gave it back to him. "It's not loaded," she said. "The time has come for you to lead me to where this *oyinbo* is located."

The terrified guard led Annie into a large, squat building, its interior dimly lit and reeking of urine, feces, and blood. On the far wall of the front room was a tall metal cage with three pale-skinned men sitting inside. They were all shirtless, shoeless, and bloodied. This had to be Little Eagle's rescue team... and the president's brother wasn't among them.

Another scream of pain sounded from behind a closed door to the right. The guard pointed in that direction—as if Annie needed any more indication that that was where the torture was taking place.

She faced the guard, who shrank back as she leaned in close to him, whispered instructions in his ear, then motioned toward the closed door.

The guard's mouth hung open and looked at Annie as if she were crazy. It was far from the first time Annie had received that look, and she was sure it wouldn't be the last. She motioned curtly toward the door, and the guard obediently walked over to it, knocked loudly, and opened it.

He stepped through and announced, "Enitan has sent you a gift."

Two men's voices spoke in unison. "A gift?"

Annie walked in after him. Two Nigerian men stood on either side of a table where a white man was strapped down. This wasn't Little Eagle himself; he must have been the other surviving member of Little Eagle's rescue team. There were fresh bloody burn marks all up and down his sides and on his chest, and, for the moment at least, he was unconscious.

Annie gave the two men a brilliant smile then turned back to the guard. "Close the door and wait outside."

The guard eagerly scrambled out of the room and closed the door behind him.

One of the torturers, who was closer to seven feet than six, gave her an appraising look that was practically a leer. "Am I dreaming this? Such a gift is hard to believe."

The other man held the tip of a metal rod in a pile of glowing coals. "We have no time for this right now."

Annie adopted an innocent look. "Enitan wishes you to proceed. I will not get in your way." She stepped over to the tall man and pressed him down into a chair. "You look tense. Let me massage your shoulders." She didn't wait for a reply before stroking the man's broad but bony shoulders.

The man groaned and leaned his head back against Annie's stomach. His partner scowled but said nothing as he waved smelling salts under the white man's nose, waking him. Then he retrieved the iron from the coals, its tip now glowing red, and held it in front of the white man's face.

The man she was massaging spoke English with a British accent. "Who is the tiny man you were guarding?"

His partner brushed the glowing poker across the prisoner's chest. The man grunted with pain, and the sound and stench of sizzling flesh filled the room.

Annie rubbed both of her thumbs up and down the back of the English speaker's neck as he said "Just tell us who he is and this will be over."

The prisoner's breath came in gasps, but he said nothing. The hot poker moved so that it hovered directly in front of his face.

Almost magically, a knife flashed into Annie's hand as she reached across the speaker's throat and sliced deeply with its razor-like edge. The blade bit cleanly through the flesh, across the gristly cartilage of the larynx and through to the other side, sending forth a fountain of blood onto the table.

Just as the torturer's eyes widened with the realization of what she'd just done, Annie leaped across the table and buried her dagger to the hilt in the man's left eye socket.

The torturer flew backward, sending the hot poker flying and lay unmoving as she twisted the blade and removed it.

The man she'd been massaging lay sprawled on the ground, a large pool of blood emptying from the twitching body.

Both men now lay dead on the ground.

The prisoner looked at her with fearful eyes, and Annie gave him a wink. "Don't worry, big boy. I'm here to help you." She began unbuckling his restraints

He spoke, his voice hoarse. "Are you from—I guess it doesn't matter. Thank you. Who are you?"

"Let's get you and your buddies out of this mess, and then we'll talk," Annie said. "In the meantime, you can call me the Black Widow."

CHAPTER TWELVE

The guard unlocked the cage, and Annie frowned at the condition of the three soldiers trapped within. It looked as though each had at least one broken arm, and one of them had an obvious compound fracture of his lower leg. These men were no doubt well-trained and strong, but they were in no condition to sneak out of this place, much less help her fight their way out.

Shifting her gaze away from the soldier with the obvious compound fracture of his lower leg, she focused on the other two in the cage. "Can you two carry him?"

The soldier with the broken leg started to protest, so she nudged his foot with the toe of her boot. The man sucked air through his clenched jaw.

She pointed at the other two, who looked at each other, figured out that between them they each had one working arm, and nodded. "We can do it."

Annie then stepped close to the guard and spoke in a cold voice. "There is another *oyinbo*. Take me to him."

Though the man was taller than her, he cowered before her. "This is all of them. There was another. But he left hours ago. Just before sundown." He closed his eyes and muttered what sounded like a prayer to Allah. "I heard they were taking him to the big man's place. They took three trucks, including the big truck with men in the back."

"What does this 'big truck' look like?"

"It was the same truck that came with him. It was... big," the guard said, spreading his hands. "A large wooden box was in the back. I saw it." He glanced nervously at the soldier who'd walked out of the torture room, he was eyeing him with animosity and looked ready to snap his neck. "I don't know anything else."

"By big man, you mean Enitan?"

The guard nodded.

"Where is his place?"

"Almost directly south. Two days' drive from here."

Annie took a step back. "Stand right where you are, and don't move. I'll be right back." She faced the soldiers. "You too. I'm going to call my people and see what I can do about getting an extraction."

She walked into the other room before pulling out her phone and placing a call. After half a minute to sync with the satellite, Brice picked up.

"Annie, what can I do for you?"

"Brice, I'm going to need a miracle. I've found the four remaining members of the rescue team. They're alive, but in poor condition. They'll need a medevac. Little Eagle and the package are heading south to what likely is Enitan's main camp."

"I'll see what I can do about getting an intercept on Little Eagle. As for the medevac, your GPS shows that you're right in the middle of that encampment. You're going to need to get those men out of there before we can pick them up."

"I have a few ideas. Just get the evac to land quietly two klicks south of here."

"Will do, but it's going to take a while. My orders are to prioritize Little Eagle's extraction, and I've got exactly one chopper in-country."

"Understood. Tell those guys to be careful—my informant says our target is traveling with an armed escort."

"Roger that. I'll send a text the moment we take possession, and I'll give you an ETA for the medevac. In the meantime, don't get dead, you hear me?"

"Stop flirting and get the job done. We'll play when I'm stateside."

She disconnected and returned to the other room. All the soldiers were on their feet now, the one with the broken leg being held upright by two of the others. Annie ignored them and walked right up to the guard.

"You had two grenades when you were patrolling. Can you get more?"

The man's eyes widened. "There's a cabinet in the supplies room. I have the key."

Annie turned to the soldiers. "We likely won't have a bird landing until dawn, and when it does, it'll be two klicks south of here. Think you can make a march in the dark?"

All four of the men nodded.

"Good." Annie turned back to the guard and gave him an icy smile. "Now. If you ever want to see your family alive again, you're going to listen very carefully to my instructions."

———

Connor looked out the window as Thompson drove their Lincoln Navigator through the section of Foggy Bottom known as Embassy Row.

As they drove past the British Embassy and hung a left on 30th Street NW, Connor asked, "Why do I get a feeling that even with a suit and tie, I'm going to be underdressed for meeting the First Lady?"

"I don't think you have anything to worry about," Thompson said. "It's just some Silicon Valley bigwig's fundraiser, and these fifteen-year-old CEO types aren't big on playing dress-up."

Thompson turned onto Benton Place and stopped in front of a gated entrance manned by Secret Service agents. Thompson lowered the window, and one of the agents approached, glancing over at Connor before turning his focus back on the driver. "Can I have the name of the attendees?"

Thompson hitched his thumb at Connor. "Connor Sloane. I'll be staying with the vehicle."

"I'm sorry, but there isn't room for guest vehicles past the gate. You'll have to drop off your passenger here and come back when the event is over."

Thompson nodded. "Roger that."

The agent then scanned a printout, nodded, and looked over

at Connor. "Mr. Sloane, welcome. You'll need to present your ID to the agent at the door. Please be aware that you'll be wanded, and no weapons of any kind are allowed on site."

"That's fine."

Thompson turned to Connor. "I'll be nearby. Just call me when you're done."

Connor nodded and hopped out of the car. The gate was already opening, and he strode through.

As he walked across the motor court, he took in the breadth of the mansion that lay before him. He'd done his research and knew the layout of the place. It was a nine-bedroom, twelve-bath home, just shy of 15,000 square feet. And of course it was located in one of the most premium locations in DC.

He passed the twenty-foot-tall pillars arrayed in front, and an agent met him in front of the giant double doors.

"Welcome, Mr. Sloane. Can I see—"

"Here you go." Connor offered his CIA credentials, which were the *official* government credentials members of the Outfit carried.

The agent flipped open the billfold, flashed a black light on the picture ID, nodded, and handed it back to Connor. Then he took a wand-like device from his belt and gave Connor a few quick swipes before passing him off to another agent, who escorted him inside.

Connor followed the man to the reception hall. The hall was huge, its white marble floor gleaming, with a massive staircase at its center that led to a balcony on the second floor. Guests were scattered about in groups, and though the attendance was robust, the crowd looked small in this tremendous space.

Connor continued following the agent past the staircase when suddenly the agent paused, pointed at one of the large paintings hung on the far wall and whispered, "Mason let me know about your objective. I'll see what I can do to help."

Focusing on the far wall, Connor nodded. Anyone observing them would have seen an agent saying something presumably about the painting on the wall. Nothing out of the ordinary.

The man led Connor through a door onto a backyard terrace. There were plenty of people already out here as well, including a young man in a polo and khakis whom Connor recognized as the tech wunderkind who had become an instant billionaire a few years back when his Silicon Valley startup had gone public.

The agent ignored the tech kid and headed straight for a group of women who were all holding glasses of wine and laughing about something. Connor recognized only one of them: the First Lady.

The agent walked right up to her and whispered something in her ear. The First Lady nodded, said something to the others, then walked with the agent straight over to Connor.

That was almost too easy.

"Mr. Sloane, you needed to speak with me?"

The woman had stopped only a foot from Connor, well inside his personal space, and it took a concerted effort for him not to take a step back. At least the agent had moved off to give them some semblance of privacy.

"Yes, ma'am," Connor said. He showed her his CIA credentials. "This may not be an opportune time, but I've been tasked with tracking down a threat to your husband."

The woman's eyes flickered and an almost imperceptible

expression of annoyance flashed on her face. "I'm sure such threats are always occurring. The Secret Service is certainly on top of this."

"They are, but—"

The woman's expression darkened. "Why would someone from the CIA even be involved?"

"Ma'am, I'm not sure if you're aware, but there have been threats—"

The First Lady's expression grew severe. "I'm only going to ask this one last time. Why is someone from the CIA talking to me about this."

Connor's heart was beating rapidly and it dawned on him that this woman was intimidating the hell out of him. He took a deep breath and whispered, "The truth is, your husband was informed of this threat and dismissed it for various reasons, including it being an election season. The Secret Service has yet to be able to identify the source of this threat, and I believe you might be able to help."

The First Lady's shoulders drooped ever so slightly as tension seemed to leak out of her and her expression changed to one of concern. "How is that possible?"

Connor pulled out a printout of the picture of her and the future president holding up a pair of croissants. "We believe the threat is coming from someone who knows your husband, and we think it might go as far back as high school."

The First Lady took the picture from his hand, and as she gazed at it, her features softened. She stared at it for a full ten seconds before turning and beckoning to the agent, who hadn't gone far. He came right over.

"Steve, is there somewhere around here that Mr. Sloane and I can talk in private?"

"In private, ma'am?"

"Yes, you know the meaning of the word," the First Lady huffed.

"Yes, ma'am."

As the agent stepped away and said something into the microphone hidden inside his sleeve, the First Lady looked at the photograph once more.

"May I keep this?" she said.

"Yes, ma'am." Connor replied. It was absolutely endearing to see the tough no-nonsense woman have a sentimental moment over an old high school image.

The agent returned. "Ma'am, if you'll follow me."

Connor and the First Lady were escorted by two Secret Service agents back into the house, down a hall, and into a library. It was furnished with two loveseats and a coffee table, and a cozy fireplace was flanked by two lavender display cases. Connor expected them to sit on the loveseats, but one of the agents walked to the corner of the room and did something with one of the display cases, and suddenly a hidden section of the wall slid open.

"Ma'am," he said, "this is an empty media room. It should provide the privacy you need."

The First Lady chuckled and shook her head as she passed the agent who'd cleared the room and looked back at the hidden entrance. "This is like something from a James Bond novel. Mansions, secret rooms, and spies. It's all a bit much for a Montana girl."

The room was small, but featured theater-style armchairs, and as the First Lady took a seat, she gestured for Connor to sit beside her. They had to half-twist in the extra-wide chairs to face each other.

"Ma'am," Connor began, but she cut him off.

"In private, please call me Kathy. Now tell me." She held up the photo. "What does this have to do with a threat against my husband?"

Connor took a deep breath. He was about to cross the line that Mason had drawn for him.

"Kathy, even though I've been told not to, I'm going to tell you everything I know. And then, hopefully, you can help fill in some blanks. This threat started in Italy…"

———

The First Lady pursed her lips in thought, processing everything Connor had shared with her. She'd taken it all in without any unwarranted reactions.

"And simply because this note," she said, "the one with the shell casing—" She paused. "Who was it signed by again?"

"Lewis Payne, but as I've said, we don't believe that's his real name. A Lewis Payne was involved in the Lincoln assassination, as was the signer of the other note."

She nodded. "I see. And because Lewis Payne's note said *mon ami*, you think this has something to do with our French class in high school?"

When she put it that way, it did sound like a stretch. But Connor had a feeling he was on to something.

"It may or may not," he said. "Really, we just want to identify anyone who might hold a grudge against the president. For
any reason. That's why I'm here." He took out his phone and
pulled up the scans from her high school yearbook. "Perhaps if
you look through some of the pictures, it'll jog your memory. If
not, it's at least a trip down memory lane."

Kathy held the phone up close to her face, then held it at
arm's length until she had the right distance. "I miss the days
when I could read things up close," she said. "I don't recommend
getting older, Mr. Sloane. In fact I give it zero stars."

She began to scroll through the images, occasionally smiling
and shaking her head as if she couldn't believe this was her own
past. At one point she held up the phone with a wry grin. "Mrs.
Levitz, that was her name. Our French teacher. God, I haven't
thought of her in ages."

She continued scanning the pages, then suddenly stopped.

"Someone who might hold a grudge..." she said.

"Ma'am? I mean, Kathy? Do you have someone?"

The First Lady sighed and shook her head. "I hope not... I
really do." She again turned the phone to face Connor. "Johnny.
Jonathan Gibbons. He and I... well, it's complicated." Her
cheeks reddened. "But no, there's no way he could be involved in
a threat to my husband. Forget I said anything."

"Can you at least tell me what made you pause on him?"
Connor asked.

The First Lady pressed her hands to her cheeks. "My word,
I'm blushing like a little girl." She took a deep breath. "Johnny
was the other guy."

CHAPTER THIRTEEN

Connor texted the name "Jonathan Gibbons" to Brice as the First Lady replayed for him a tale that had happened over a quarter century ago.

"As you probably know, the president and I dated through high school and college. But when he went off to Harvard, I went to MSU. We pledged to get married as soon as we were done with school."

"MSU—you mean Michigan State?" Connor asked.

Kathy smiled. "No, the other one. Montana State. I was scared to go far from home, so I opted for the local school in Bozeman. And I didn't exactly have the same high-flying aspirations as my future husband." She smiled. "We saw each other when we could, holidays and other breaks, but during our junior year, he sent me a Dear Kathy letter. I couldn't believe it. He didn't even have the guts to *call* and break up with me. He dumped me in a *letter*.

"I was furious with him, I have to say. I cried for days. He was my first love, you know. My only love. The only boy I'd even kissed. In my mind, I had lost the love of my life. He wouldn't respond to my calls, never returned a letter, nothing. He didn't even come home for the holidays, and trust me, I checked.

"Anyway, after a while I forced myself to forget he'd ever been in my life. I burned his letters, everything he'd ever given me. I burnt him completely out of my life. We were done. And that was when things started with Johnny."

She smiled sadly. "We'd known each other since high school, but not well. The same classes now and then. French classes, if you want to know. But he was also attending MSU, and... well, I suppose he was a familiar face, a shoulder to cry on. Though I didn't cry so much as scream and curse. You know the saying, 'a woman scorned'? I was *really* mad."

"And so you started dating?" Connor asked.

She shook her head, then nodded. "Yes and no. We were just friends. I wasn't really into him, but I could tell he didn't feel the same. The truth is ... I'm afraid I may have led him on. He was the distraction I needed at the time. And so, in time... yes, we dated."

"And how did it end?"

"Quite vividly—and unexpectedly. One afternoon very near the end of senior year, I was working on a paper for school. I still lived at my parents' house at the time. And there was a knock on the door." Now she smiled widely. "When I opened the door, I nearly passed out. My future husband stood before me, a graduation cap tilted back on his head, a bouquet of roses in his hand. And he got down on one knee."

"You're talking about the president," Connor said.

"I am. And I know what I said—about how angry I was at him. But at that moment, all that pain and anguish that man had put me through just vanished. I don't know why, I don't know how, but somehow, it just didn't matter." She chuckled. "There's just something about that man. I couldn't say no."

"And Johnny? How did he take all this?"

Kathy looked embarrassed. "To be honest, I never saw him again. I was supposed to go on a date with him that evening, and I was going to tell him what had happened, but he didn't show. My fiancé—oh how I loved calling him that—he showed up instead, and explained that he'd spoken to Johnny. He said they'd talked over some drinks and had come to an agreement. I didn't ask questions. I know it sounds terrible, but I didn't really care. It *does* sound terrible. It *is* terrible. But I was young and in love. And until just now, I haven't really thought about Johnny again. I should have spoken to him, explained it myself. But I didn't."

She shrugged. "I don't know why I'm telling you all this. That was so long ago. And besides which, Johnny was a Quaker. A total pacifist. So he couldn't be the person you're looking for."

Connor smiled. "I understand. And I appreciate you taking the time to speak with me. I'm sorry to keep you from your event."

Kathy rolled her eyes. "Trust me, I'd rather hide out here all night." She rose from her chair, and suddenly she was the First Lady again. "But if you'll excuse me, Mr. Sloane, I do have some hands to shake."

As Connor headed outside, his phone buzzed with a text from Brice:

Jonathan Thomas Gibbons, MOS 11B (Infantry)
Completed Sniper School
Two deployments to Afghanistan
Fifteen confirmed kills
Injured on 2nd deployment with a TBI
Three-month recovery from a coma in Walter Reed
Flagged as non-deployable
Honorable discharge with 80% disability
Call me when you're done with her. We need to talk.

Connor felt a tingle race up his spine.

He texted Thompson that he was leaving, and the black Navigator rolled up to him the moment he reached the street. He climbed in, and they took off.

"Well?" said Thompson.

"It turns out that at the time the president proposed to the First Lady, she had a boyfriend who had taken French class with them both. Jonathan Gibbons. She immediately dumped him like a hot potato, although it sounds like the president himself handled the dumping. She hasn't seen or heard from Gibbons since, and he ended up going Eleven Bravo and became a sniper with fifteen confirmed kills."

"That sounds promising."

"That's not everything. He got some kind of head injury that sent him into a coma for three months. After recovering, he couldn't pass muster, and he got discharged."

Thompson winced. "Ouch, that sucks. So we've got someone who knows the president, may be harboring some jealousy from way back when, is a sniper with confirmed kills, and has a head injury, so who knows what's going on up there."

"That about sums it up."

Connor's phone rang—Brice—and he picked up.

"Connor, I need you to get in here. I've ordered up a fresh set of FBI credentials for you, which I'll have within the hour. These will replace the ones you were given in Germany. They should give you cover to pursue this guy domestically and not get hassled."

Connor grinned. "Good, do we know where he is?"

"Unfortunately, Mr. Gibbons has missed the last two of his VA counselor meetings. We can talk about the details when you get here."

"Roger that, I'll be there in a bit."

Connor hung up and turned to Thompson. "Did you ever talk to a VA counselor when you left the service?"

Thompson stared ahead at the traffic, his thumbs tapping on the steering wheel. "A couple times, just as a routine transition thing to civilian life, but I stopped after a bit. I got picked up by the Outfit and didn't think it was doing me any good. You?"

Connor shook his head. "Never did. How often did you meet with your counselor? Every week?"

Thompson snorted. "Are you kidding me? Those guys are usually so backed up, unless you're a high-risk suicide type, you're lucky if you get something more than once a month."

"Brice says Gibbons has missed his last two meetings. So if he's been out of pocket for a couple months…"

"That's plenty of time for him to have done what our guy did."

"Exactly."

Connor's heart thudded in his chest. He recognized the feeling of adrenaline being dumped into his bloodstream, and understood why. For the first time in a long while he had a legit target to chase after.

As Annie crept toward the camp's gated entrance, the only sounds were the hum of a generator and the incessant chirping of crickets. She peeked around the corner of a building, and her glasses picked out two seated guards. One appeared to be asleep, while the other was halfway there, church-nodding.

While the guard church-nodded, she pulled up one of her sleeves and drew back on a lever attached to a wrist-mounted metal tube. When it clicked into place, she repeated the same motion on her other wrist. She then loaded the tubes and lowered her sleeves, concealing the tools of her trade. She glanced over her shoulder and the glasses instantly switched to night vision, giving her a clear view of the four rescued soldiers and one coerced guard. As instructed, they remained hidden in the shadows.

Annie looked up at the watchtower, confirming yet again that there was nobody up there. These people didn't take their security very seriously. Then she stood and walked brazenly to the entrance. One guard was alert enough to hear her coming and raise his head, and when he did, she met his gaze and smiled. Annie imagined his mind racing, trying to remember who she might be: maybe a relative of one of the men, maybe a prostitute from a neighboring village, or maybe...

That was enough time for her to get in range, with a flick of her wrist, she sent the dart flying and turned her attention to the other guard whose chin rested against his chest, asleep.

Without hesitation, Annie pointed at the man's head and let the second dart fly.

With just the slightest sound of a hollow thunk, the metal projectile penetrated the side of the man's head, the four cutting edges of the arrows expanded inside the skull, doing maximum damage.

As the guards' bodies convulsed, she dragged them one by one into the nearby scrub. She'd left behind no blood, no signs of a struggle. Exactly as she'd intended.

She returned to the soldiers, still hiding, and approached the least-injured man. She gave him the two handguns she'd gotten from the guards, a worn pair of Beretta Model 92s.

"For later," she said. "Each of them has one in the chamber already."

She turned to the others and motioned for the rest to follow her.

The soldiers had splinted their teammate's broken leg, but he was still unable to put any weight on it. They managed to follow with a minimal amount of noise, albeit at a slower pace than she'd have liked.

Moving past the gate, the least injured soldier glanced back and forth at the empty chairs sitting just outside the camp, shot

Annie a knowing grin and focused his attention on the Nigerian guard.

It took them almost ten minutes to cross the quarter mile of African scrub as Annie's anxiety deepened. With the assistance of the glasses, she should already see the thermal images of Achoja and Debare.

But there was nothing.

She turned to the men with her and whispered, "Wait here. I'll be right back."

Breathing in deeply, she fell back to her tracking skills, looking for the path she'd taken toward the camp.

It took a few minutes with the help of the night vision given by Brice's glasses before she spotted the crushed grasses from her footsteps.

As she traced her footsteps back to their origin, her skin tingled with the preternatural knowledge that something was wrong. The smell of copper was in the air.

Blood.

Blood and no heat signatures could mean only one thing.

And just as she had that thought, she almost tripped over the body of Achoja.

He'd been garroted. A metal wire had been wrapped around his neck and pulled so tight that he'd almost been decapitated. Annie had no doubt this was Debare's doing; he had the strength to accomplish the task, and she'd always figured he wasn't playing straight with her or Achoja.

She pressed her fingers to her lips, then placed them on the dead man's lips. "I hope you've found a happier place."

After retracing her steps to the ravine and then returning to the men she'd left behind, Annie let out a low two-toned whistle and whispered loudly, "I'm here."

The men were all staring about wide-eyed as she stepped out of the brush, making a point of scuffing her feet on the ground.

"Guys, plans have changed. The jeep I thought would be here isn't." She dug a compass from her pack and handed it to the soldier she'd given the guns to. "Keep leading the others south, stay off the road, and I'll talk to my people and have a bird find you. Any questions?"

The soldier hitched his thumb at the guard who was still with them. "What about him?"

Annie grinned. "He'll stay with me. I've got plans for him."

The soldier with the broken leg spoke. "You've saved our asses, ma'am. How can we get in touch with you back in the real world to thank you properly?"

"Just get those asses on the bird when it lands—that's all the thanks I need. Now get moving."

The weapons cabinet in the supply room didn't have much in the way of heavy weaponry, but it did have an assortment of handguns, a few AK-47 automatic rifles, a decent supply of ammo, several M18 smoke grenades, and two boxes of what looked like M67 American grenades.

Annie was shifting the boxes around when she caught sight of something that made her smile: they looked like four old-style WWII German stick grenades. They had a handle with a cylinder on one end, a long lever-like spoon running up the side of the handle, and a telltale pin with a metal ring on it. Except these had Russian lettering on them.

She looked up at the guard. "Why do you have anti-tank grenades?"

The guard was wringing his hands as he glanced between her and the door. "I don't know," he said. "We get what we get. Those I have never used before. They're for tanks?"

Annie imagined someone throwing one of these things, expecting a large boom, and not getting exactly what they expected. No, these things were good for one thing in particular.

She grabbed an empty box and loaded it with the stick grenades and several smoke grenades, then grabbed a roll of duct tape that she found on a high shelf.

"Please hurry," the guard whispered. "A woman shouldn't be in here. I won't be able to explain."

Annie finished loading up her pack and stood. "Then let's go finish this. And afterwards, you'll be free of me."

Annie duct-taped all four of the anti-tank grenades to the western wall of the encampment. Together, they were sure to blow a huge hole in the wall. She'd instructed the guard to yell like a stuck pig that Sijuwade's forces were attacking, and then with use of the smoke grenades she hoped to steal a truck and race after the president's brother—and the nukes he was babysitting.

She pulled the pins from the anti-tank grenades, flipped away the spoons from the handles, and moved away from the wall. These grenades weren't on the same kind of fuse as standard grenades; at this point, with the pins pulled, any significant motion would kick start a two-second counter.

She turned to the camp's gas-fueled generator. She'd already taped an M67 grenade to it, and had wrapped a wire around the fall-away spoon. The remote activation device she'd attached to the wire blinked with a red LED. Everything was in place.

And then she noticed movement near the center of the camp. She quickly blended into the shadows. A couple hundred feet away, her captive guard was holding himself in an awkward and stiff manner, talking to someone who must have noticed him working near the refueling truck. The guard made large sweeping motions with his hands and pointed to the north. And when his companion turned to look, the guard smashed the butt of his AK-47 against the back of the man's head.

Effective, but not unobtrusive. It was time to move. Quickly.

Annie pulled the pin on the M67 and hugged the shadows as she raced to the center of the camp. The guard was dragging his former brother-at-arms behind one of the vehicles. Even in the darkness, her glasses showed the trail of blood. There was an art to knocking people out with a blow to the head. A little too light and it doesn't do anything; a little too hard, or with a sharp edge like from the buttstock of an AK-47, and your target's skull gets crushed.

"I killed him, may Allah forgive me," the guard said, sounding panicked. "He didn't believe my excuses for checking on the vehicles."

Annie poked him hard in the chest with her index finger. "Remember your children, and focus. Do you remember what I told you to yell?"

The man nodded vigorously. "I do."

"Good." She pulled the remote from her pocket and nodded at the Humvee they were standing next to. "Is this the truck we'll take?"

"Yes. It's fully fueled and has spare fuel in the back."

"Then let's go."

Annie walked over to the passenger's side, stepping over the dead man, and opened the door, but she didn't get in just yet. The guard leaned into the Humvee and flipped the switch to "run," and the "wait" light turned on as the batteries heated the glow plugs to help start the diesels. When the "wait" light blinked off, the guard gave her a thumbs-up. The truck was ready.

Annie pulled the pin on the first smoke grenade. She tossed it and heard a slight pop, almost as loud as the pop of a soda can, and smoke began pouring out the bottom of the metal cylinder. She quickly repeated the process three more times, throwing the grenades in different directions. The clock was ticking, and she needed everything to happen at almost the same time.

She pressed the button on the remote and held it down as she jumped into the Humvee and extracted another remote from her right pocket.

Right now the wire wrapped around the spoon of the M67 would be starting to glow red hot as the remote triggering device sent an electric charge through the loops of metal. When the wire became white-hot and melted—a loud explosion flashed on the other side of the camp and any lights that were on flickered and died.

A loud metal screeching sound erupted from the generator

and Annie tossed the remote she'd just used in the back, leaned across the empty driver's seat and yelled. "Get in and drive!"

The guard dove into the truck, flipped the switch to "start" and the diesel engines roared to life.

As the guard put the vehicle into gear, gunned the engine, and aimed for the entrance, Annie yelled, "Go faster!"

The guard's eyes were huge and he began praying loudly in Arabic, trying to drown out the screeching sound of metal scraping against metal as the generator died a seemingly painful death.

Annie mashed her finger down on the second remote and held it there.

The generator was on fire, and through the streaks of smoke, she saw the gaping hole in the camp's protective wall.

There was a sudden *whoomph* as the grenade she'd had the guard plant near the refueling truck exploded, bathing the camp in fiery daylight, and at the same time the western wall exploded as well. The Humvee was peppered with debris as they raced through the entrance, leaving chaos behind.

"South," Annie barked.

The guard gripped the steering wheel tightly as he drove through the near pitch-black of the African night. "It is good? I can be free now?" He tapped at the suicide vest on his chest. "You can take this off?"

Annie's phone vibrated. "One second," she said, putting it to her ear. "What's up?"

"I sent you a text earlier. You didn't call."

"I've been busy. What's up?"

"We've got Little Eagle, and I just got word that the chopper picked up the injured soldiers you found."

Annie looked up into the night sky, wondering if the helicopter was nearby. "Great. So do I get an extraction?"

"Actually, I've got some good news and some bad."

"Of course you do." Annie massaged the back of her neck. "What is it?"

"When we got Little Eagle, the truck carrying the bombs wasn't with his caravan. Based on the in-air debrief of our guy, he managed to dispose of one of the nukes, which is the good news—"

"Dispose how? I saw one of the high-explosive tiles to one of those things in the crashed plane."

"All I know is that evidently the business end of the nuke was dumped somewhere over the desert dunes of Chad and blown into smithereens. Not pretty, but I suppose effective. At least for that nuke, Humpty Dumpty isn't being put back together.

"The bad news is that Enitan's men have a bomb that's been modified to be idiot-proof. If someone wants to blow it, it's a matter of a few button presses and that's it. Mason said that if it were up to him, he'd let the Nigerians deal with the situation, but we've gotten orders from the top: we can't let a working thirty-five-kiloton nuke get into some warlord's hands."

Annie felt a wave of nausea wash over her. "And you want me to somehow wave a magic wand and steal it back?"

"Not exactly. But if you can get to the bomb, Little Eagle claims that he can guide you on a way to make it inoperable in less than five minutes."

"Brice, I don't even know where it is."

"But I do. Little Eagle put a tracking device on it, and I now have three different satellites tracking it. It's about five hours ahead of you, due south."

Annie took in a deep breath and let it out slowly, trying to calm herself. "I'm heading south now. Talk to you later."

She hung up and turned to the guard. "I want you to show me how fast this truck can go. And when we get to where we're going, you're free."

That last promise must have been the motivation the man needed, because the engine roared and the truck raced ahead into the darkness.

CHAPTER FOURTEEN

This was the first time Connor had ever been in Montana, and as he drove his rental car along Frontage Road, he was amazed at just how different this part of the country was compared to the East Coast. Other than the occasional tiny building off in the distance, there was nothing but flat prairie as far as the eye could see.

The only data Connor had been given before going wheels up was that the last known sighting of Johnny Gibbons had been at the local bank in Bozeman, where he'd drained his account. That was a several weeks ago, which was still before the first killing in Italy. Brice had gotten no computer hits on the international flights coming or going, so this might be a real long shot. But it was the only shot they had at the moment.

The car's phone buzzed, and Thompson's name came up on the heads-up display. Connor tapped a button on the steering wheel to take the call.

"Hey, Thompson. I'm en route."

"Do you have your service weapon on you?"

"I do. The FBI credentials were the magic pass. The airlines didn't give me any grief."

"Good. Because Mason has gotten a judge to sign off on a search warrant. I'm forwarding a copy of it to your email. You're authorized to go on property if you think it's safe. But don't cowboy this, you got me?"

"Roger that. I'm just going to surveil the location and report what I see."

"I hope so. Also, just so you know, there's not much backup available in the Bozeman FBI field office. But if the shit hits the fan and you ring the bat phone, I can have upwards of one hundred agents at your location in two hours."

"That's good to know. Thanks."

"Keep me posted. Everyone here is breathing down every-one's neck right about now. So don't screw this up."

Connor frowned and shook his head as he hung up. Thompson always rode him like he owed the man money.

As he drove down the rural road, he knew that this wasn't going to go as he'd envisioned it. This place was *really* rural. Any car that wasn't normally there—like his—would stand out. Hell, with the lack of trees and cover, even if he left the car behind and walked the rest of the way, he'd stick out like a sore thumb. And as he turned right onto Watts Lane, the situation only grew worse. He'd entered a tidy one-road neighborhood, the kind where everyone knew everyone's business.

Paying attention to the numbers on the mailboxes as he drove down the street, he passed the Gibbons home, and a hundred yards later, the road dead-ended in a cul-de-sac. It was the middle of the day, he was in an obvious rental car, and there was no way for him to *not* look conspicuous. Nonetheless, he parked in front of the next house down the street, where he still had a good view of the suspect's home, and pulled out a set of binoculars.

The Gibbons's house was a small single-story home. From the property records he'd pulled up, the home had been built about thirty years ago, and Johnny had inherited it from his parents. The grounds looked unkempt, with weeds and grass growing knee-deep, and from what he could see of the back yard, it hadn't been maintained in years. Connor couldn't see inside the house, as all the windows were blocked by closed blinds. There was no car in the driveway, but there was an unattached three-car garage, so an empty driveway meant nothing.

Connor sensed motion to his left, and turned to see the neighbor across the street heading in his direction. He groaned. He was without a doubt getting a visitor.

She looked to be in her forties, dark brown hair, wearing jeans and even though she didn't look overweight, most of her weight was gathered on her bottom half.

Connor lowered the driver's side window as she approached. "Can I help you?"

The woman looked amused. "I was going to ask you the same question. Are you lost?"

"Actually, ma'am—"

"Please, I hate ma'am. The name's Brandy."

"Brandy." Connor pointed at the Gibbons house. "I'm actually looking for the owner of that home."

Brandy put her hands on her hips. "Have you given any thought to knocking on the door?"

Connor chuckled. "I'm sorry, I should have started with this." He took out his FBI credentials and showed them to her.

The woman nodded, unfazed. "I've lived here since that house was nothing but a field. Is there anything in particular you want to know?"

"When's the last time you saw the owner?"

Brandy crouched, bringing herself to eye level with Connor. "I suppose that depends on what you mean by the owner. That's the Gibbons's home, or was. A nice family. I even dated their son Johnny for a couple months back in high school. But a few years after that the parents both got sick with cancer, and I heard something about the ranch being in trouble. Johnny was back from college then, working at a local store, but after they died, I guess he moved, because I didn't hear from him for years. Instead we had a series of renters coming through."

"You say you didn't hear from Johnny Gibbons for years. So you did hear from him again?" Connor asked.

Brandy nodded. "A few months back. The house had been empty for a while, so when I noticed that someone new had come in, I brought over a casserole to welcome them. To my surprise it wasn't another renter, but Johnny. But it wasn't the same Johnny I knew. He didn't even smile when he saw me, which I admit hurt my feelings a bit, and not only did he refuse the casserole, he practically slammed the door in my face."

"And since then? Is he still around?"

"Well, I haven't been looking for him, if that's what you're asking. I can take a hint like any girl. But I pay attention to what's going on around here. As you can tell. And I'm pretty sure the house has been empty for a while now."

"Momma!" a voice shouted from across the street. "The timer's going off!"

"Oh, shoot," Brandy said, straightening. "I've got a roast in the oven. If you're still around at dinner time, you're more than welcome to join us. My husband should be getting home in an hour or so."

Connor thanked the woman for her time and watched her go. Then he shifted the car into gear, drove up to the Gibbons home, and parked on the driveway. It was time to exercise the warrant.

He started by walking the perimeter of the property—or at least, what he guessed was the perimeter. Because the surrounding land was largely undeveloped, and there was no sign that any sod had ever been laid in the back, it looked as if the Gibbons land stretched on forever. There was probably a property marker hidden somewhere in the scrub.

As Connor looked around, not even sure what he was looking for, he spotted something hanging from a pine tree about one hundred yards behind the house. As he walked up to it, he saw that it was nothing but a cut rope. But as he thumbed its frayed texture, he could tell that it hadn't been cut with a knife; the fibers were too unevenly severed. And on the ground beneath it were irregular fragments of those very same fibers.

It was almost as if the rope had been blown up, pieces of it tumbling to the ground and—

Connor smiled. The rope hadn't been blown up. Someone had shot it.

He'd once seen a video of Jerry Miculek, a professional

shooter, shooting a hangman's rope with a civil war era rifle. It wasn't easy to do, even for Jerry. But for a trained sniper, with the right gear…

As Connor studied the end of the rope, something made him spin on his heel and draw his weapon, his heart thudding heavily in his chest. But he saw nothing. The sliding glass door at the back of the house was closed, the vertical blinds remained motionless. Slowly, he holstered his weapon, not sure what had freaked him out. But his senses remained on high alert.

He walked a straight line toward the sliding glass door.

"Mr. Gibbons!" he shouted as he approached. "Mr. Gibbons, I have a message for you from a friend!"

He stopped ten feet from a small concrete slab just outside the sliding glass door.

"Mr. Gibbons!" he yelled again, as loud as he could, then waited for a count of thirty. There was no movement of the verticals, no sounds, nothing.

As Connor took a step toward the door, he caught a golden glint in the scrub beside the concrete. Crouching low, he saw what it was: a spent shell. And a huge one, a .50 BMG. It wasn't tarnished at all, telling him that it had been used relatively recently. It certainly hadn't gone through a Montana winter.

Connor pulled on a pair of surgical gloves, picked it up, and put it in a Ziploc bag. The casing belonged to a much larger bullet than what had been used in Europe, but it was still potential evidence.

Then he looked back at the tree. Had the rope been shot from this distance? If so, that was some impressive shooting. Connor knew there was no way he himself could have made that shot, not even on his luckiest day. If Gibbons had taken that shot and made it, he could have made any shot he wanted.

The man clearly had the skills. And fifteen confirmed kills. But there were probably hundreds of people in the military who could have made the same shot. Maybe...

Connor took a moment to type up a few notes on his phone and sent them to Brice—his notes from the talk with Brandy, and a photo of the .50 BMG shell casing. Then he walked to the glass door. It was locked, but as Connor looked at the empty bottom track of the slider, he smiled. Most people didn't realize that the so-called locking mechanism on most of these doors wasn't even a lock, but a latch that could easily be bypassed.

He grabbed the bottom of the handle with one hand and pressed upward along the frame with the other. With a grunt, he lifted the door into the upper track, and it slid open.

He called out once again. "Mr. Gibbons! I have a message from a friend of yours." Then he pushed aside the verticals and stepped inside.

His phone vibrated with a text from Brice. *I'm working on what you sent me. Can you video conference me in?*

Connor inserted an earbud and made a video call.

"I've just entered the back of the house," he said. He tapped on his glasses to activate the video interface so Brice could see what he was seeing. "Have you got something for me already?"

"Just a little. It looks like Gibbons fired the property management company sometime after he got discharged. That was three months ago, and there've been no payments on anything since then. The utilities are scheduled to be cut off next week."

"Sounds like he isn't planning on coming back." He panned his gaze across the kitchen, which was neat and orderly. The counters were cleared off and there was nothing in the sink.

"Or maybe he's just not thinking clearly. He failed a battery of psych tests before his discharge. Not only that, he got into a fight off-base. According to the police records, he just walked into a restaurant, picked out some dude seemingly at random, and proceeded to beat the crap out of him. Sent the man to the hospital. It took four customers to get him off the guy."

"I'm surprised he didn't land in jail."

"He got a sympathetic judge. He's on two years of probation."

Connor walked past the empty living room and entered a hallway.

"Hey, can you turn on lights. The video feed is looking pretty dark on my side."

He flipped on the nearest light switch and only one of the two hallway lights turned on. "Mister Gibbons!" Connor called the man's name as he pushed open a door revealing a small bathroom.

Down the hall Connor peered into the room on the right, it was an empty bedroom. "I don't know. This is starting to look like nothing."

Connor walked to the end of the hallway and pushed open a set of double-doors. They yawned open and he pulled his gun from the shoulder holster.

"Lights. Turn on the lights."

He flipped both of the wall switches to their on position and the master bedroom's light flickered to life as the ceiling fan groaned and slowly began turning.

There was a rolled-up rubber mat in the corner of the room. "Someone was definitely here."

With Connor holding the gun in a modified Weaver stance, he stepped into the bedroom, leading with the gun and walked across the room to a door that stood slightly ajar.

Pressing the barrel of the gun against the door, it slowly swung open revealing the master bathroom.

It was empty.

He holstered the weapon and turned on the lights. On the counter was a two-foot-long cardboard box. Connor walked over to it and peered inside.

"What the hell is that?" he said aloud.

"Pick up some of the items." Brice said. *"Let me see it from from all angles."*

When Connor did as he was asked, Brice spoke again. *"That looks like a skullcap."*

Connor picked up the skullcap with his gloved hand. It had almost been torn in half, as if it had been ripped off someone's head. "Not what I expected to find." Poking through the rest of the box, he frowned. "And a bunch of used makeup."

"I can't see from this angle, can you—"

"I got you." Connor moved the phone over the box so Brice could see.

"I see an empty bottle of spirit gum. A bunch of used stippling sponges. Brushes, shaders, foundation. A packet of crepe wool..."

"Crepe wool?"

"That yellow packet with the clear window labeled 'plaited' on the top. That's a type of wool. It's used by makeup artists."

Connor understood. "You're saying this is stuff for disguises. Do you think Gibbons knows how to use this stuff?"

"Anything's possible."

Connor dug deeper and found a piece of card stock underneath the makeup supplies. He pulled it out, and when he flipped it over, he and Brice said "Holy shit" at the same time.

It was an eight-by-ten glossy photograph of the president. From back in high school.

And a large red 'X' was drawn across his face.

CHAPTER FIFTEEN

It was approaching midday as Annie weaved the last of the shrubs into a screen that obscured the Humvee from the road. She'd already disconnected one of the batteries stored under the passenger seat so that if someone did happen to stumble onto the truck, they wouldn't be able to steal it unless they were familiar with its operation and maintenance.

"Excuse me, but what about this?" The guard pointed at himself, the suicide vest obviously still being top of mind to the man she'd in effect kidnapped.

Annie pointed to the south. "Have you been in this camp before?"

The man nodded. "It's not the same as the one you destroyed. This is more like a town. It is Chief Enitan's home."

"What kind of security is at its entrance?"

He tilted his head slightly and furrowed his brows. "You're

not understanding my meaning. There's no walls. It's a normal town."

Annie pressed her lips together as she studied the man's body language. He believed what he was saying. Nonetheless, with her tenuous grip on this man's loyalties and her naturally untrusting nature, she wasn't about to take what he said on face value. Especially since they'd stopped a good half mile from the first sign of the town's entrance. "There is something that was brought into this town. How do you suggest we enter?"

The man closed his eyes and looked up into the sky. His lips moved in prayer and Annie felt her impatience growing.

"Well?"

"If *we* go, then I suggest we just walk in. I told you, there is no outer security." He sighed and focused his gaze on Annie. "Unless you are planning on stealing from Enitan's home, there isn't a danger in this place. It is a home to many of Enitan's people."

Annie motioned toward the south and said, "Well, you lead the way. I swear to you, there's one last thing I need, then I leave the town, and leave you for your freedom."

The guard nodded and began walking south at a casual pace, the empty AK47 slung over his shoulder.

Along the way they passed a waylaid wagon filled with watermelons. One of the men at the head of the wagon was yelling at the ox since it had pulled the wagon into a rut and was munching happily on a nearby flowering shrub that was apparently very tasty.

As they approached the town, Annie glanced at the app that

Brice had pushed to her phone. It was a piece of tracking software that was about as simple as anything she'd ever seen, making it fairly idiot proof. It had an arrow and a number noting the distance. She was within a quarter mile of a thirty-five-kiloton nuclear bomb.

Great.

After her last brush with a nuclear weapon, Annie had learned all sorts of details about how destructive those things could be. It was an obsession of hers, wanting to know everything about an enemy. That obsession had been useful to her in the past. But this time around, she almost wished she didn't know what she knew. If that damned bomb blew up right now, she wouldn't even be a grease spot. She imagined herself like Sarah Connor in that scene from one of the *Terminator* movies. The doomed Sarah was near a playground, holding on to a chain-link fence when a nuclear bomb exploded nearby. As the heat wave smashed into her, she was transformed from a living human into a fiery skeleton, and then exploded into dust.

Annie knew that was only a movie, but the truth was just as ugly. At thirty-five kilotons, anything within a mile of the bomb would be dead almost instantly. And anyone caught within two to three miles would wish they were dead.

The town came into view, and sure enough, it looked like an ordinary town, much like the villages she'd driven through except that this one was larger, probably housing hundreds of people rather than dozens, and everything was in better condition. It looked like a healthy and thriving town.

She told the guard to wait for one second, then pulled out her phone and stepped off the road far enough that she wouldn't be overheard. She dialed Brice's number and waited for the line to connect.

"Brice, I'm in spitting distance of our target. Just outside a town that's supposed to be the warlord's home."

"Great. Little Eagle is still in the air heading back to the States. Let me see if I can get a patch in to him. Hold on."

Annie paced back and forth, occasionally tossing her companion a glance. The guard was wringing his hands and averted his gaze whenever anyone walked past him. He looked guilty as hell.

The line was suddenly filled with crackling sounds.

"Ryan?" Brice said. *"Are you still on?"*

"Yup, I'm here. Somewhere over the Atlantic. Is the agent on scene?"

"I'm about a quarter mile from the target," Annie said. "I need to know what I have to do to not get everyone around me killed."

"A female agent? I hadn't expected that. Are you the only one on site?"

Annie gritted her teeth. "Yes."

Brice quickly interjected. *"Let me fill you both in on our instructions, which come direct from the Secretary of Defense. There is no option to leave the bomb behind. The warlord in possession of it has already made plans for its use. We can't let that happen."*

"Roger that," said the president's brother. *"And I'm sorry but... don't take this the wrong way, I'm not trying to be an asshole, but I think if we only have one person on site and espe-*

cially if she's a woman, our choices may be limited. We may have to set the timer and let nature take its course."

"Hold the hell up, cowboy," Annie said with a snarl. "I'm standing a hundred yards away from a town filled with kids and families and shit. I may be a lot of things, but I'm not about to blow up an entire town on your say so."

"Hold on, Annie," began Brice, but she cut him off.

"Shut the hell up, Brice. I'm talking to the cowboy. What's the other option, cowboy? Because the one you just talked about isn't happening."

"The other option requires you to carry out over one hundred and ten pounds of highly enriched uranium from whatever hell-hole it's hiding in. And I can't even be sure that's the size. For all I know it might be twice that weight."

Annie willed herself to focus less on the asshole she was talking to and more on what the asshole was saying. "I'll figure something out. How much of a procedure is it to take this thing apart and know what I'm looking for?"

"Luckily, I managed to dispose of the more advanced design before our plane got shot down. The one that remains… well, I'd rather walk you through it, but just in case we can't get a phone connection when you need it, let's go over the details."

"I'll take notes," Brice said.

"Thanks, Brice."

"This particular nuke is a really simple gun-style design. Basically a glorified gun barrel. You're familiar with how a bullet is lined up at the back end of a barrel and there's some target you aim at with the business end. This is basically the same thing, but

instead of a bullet with a shell casing, you have a doughnut-shaped chunk of highly enriched uranium on one end and your target is a cylinder of the same stuff on the far end of the barrel.

"You're trying to put the doughnut hole back together with the doughnut. When it's go time, cordite or some other type of high-explosive acts like the equivalent of a blasting cap and shoots the doughnut down the barrel. The doughnut is going well past supersonic speeds, and if you actually saw it in slow motion, you'd see it starting to sparkle and get angry as it gets closer to the doughnut hole made of uranium. At about a foot apart it goes critical, and if designed properly it only goes supercritical when the angry doughnut impales itself on the doughnut hole at the end of the barrel. At that moment, you better hope nobody is nearby, because everyone within a two-mile radius will witness a very big boom."

Annie could picture the design he described, and she allowed herself a small hope that things might prove to be simple. The last bomb she'd tackled had been a nightmare.

"Okay, so what are my steps? Crack open the case, and remove the doughnut and the doughnut hole?"

"Actually, it's even simpler than that. The case is held shut with ordinary Phillips-head screws, so no cracking required. The propellant is wired to the triggering harness, but you can just yank those wires and be done; there's no fancy anti-tampering switch. The barrel is sealed somewhat like a pipe bomb, with the end caps being screwed on. Unscrew the far end and you'll be able to extract the target cylinder. Just be careful. If you bring the doughnut and its hole together, even if they don't touch, it might go critical, and before you even realize you made a

mistake you'll be vaporized. It won't be a full-yield explosion, but even a tiny explosion isn't something you want to experience."

Annie swallowed. "How far apart do they need to be?"

"To be safe? I'd say you don't want them anywhere closer than two feet. But the further the better. That's why I'm doubting if this is feasible for you, no offense. Most men couldn't reliably carry two heavy weights by themselves and ensure they're kept far apart."

Annie closed her eyes and breathed deeply in and out. He wasn't wrong.

"Annie, do you have any other questions?" Brice asked.

"Do I need to worry about radiation?"

"No. It's mostly alpha particles that won't go through your skin. Just don't touch anything and lick your fingers."

"That won't be a problem. Brice, do you know if I have enough time to wait until it's dark here?"

"Like any intel, there's no sure thing, but the computers did intercept what we believe to be info on the warlord. Enitan is supposed to arrive at your location this evening local time. I have nothing that indicates any other movement before tomorrow."

Annie nodded. "Okay, cowboy, is there anything else I should know before I risk my ass on this debacle of yours?"

"I don't think so. I'm guessing I'll have landed by the time you try this, so please reach out, and I'll walk you through it, or help in whatever other way I can."

"I can assure you that I'll take you up on that. Brice, the next time I reach out, I'll be sitting in front of the nuke. Be ready."

"I'll be right here waiting on your call."

As Annie hung up, she looked over at her nervous and increasingly reluctant assistant.

"He is definitely not going to like what I'm about to ask him to do next," she muttered.

Sitting on one of the covered benches just outside the Stanford Residential College on the campus of the University of Miami, Johnny pretended to be flipping through a textbook he'd found on the grass, but really he was watching the school maintenance workers who were cordoning off the intramural field. Of particular interest was a crew of Secret Service agents, some of them with K9 units, who were obviously clearing the location. Signs everywhere stated that the field was off-limits to all student traffic due to an upcoming event, and even though that event wasn't specified, everyone knew what was going on.

The president was coming to the University of Miami to give a speech.

At the center of the field a raised stage had been erected, with a small set of stadium-style seating behind it. Those seats would no doubt be reserved for a handpicked smattering of whatever demographic the political machine wanted to cater to. Politicians were all scumbags. But some were most certainly worse than others.

One of the Secret Service agents pulled out what looked like a metal detector and disappeared beneath the stadium seating. Several other agents walked along the raised stage where a podium had been set up, and at each corner of the stage an agent stood watch over the non-existent crowd. Johnny spotted movement up and to his left, and glanced up to see an agent on the roof of the nearby Hecht-Stanford Dining Hall.

Lots of forethought was going into this. The security around the president would be tight.

Johnny smiled.

It wouldn't be enough.

CHAPTER SIXTEEN

Connor sat in a conference room with Thompson, Mason, and four other Outfit agents he'd only just met, all listening to Brice's presentation.

"As you all know, our current top suspect is a former sniper who has been out of sight since before the assassination of the Mayor of Turin. But after running through all the video footage we have coming and going from any US airport, I came up with nothing. And even though our guy couldn't have financed it, I included all of the private terminals that had video feeds, and again came up with nothing. It wasn't until Agent Sloane collected some evidence from the suspect's home in Montana that we realized that maybe our guy was traveling not only under an assumed name, but using an elaborate disguise."

"Marty," said Mason, "I thought your computer wouldn't get fooled by a disguise. Am I mistaken?"

"Well, generally that's true. But if your goal is to fool the computers, it's possible. The software inevitably has to use certain things that aren't normally malleable, like the distance between your eyes, shape of your nose, the ratios between different parts of your face. But with enough prosthetics and certain latex pieces, even some of those things can be altered. I can make Barack Obama look like Jackie Chan given enough makeup and time.

"Anyway, I messed with the algorithm and took into account some of the more likely changes in facial structure. I also set some parameters to limit the search to departures from the US sometime before the mayor's assassination and arrivals in the US sometime after the attempt on the German chancellor.

"After borrowing some of the computing horsepower from the Utah Data Center so that we could make a ridiculous number of runs through the video, we came back with way too many possible hits. The problem is, with prosthetics, it's almost impossible to predict what a suspect might look like.

"Nonetheless, I tried to winnow down the list. I removed those accompanied by children, people who were obese and unlikely up to the task, anyone with a medical history that might preclude them. Males only between the ages of thirty and fifty. We were down to a couple hundred possible ones. None of them had a military or law enforcement history. I started looking at each of the records one by one, and none of them made any sense. And then I stumbled into one that puzzled me. I set him aside and moved on, and eventually I had three people that I couldn't account for."

He clicked on the mouse, and three faces showed up on the screen on the wall of the conference room.

Connor had memorized Gibbons's face, but he'd never have guessed that any of these images were his guy. "Who are these people?" he asked.

Brice smiled. "Those three faces belong to people who don't exist."

"What do you mean, don't exist?" Mason said.

"They have legit passports. They're attached to legit social security numbers. They were definitely on the plane, and we have video footage of them. But none of those three people have ever worked a day in their life. Their current address is unknown. It's not like homeless people take international flights all that often." Brice patted the air as he looked at Mason. "I already know what you're thinking. We probably have people gaming the passport and social security system, and that's an issue I've now got on my board. Nonetheless, these are the faces I've found through my searches."

"Which airports?" Mason asked.

"One in LaGuardia, one in Miami International, and one in Dulles."

Thompson drummed his fingers on the table. "The images seem really sketchy. I'm not sure those are actionable. I want to take a step back. This Gibbons guy—can we pin down the motivation? I'm familiar with the background here, and to be frank, the case against him seems flimsy."

Brice clicked the mouse again, displaying a wall of text. "Thank you for that well-timed segue. Based on some of the latest data we received, I did some digging into Gibbons's family background and finances, and any possible links to the president or his family. Since everyone here has been briefed on the First

Lady's description of events, I'll unroll the data in chronological order.

"It seems our suspect's parents had a family ranch that was mortgaged, but they were keeping up with the bills until the suspect was midway through college. At that point there's records of some late payments. Things continued like that until shortly after the suspect graduated school. The local bank, Bank of Montana, sold their interest in the loan to a private equity firm. That equity firm was owned by none other than the president's father."

Connor raised his eyebrows.

"The previous bank had a rather interesting clause. It allowed them to demand payment in full for the balance of the loan if a loan had been late more than three times in the span of two years. The Bank of Montana never exercised that option."

"But the president's father did," Thompson said matter-of-factly, a look of contempt on his face.

Brice nodded. "That's right. And when Gibbons's parents weren't able to secure another loan to pay off the balance, the equity firm took possession of the ranch. The Gibbons family lost any equity they'd had.

"That's when things went from bad to worse. Both parents were diagnosed with terminal cancer. Jonathan Gibbons had been working as an accountant, but he moved back home to take care of his ailing parents. I imagine his life was hellish for quite a while, working two jobs and keeping things maintained while his parents hung on for a few more years. When they eventually passed, our suspect joined the military, leaving the house to be rented."

Thompson nodded grimly. "We have to assume that Gibbons's parents told him what had happened and how things had transpired. The motivation for Jonathan Gibbons gets stronger all the time. I don't think I need too much more convincing."

"Marty," said Mason, "send me a copy of those faces. I'll make sure the Secret Service is aware, just in case. I'll also make a few calls." He turned to Connor and the other agents. "Get your bags packed. You're going to be part of the travel shift that accompanies the president to his campaign stops. I'll make sure you get briefed in the air so that you're ready. And right now I'm going to call Jim Murray to tell him he's got four new worker bees and a whole lot more to worry about."

Connor positioned himself at the base of the steps to Air Force One, facing a long line of cars, including the Beast, the president's eight-ton armored vehicle. A warm breeze blew across the tarmac, carrying the scents of jet fuel and the salty air of the ocean, which was less than five miles away. Connor had never been to Miami before, and under different circumstances he might have enjoyed it.

The lead agent's voice came over his earpiece. *"Bonanza leaving Air Force One."* Bonanza was a nickname for the president's home state, so the code word for the president made some sense, even if it sounded a bit silly to Connor.

He heard the president's footsteps coming down the stairs, and as one of the other agents opened the rear door of the Beast,

Connor saw that the door was almost a foot thick. No wonder the car weighed so much.

The president jogged to the car, waved to the few dozen airport workers who'd gathered to see what was going on, and got in the limo.

"Bonanza is in the Beast. Local PD has cleared the path. Take your assigned positions."

Connor went to one of the large Lincoln Navigators along with two other agents. The driver spoke into a mic hidden in his sleeve. "Car three is ready."

About two minutes later the response came over their earpieces. *"Site two security, shotgun. Depart site one en-route to your location."*

The motorcade proceeded out of Miami International Airport and onto Le Jeune Road.

"Shotgun site one security, copy your departure, ETA ten minutes."

It felt eerie to drive through the streets of Coral Gables without traffic, ignoring the red lights, and never having to slow down for even a moment. It would be easy to get used to this.

The motorcade turned right on Ponce de Leon Boulevard, and the leader spoke again.

"Almost at destination."

"Drivers, local PD has closed San Amaro Drive. Bonanza's entering from the north corner of the field."

"Site two security, shotgun, arrive."

"Site two security copies arrival 1828 hours."

"All post at site two, Bonanza has arrived."

The motorcade slowed until the main limo was in position,

and then all at once two dozen agents, Connor among them, stepped out of their vehicles. They were met by other agents who were already there, probably the advance team who'd done the initial security screening.

Well over a thousand people had gathered to hear the president's speech, and it dawned on Connor just how difficult this task was. How could they possibly spot one bad guy in this crowd—especially one who was skilled with disguises? He activated his glasses and panned his gaze over the crowd. The lenses automatically draw a thin outline around each person, providing a color-coded threat level.

Connor assumed his assigned position along one of the aisles in the crowd. He scanned the folks nearest him, looking for anything out of the ordinary. The glasses were having trouble isolating individual faces in the crowd, and when they did, he was getting a constant threat level of yellow. Not useful. Besides which, their suspect was a sniper, and there was no way he would be in the crowd.

Suddenly the crowd began cheering so loudly that Connor felt the vibrations in his chest. Apparently the president had arrived on the stage.

Connor flipped his mic to the Outfit's channel, so that only the other team members would hear. "This is Sloane. Is one of you checking on the counter sniper teams? If our guy wants to take a shot…"

"This is Jenkins. The Secret Service guys have doubled up on the rooftops. They're on alert."

The president began talking to the crowd, his voice booming

from speakers arrayed across the field. Connor scanned the area. If he were a sniper, where would he take the shot? Across the field were several buildings, and all of them had people on them, but these were presumably agents. He saw the glint of sun reflecting off a spotter's scope. Definitely one of the counter sniper teams.

"We are ten minutes in with a planned ninety-minute speech."

Connor shrugged his tensed shoulders, trying to loosen them up. This job that the Secret Service did... no thanks. This was going to be the longest ninety minutes of Connor's life.

Johnny sipped at his Muhammad Ali and grimaced. "What the hell? People drink this shit?"

Carter, sipping his own fruit drink, laughed. "This is DC, what do you expect? Especially from a place called Turning Natural. You're the one who picked this hippy-dippy place." He turned on his stool and looked up at the board. "Mango, blueberry, raspberry, pineapple, BCAA, and glutamine. I have no idea what those last two are, but I'm sure it'll grow hair on your chest."

"I've got enough hair for you and me both. How is it that I always end up ordering shit I regret?"

His old army buddy smiled. "I remember back in the day, while everyone else was getting themselves trashed on the twelve bottles of Jordanian whiskey that someone had smuggled inside the wire, your ass convinced me to go with you and find something better. How sick did we get on that rotgut gin that that old toothless man sold us?"

Johnny laughed. "We're lucky we didn't go blind drinking that stuff." He raised the plastic bottle of Muhammad Ali and chugged. After the last gulp, he slammed the bottle on the counter and shuddered. "Okay, I need a beer to wash this crap down. You up for O'Malley's tonight?"

Carter shook his head. "I can't. I've got work tonight."

"Where are you flying off to this time?"

"You know I can't say." Carter glanced at his watch. "In fact, I have to get going. A rain check on O'Malley's?"

"Of course." Johnny fist-bumped his friend and said in a mock whisper, "Say hi to the president for me."

With a sidelong grin, Carter got up and left.

Johnny knew where his friend was going. Everyone knew the president's speech was scheduled for tonight. They had tried to keep it under wraps, but CNN and the rest of the stations had made the schedule loud and clear. And conveniently, that speech would take place no more than six miles from here.

Johnny whistled as he left the shop and turned off Martin Luther King Junior Avenue, away from his cash-only, one-bedroom rental. Down the street, he could see Carter walking away. One of Johnny's oldest friends in the world. A fellow sniper who'd flipped out of the army and had made good for himself.

It was such a shame… Johnny really liked Carter.

CHAPTER SEVENTEEN

Somewhere nearby a baby cried, startling Annie awake. In the darkness, she breathed in the scents of mud, urine, and straw. The guard had posed as her husband and rented this empty supply room from a local merchant. It was disgusting, and Annie was nostalgic for real civilization. She imagined herself taking a warm bath with bubbles, a nice uninterrupted sleep on a plush mattress, a slice of cheesecake…

She looked over at the guard, who was splayed out on the straw-strewn mud floor, snoring lightly. She knew better than to lie on the floor like that; it was almost certainly infested with all variety of bugs. By contrast, she'd fallen asleep wither her back against the corner of the room.

She levered herself up from her crouching position, her legs complaining as she stretched and twisted, and nudged the man with her toe. He grunted and lurched into a sitting position. Not surprisingly, he began scratching himself as he got up onto his feet.

"Let's get something to eat, and then we can see what there is to see," Annie said.

She opened the door into the merchant's store. He looked up as they exited.

"It good for you and your bride?" the man said to the guard. "That's a place where many new babies have been made." He let out a barking laugh.

Annie contemplated whether killing the gap-toothed merchant would be worth her time. But the guard pulled her away. "Let's get some puff puff. I can smell the oil nearby."

They stepped out into the street and saw that it was getting dark. They'd slept for longer than Annie would have thought possible. Still, the timing was good. They followed the smell of fryer oil, and when they found the boiling cauldron, the guard ordered them ten puff puffs.

The puff puff merchant had interesting markings on her cheeks. To the uninitiated these might look primitive, but Annie knew they were traditional markings that some in the Yoruba culture still took part in. They were typically etched or burnt into the skin when you were very young, even as young as six months old. She didn't know the tradition well enough to understand what they signified, other than that different markings usually identified where someone was from, almost like gang tattoos.

Using a metal spider, the woman scooped ten brown balls out of the oil. A second woman with a mixing bowl of dough was forming new balls and tossing them into the oil.

"They are still very hot," the guard said, handing Annie five puff puffs.

Her stomach grumbling, she blew on one of the balls, then took a bite. It tasted exactly how it looked. It had a dense texture, a bit bland, but it was fresh, hot, and filling. Tossed in powdered sugar, it would make an excellent doughnut hole.

The thought of a doughnut hole shifted her thinking back to the bomb.

She pulled up the tracking app on her phone and motioned for the guard to follow her as she tracked the arrow to its destination. With night falling, the hustle and bustle of the central market was dying away. Annie tossed the last of the puff puffs into her mouth while she left the market area, walked through several alleys, and found the arrow directing her to a large house. Just as she was approaching it, two Range Rovers pulled up in front, and she quickly stepped back into the shadows.

The vehicles' doors opened and several armed men stepped out, followed by two kids and a man in a flowing blue outer dress with trousers, an inner jacket, and a cap. This was a traditional Yoruba outfit called an *agbada*.

Her companion tapped on her shoulder and whispered excitedly. "That's the great man. That is Enitan. I can't believe I see him so close. And his children."

Several of the armed men walked over to a neighboring building, but the largest of them took up a position in front of the home. Annie double-checked her app. The house was definitely where the bomb was.

"Remember when I said there's something very dangerous in the town, and I'm trying to remove it?" she whispered.

Her companion nodded.

She nodded toward the house. "It's a bomb. A bomb powerful enough to destroy this entire town and far more. And it's in that house. Enitan doesn't understand how dangerous this is. We have to get rid of it, and I'm going to need your help."

The guard's eyes widened, and he shook his head. "I can't steal from Enitan. I cannot. It's *haram*."

Haram. It was a reminder that the guard was a follower not only of the warlord, but of Islam. *Haram* was the Arabic word for forbidden, especially as it pertained to Islamic scripture.

"Is it *haram* to kill innocent lives?" Annie asked.

"Of course."

"What about the killing of children?"

The man gave her a look of revulsion. "That is especially *haram*."

"Then let me tell you why we rushed at such a crazy pace to get here. If I don't find this bomb and remove the dangerous parts of it, then it will destroy this town before the sun goes up."

"You can't be serious. Are you?"

"It's also *haram* to be deceitful. I wouldn't lie about this."

The truth was, Annie couldn't care less about lying if it got the job done.

"You must tell Enitan," the guard said. "He will certainly listen."

"He won't. Another man I worked with tried to tell him, and he had him killed. Enitan believes that he can control this bomb to defeat his enemies. It's not true. It will defeat him instead."

The guard looked tormented. He looked back and forth between Annie and the home, wringing his hands. Finally he spoke. "I can't raise my hand against Enitan."

Annie shook her head. "I won't ask you to. I just need you to help me carry something. It will save this town."

"Just carry something?"

"Yes."

"And after this last thing, you will remove this burden from me?" He tapped at the vest under his shirt.

"I will."

The guard nodded. "Then I will do this. And no more."

———

It was about an hour since the guard at the front door had been replaced by someone new. Annie had watched the exchange, one guard handing the shotgun to the other and going to the building next door, which she assumed was the equivalent of a barracks for Enitan's personal guards. The muffled hum of generators sounded in the distance, producing whatever electricity was available in the town, and there were some lights on in the market area, but otherwise the town was silent and covered in a veil of darkness. Only a single dim bulb lit the front porch of Enitan's house, under which the guard remained awake and alert, though he was wearing headphones and bobbing his head lightly to whatever he was listening to.

Annie's companion hid in the shadows with her. The man seemed to fear both the wrath of Allah and Enitan, but it was his love for his family, and her threats against them, that had made him reliably cooperative. She just needed to rely on him a little bit longer.

She gave the man a nod, and he returned it. It was *go* time.

Annie stumbled into the clearing in front of the house, her arms flailing, and fell face-first into the dirt. As she staggered to her feet again, panting heavily, Enitan's guard rose to his feet and approached warily, holding the shotgun across his chest.

"Woman," the man hissed in a low voice. "What's wrong with you?"

Annie held up her hands in a pleading motion, then staggered once more, falling forward into the man. As her shoulder hit his chest, she raised both hands and released two spring-loaded darts into the underside of the man's jaw. One dart pierced the roof of the man's mouth; the other penetrated the back of his throat.

Annie barreled into the wide-eyed guard, launching him from his feet.

The two of them landed heavily in the dirt, the air whooshing from his lungs with a sickening gurgle.

Hearing the crunch of bone as Annie buried a dagger into the side of the man's head, she rolled off of him, ripping the shotgun from his grip and clamping her hand over his mouth and nose.

She pressed down onto his face with all of her weight as he convulsed, kicking dirt and dust everywhere. It took a full fifteen seconds before his convulsions subsided.

Annie rose and looked back at her companion, who had a look of horror on his face. He was probably wondering if he'd attached himself to a she-demon. She just hoped she hadn't done anything to lose his coerced loyalty.

She dragged the lifeless body away into the darkness, ran her hands under the man's overcoat, and found a second gun in a shoulder holster. It was a small-caliber Walther PPK with an attached silencer. Something she wouldn't have expected to see in this part of the world.

Realizing that her heart raced faster at the discovery of the weapon than when she'd killed the man, Annie pressed her lips together to suppress a laugh. Nobody needed to tell her that she wasn't right in the head.

She continued searching the man, and came away with a set of keys, a box of subsonic .22 caliber ammunition, and a handful of loose shotgun shells. She wiped as much of the blood from her hands as she could on the man's clothes, then motioned to her companion to remain where he was. Even if the man were guaranteed to be entirely loyal, she knew better than to take someone like him into a place that required stealth.

As she made her way to the front door, all of her senses were tingling. She knew from experience that entry into an unknown building was usually the most dangerous part of a mission. With the silenced pistol in one hand, she stepped onto the front porch and tested the door. It was locked. Digging the keys from her pocket, she picked the one that looked most likely, and slowly, silently, inserted it in the lock.

It worked.

Her heart thudded in her chest as she cracked open the door and entered the darkness of the home.

As she closed the door behind her, a man's voice spoke in the darkness. "What are you doing in here?"

She spun around, and her glasses highlighted a living room. A man was halfway sitting up on a sofa and looking suspiciously in her direction.

Annie pulled the trigger twice.

Both shots were no louder than the cycling of the tiny gun's slide.

The guard's body tensed and fell back onto the sofa as Annie panned her gaze across the pitch-black backdrop.

There was nobody else in the room.

Annie pulled up the app again. To her surprise, it claimed that the bomb was now only two feet away. But there was nothing two feet away from her but empty floor.

It must be on a different level.

Moving cautiously, she found a staircase and climbed to the second floor. The stairs emptied out into a long hallway with several doors, most of them closed. The lights were off up here as well, but her glasses displayed her surroundings in a vague grayish hue.

Annie started down the hallway. As she approached an open doorway, she peered around the corner. Just an empty bathroom.

She continued forward.

As she approached the next door, a floorboard creaked beneath her foot. She froze. Had that been loud enough for others to hear it?

After what seemed an eternity, she continued on and pushed open the door, which was ajar. This was one of the children's rooms. A boy clad in pajamas was splayed sideways across his bed, unmoving.

As she moved farther down the hall, the glow of a light appeared under the door at the very end of the hall. Suddenly the door opened and a man appeared, wearing only boxer shorts, his eyes wide with shock at the sight of the intruder in the hall.

Annie raced forward and shot four times, aiming for the

man's head. She caught the man as he collapsed and pulled him back into the bedroom behind him, which was empty.

And then she looked at the man she'd just shot.

Enitan.

The man whose people had butchered the soldiers who come to rescue Little Eagle.

Good riddance.

She pulled up the app once more. And again, it told her she was almost directly on top of the bomb. But again, there was nothing here.

The house had only two stories. Which meant there must be a basement. A very unusual thing in this part of the world, especially in such a remote place, but there was no other explanation.

Closing the bedroom door behind her, she went back down the stairs and began searching the lower floor. Finally she found it: a set of stairs going down. She followed them into a large basement filled with supply crates, most of them labeled as containing types of munitions. But at the center of the room, one large crate sat apart from the others, held together with canvas straps.

The app was pointing directly at this box.

Annie removed the straps and carefully lowered the wooden sides of the crate to the floor. She now found herself standing before a plain metal cylinder with a keypad at its top.

The nuke.

She inserted her earpiece and double-tapped her glasses. Within seconds she heard Brice's voice. *"Annie, what's your status?"*

"I'm standing right in front of it. Get our friend on the line."

CHAPTER EIGHTEEN

Johnny looked down sadly at his friend. Carter was lying on the floor, a bullet hole in his forehead.

"I would have said you didn't see that one coming, but you did." He sighed. "I'll see you in hell, my friend."

He undressed the man at his feet, making sure that the lapel pin on the suit jacket remained in place—that would identify him as an agent to the other agents—and paying careful attention to how the various microphones and transmitters were attached. Once he had everything laid out for him to use, he dragged Carter over to the bathroom and began his process of transformation.

Johnny looked in the mirror and chuckled. He'd dyed and styled his hair to match Carter's, and he'd applied several latex pieces to make his face more closely match Carter's face, but he still looked like a slapped-together Frankenstein's monster. Still, that was to be expected. Now was when the magic really started.

He'd been obsessed with professional makeup artistry ever since seeing a show on the topic when he was a kid, and he'd practiced in private for years. His parents hadn't understood; in fact, at one point his dad asked him if he was gay. But it wasn't that at all. It was just the idea of looking like someone else. That had always fascinated him.

He used a stippling sponge to dab several layers of liquid latex along the edges of his prosthetics. That made for a more seamless appearance. He then applied a colored mask grease with a stippling motion over the entirety of his face, making his skin tone closer to Carter's. With a liberal application of translucent powder, he removed the shine from any exposed glue.

Then he studied himself in the mirror once more, looking from the reflection down to his dead friend on the floor. He was getting closer. He just needed a few more age lines and other small details.

He used a wedge-shaped sponge to apply a thin coat of foundation across his forehead, on his cheeks, and along his throat. This changed the opacity of his skin and acted as a base layer to apply his other changes. Grabbing a makeup brush with a plum-colored shader, he applied shadow under his eyes, on the hollows of his cheeks, and along some lines on his neck. Using another brush, he applied highlights to his cheekbones, nasal folds, and forehead wrinkles. He softly blended the wrinkles to ease the contrast between the highlights and shadows. He dabbed on a maroon effect, which gave the illusion of broken capillaries on his nose. As a final touch, he did a few makeup tricks to simulate Carter's bushy eyebrows.

This time when he looked in the mirror, he smiled.

No, the smile was off. Well, there was nothing he could do about that. But as he stared at his reflection, adopting his best somber Carter expression, Johnny felt a wave of satisfaction wash over him.

This was going to work.

"Cowboy, can you see what I'm seeing?" Annie whispered.

"Yup, I see it clearly. Just remove the casing like we talked about."

With a screwdriver in her hand, she began working on the case. "Are you sure this isn't going to make it blow?"

"I'm sure. I have the advantage of having x-rayed the unit before, so I know what's inside. The trigger mechanism is a joke."

Annie made quick work of the case, and removed it to expose yet another metal cylinder. Only this one had no screws, just end caps. A glorified pipe bomb, just like Little Eagle had said.

"You see those two wires leading from the timer mechanism and into the metal pipe? Just pull them loose from the pipe. Do it one at a time if it's easier, but it doesn't matter either way."

"Okay…"

Annie's heart was racing, and she felt sweat dripping down

the back of her neck. She held her breath as she grabbed the insulated wire and pulled.

It popped free without much effort. When nothing exploded, Annie let out a sigh of relief and pulled out the second wire.

"Good. Now unscrew the top. The entire timing mechanism will rotate with it. Remember, this thing is heavy, so be ready for the weight. Also, lefty-loosey, righty-tighty. Whatever you do, counterclockwise is the direction you want."

The end cap had knurled ridges along its circumference that made it easy for her to grip. Yet she couldn't help but feel a bit of panic as she gripped the cap and began twisting it. That panic only increased when it didn't move. She exerted more pressure, and still more pressure, and for a moment she was worried that she might not be able to remove the cap at all.

And then it shifted.

After that initial movement, it loosened up and got easier to turn.

"You're doing great."

The moment the cap came off the last thread, Annie felt it tilt slightly. "Do I just lift it straight up?" she asked.

"Yes. And do us all a favor, don't put it down near the cylinder. Take several steps back before you set it down."

Annie began lifting the end cap up. It was heavy. Definitely more than fifty pounds. She strained as she slowly withdrew a cylindrical object from within the tube.

"Okay, several steps back."

"I know," Annie snapped.

She moved about ten feet from the bomb, then set her burden down.

"If you have the time, I can walk you through separating the uranium from the propellant and the rest of the end cap. It'll make it lighter. But that'll take about ten minutes."

Annie shook her head. "No. This has to be quick."

"Okay. Then go back to the bomb, turn it upside down, and repeat the process with the other end cap."

Annie tilted the cylinder onto the ground and was about to lift up the other end when Little Eagle's voice shouted into her ear.

"Shit! That's not good."

Annie saw it too. A bulging seam along the base of the end cap. "That looks like a weld," she said. "This thing isn't coming off."

"That's what it looks like to me as well. Shit."

Annie sighed. "Okay, cowboy, what now? This end of the pipe probably weighs three hundred pounds. There's no way I can get it out of here."

Brice cut in. *"Ryan, what if we evac the piece Annie separated, leaving the rest behind? Would that work?"*

"That's a good compromise," Little Eagle said. *"And I think it's our only option. Annie, if you can get away from there with the other end cap, we've made the best of a bad situation."*

"One second." Annie peered into the pipe and spotted what Little Eagle has described as the doughnut hole. She opened her pack and retrieved her last grenade. "Guys, if I put this inside the tube with the uranium it won't do anything funny, will it?"

"Is that an M67?" Little Eagle asked.

"Yes. I was thinking of remotely detonating it. I've got one last remote detonator circuit I can use."

The president's brother began chuckling. *"I like it. 6.5 ounces of comp B explosive will probably shatter the uranium cylinder. That's excellent."*

Annie made quick work of wrapping wire around the spoon of the grenade, twisting it tightly and attaching a receiver to it.

"That looks pretty good." Brice noted.

Dragging the pipe across the dirt floor, she brought it to the opposite side of the basement where there were no other boxes. She was very conscious of the kids two stories above her, and didn't want to blow the entire house apart. With one arm, she carefully lowered the grenade into the pipe, checked to make sure the wire was still secure, and then pulled the pin.

"Okay, little lady. Now get your ass out of there."

Cowboy was a real asshole.

Annie walked over to the end cap she'd removed, wrapped her arms around it, and started back up the stairs. "Brice, I'm assuming you'll get me out of here."

"I've already sent the request, and the chopper will be lifting off any second. I'll ring you back when it's just about there."

Annie burst out of the house and staggered across the clearing.

Her companion stood wide-eyed as he watched her approach. "Is that the bomb?" he asked.

"Part of it."

Panting, she hefted the heavy metal bundle into his arms and said, "Bring this and follow me."

By the time they exited the town, Annie's companion was breathing heavily. She motioned to the north. "Just keep going that way. I'll be right behind you."

He staggered north, and Annie stepped up behind him and smothered his face in a chemical-soaked cloth. Thanks to his rapid breathing, it took him only two seconds to pass out and fall to the ground, dropping his burden.

Annie set his back against the nearest building, ripped open his shirt, and with a few quick cuts with her knife, removed the makeshift suicide vest, which had been an inert sample that she'd taken from Brice's supplies. She patted the guard's cheek and said, "Thank you for your assistance. You're now free to go."

She dug the last of her transmitters from her pocket, pressed the button on the remote and held it down.

Somewhere in a basement below Enitan's home, the wire wrapped around the spoon of the M67 started glowing red hot as an electric charge surged through the loops of metal.

In the darkness Annie heard a muffled explosion and smiled.

She double-tapped her glasses and called Brice.

"What's the update on that chopper?"

"I was just about to contact you. It's on its way."

"Well tell them to come right to me. I can't carry this thing very far."

"Roger that. I'll have them drop right on top of you."

Two minutes later, Annie heard the *whoomp whoomp* of the helicopter. It set down, and three men hopped off. In short order they had dragged both Annie and the fragment of the bomb on board.

Annie, exhausted, lay on her back as someone put an oxygen mask over her face. The helicopter was in the air again, and she heard a voice say, "Director Brice, we have Agent Brown and the package. We're en route to base."

The Miami speech ended up making Connor very aware of how much this kind of security duty sucked. Knowing that any event could be the one where someone tries to take the president's life, yet you were almost assured nothing would happen. It was really hard to keep up the necessary vigilance and he now had a lot more respect for what the presidential security detail entailed.

And today was just another day. This one was theoretically simpler, because it was local. DC's Capital One arena was literally walking distance from the White House.

Connor was stationed near the podium when he heard across his earpiece, *"All post at site two, Bonanza has arrived."*

That meant the president was on the premises.

The feel of this place was very different from Miami. The enclosed space of an arena made the whole sniper thing seem impractical. Everyone had gone through a magnetometer, and he wracked his brain on where a possible attack could come from.

"Bonanza moving to greeters."

A rustle of excitement sounded at the far end of the stadium. Some of the audience must have spotted the president.

"Bonanza moving to off-stage announce."

One of the many politicians in the arena jogged up to the

podium. Connor kept his head on a swivel, and his glasses high-lighted the politician in green.

Green meant Brice's gadget was able to recognize whoever it was and connect it to an identity with security clearance.

The politician began speaking to the crowd, his voice broad-casting through the stadium. Connor panned his gaze across the sea of people. Yellow outlines—people for whom the glasses didn't have an identity.

Yellow wasn't bad, it was just an unknown.

The politician's voice took on a more excited tone, and Connor spotted the president and his entourage of agents approaching, all with green outlines. The agents had their hands held forward in the ready position. To the untrained eye, the agents were simply gripping the front edges of their suit jackets, but there was a purpose behind that. If any threat appeared, their hands were in a position to respond as quickly as possible.

The politician at the podium called out the president's name, and the president passed not more than a few feet from Connor as he climbed the stairs to the stage. The two politicians shook hands, the president using a firm two-hand grip, as he always did. The agents on each corner of the stage faced the crowd, looking for anything out of the ordinary.

Everyone on the stage had a green outline.

Except for one.

One of the agents was outlined in yellow.

A tingle raced through Connor as the yellow agent reached into his suit jacket. Without thinking, Connor took the steps three at a time and yelled, *"Code red!"*

He launched himself at the suspected agent just as he pulled out a gun.

Connor slammed into the man just as the gun went off.

Chaos erupted as a knee slammed into his head.

The world went black.

CHAPTER NINETEEN

The conference room was filled with all variety of agents, some familiar to Connor, some not. He gave Annie a fist bump when she arrived, feeling surprisingly happy to see her stateside and in one piece. He'd heard about what had happened, and it sounded like it had sucked.

There was a box at the center of the conference room table from "Renault's Bakery." That sounded promising.

Mason walked in and scanned the room. "Good," he said, "it looks like we're all here. Let's get started."

Connor hadn't experienced Mason's after-action report meetings, but he knew Mason had a reputation for being a real hard-ass about making sure people owned up to their screw-ups. Thompson had run the only AAR Connor had gone through with the Outfit, and he had been a hard-ass too. Connor still stung from the rebuke he got for letting the "bad guy" get away. It didn't matter that everything else went as well as possible.

"I've read all of your personal reports," Mason continued, "and I think some of you have been particularly generous with your credit and fairly stingy on the critique. Can I get a volunteer to talk about where they went wrong?"

Connor raised his hand.

"Go ahead, Mr. Sloane."

It had been six weeks since the attempted assassination of the president—and Connor's failures had been eating at him the entire time.

"Sir, I had all the pieces of information laid out in front of me. I knew our guy was a sniper and that he'd used those skills for his kills over in Europe. Because of that, I was so focused on some long-distance shot that I blinded myself to any other possibility. That led me astray. It was only thanks to Brice's technology that I managed to spot the assassin at the crucial second. And got my bell rung for my trouble."

"Well, a concussion is a fair exchange for helping avert a presidential assassination." Mason chuckled. "But you're right, sometimes we let the data blind us to other possibilities. The group should take that into consideration as we move forward. Facts are facts, but it all depends on how we interpret them."

"Director Mason." Brice raised his hand. "I'm partially to blame for some of the evidence issues. Before the event, we had narrowed down our suspects to three people who all fit certain parameters: they'd left the country before the Italian mayor was killed, returned back to the states after the German chancellor's assassination attempt, and had valid identification but no life history. As it turns out, none of these men proved to be Jonathan Gibbons.

"It wasn't until three weeks after the assassination attempt that I finally managed to identify one of these men as Karl Himmler, a professional assassin. Knowing that Gibbons had withdrawn every last cent from his bank account several months ago, I did some digging to figure out where those funds went. It turns out, most of them were wired by Western Union—to Karl Himmler."

"Wait a minute," Connor exclaimed. "You're saying Gibbons never went to Europe at all? He hired an assassin to go to Europe just to throw us off the trail?"

Brice nodded. "Can you imagine if that guy didn't have a screw loose? That's some next-level planning."

The meeting continued as others talked about the mistakes they had made and things that everyone could do to improve next time. They were approaching the one-hour mark when Mason called on Annie.

"Agent Brown, you're usually pretty good with using your critiquing skills. Perhaps you can tell everyone how *I* screwed the pooch."

Annie chuckled and smiled in that predatory fashion she seemed to have perfected. "Let's start with your insane idea to have a beige man try to help me retrieve the president's brother in Nigeria of all places. When we're dealing with the kind of sketchy people you like to hook us up with, him being beige wasn't helpful at all. It was drawing too much attention to us."

Mason shifted his gaze to Connor. "Your thoughts on that, Mr. Sloane?"

Connor shrugged. "She has a point. And on top of that, she

had the language skills for that part of the world, and mine weren't up to par."

Mason nodded. "Good points. But as operators, we all know that you'll be put into less-than-ideal circumstances. You need to improvise, adapt, and overcome." He returned his attention to Annie. "I would have thought that given your partner's lack of melanin, you two would have come up with a plausible backstory. His not having the language skills could have fed into that."

He looked around the room. "You all know that we don't have infinite human resources. We pick all of you for very specific sets of skills. You won't always have the ideal ingredients for the mission you're on. But you're expected to make the best of the situation."

He nodded to Annie. "Anything else?"

Annie seemed a bit pensive and uncharacteristically somber. "Well, it's off-topic, but I suppose this is as good a time as any to say this. I'm quitting the business."

Connor's jaw dropped, as did nearly everyone else's. Annie had a reputation that bordered on mythical within the walls of the Outfit.

But Mason was smiling. Of course he wasn't surprised. That bastard seemed to know everything before anyone else did.

"Can I ask why?" Connor said.

"I did survive two nuclear bombs, Sloane. I think that's a sign from above that I don't need to press my luck. But in addition..." Annie reached across the table and grabbed Brice's hand. "We're pregnant."

Connor was stunned.

Mason chuckled, "With all the death that you've left behind—"

"I don't kill children." Annie interjected with as forceful a voice as possible without yelling.

"I know that." Mason continued. "I was saying that with all the death that you've left behind, it's good to see you turning a new leaf and creating life."

"What does this mean for you, Brice?" Connor asked.

It was Annie who answered. "Brice is staying with the Outfit. Someone needs to support us." She gave Brice a wicked smile. "I'm sure you'll remember your obligations. If you cross me, just remember what Black Widows do to their mates."

Everyone in the room laughed, and Annie leaned over and gave Brice a lingering kiss.

Only then did Mason open the bakery box that had been waiting at the center of the table. Inside was a cake with the words "Congratulations Marty and Annie."

Annie leaned over to Connor and whispered in his ear. "Better be careful. I hear that Mason's got a girl who's ready to pick up my mantle."

Mason looked at the two of them and grinned. "Are you telling him about Ainsley?"

"Ainsley?" Connor said.

Annie smiled. "I think it's better that he finds out on his own."

AUTHOR'S NOTE

Well, that's the end of *The Death Speech*, and I hope you were entertained by it.

Since this is book two of a series, I'll presume that I've introduced myself to you before and won't make you suffer through that sort of tedium again.

However, I did want to talk a bit about my contract with you, the reader.

I write to entertain.

That truly is my first and primary goal. Because, for most people, that's what they want out of a novel.

That's certainly what I always wanted. Story first, always.

Now, don't get me wrong, there are all sorts of perfectly valid reasons to be reading, and in fact, I get a huge kick out of it when people tell me that they kept on having to look things up to see if they were real, and being shocked to learn that they were.

For me, I do take pride in trying to give people entertainment, while attempting to stay as true to science and technology as possible.

The nice things about having a growing audience is that I get to interact with people from all walks of life. In this particular tale, I did have the privilege of talking at length with several people who chose not to be named because they currently work either as a staff member in the White House or are active Secret Service agents.

The world of DC is quite different than what most of us would ever experience, and that unique experience is what I try to bring with my stories. Bring to the reader a world that they maybe aren't aware of, whether it's procedures, behaviors, or people that aren't your run-of-the-mill characters that we interact with in our daily lives.

I try to keep things as real as possible. And even with the things I described, and the scenarios I talk about, my litmus test when talking with the experts is never a black and white: would this work? I'm obviously not writing a how-to on assassination or other things, but I shoot for the plausible. If I can get the experts to buy into it being possible, then I've done my job to the best of my ability.

Also, since my readers come from all walks of life, I do as much as I can to avoid taking positions on what might be political matters or polarizing science topics such as GMO. I let the characters play out their roles and make no advocacies. However, I do endeavor to lay out the facts as they exist for the reader to ultimately draw their own conclusions.

So far, I've covered broken arrow incidents (See Perimeter for that), the potential disasters of uncontrolled genetic modification (Darwin's Cipher), and in this novel, a very small peek into the security systems of governments.

I shouldn't ignore that an entire thread of this story took place in what might be considered areas that government really doesn't apply. Even though many parts of sub-Saharan Africa are no different than what you or I may experience in whatever part of the world we live in, some areas are very very different. I've been in tribal-controlled parts of the world where armies go to flounder and eventually leave. I've seen how some of these things play out, but in the case of sub-Saharan Africa, I did again leverage my resources.

I have readers in Nigeria and the surrounding areas. Talking with them is a research project into a world that straddles both the new world that we know and the old. Ancient traditions and new ones. I tried to bring a little piece of that into the story for people to experience, and I hope I did it justice.

When picking this book up I don't think anyone would have expected a good portion of the book to take place outside the continental US. I really do try to keep everyone on their toes. I apologize for nothing. ;-)

Some people have called my choices eclectic, unexpected, but the vast majority of feedback I've received to date has been positive. So, thank you for that. Posting reviews is, of course, the easiest way to let me and others know what you thought of this novel or any of my work. Word of mouth is precious to us poor authors.

However, even though I enjoy writing about events, history, science especially, my primary goal always circles back to entertaining.

I do hope you enjoyed this story, and I hope you'll continue to join me in the future stories yet to come.

Mike Rothman
July 15, 2021

I should note that if you're interested in getting updates about my latest work, join my mailing list at:

https://mailinglist.michaelarothman.com/new-reader

If you enjoyed this story, you're likely to also enjoy my Levi Yoder series. If you'll indulge me, below is a brief description of Perimeter, book one of an ongoing series, followed by a sample of how it begins:

Levi Yoder is a member of the Mafia and a fixer of people's problems.

Unfortunately, Levi can't fix the problem he's facing.

Having been diagnosed with a terminal case of cancer, Levi readies himself for death, but what he didn't prepare himself for was waking up one morning and learning that he's in complete remission.

PERIMETER is a story of a man thrust back into a life he'd assumed was over.

When he finds that he and the rest of his family are targets of what the CIA claims are elements of the Russian mob, Levi reluctantly agrees to help in whatever way he can.

As Levi immerses himself in the seedy underbelly of

international organized crime and politics, he learns that he's being targeted for something his now-dead wife did.

It's quickly evident that the people he knows can't be trusted and the problems he needs to fix may be beyond his substantial skills.

PREVIEW OF PERIMETER

"Mr. Yoder, I'm sorry to have to tell you this." Dr. Cohen looked concerned, hesitant, but he spoke quickly, as if to get it over with. "You have stage-4 pancreatic cancer."

That was certainly not how Levi had expected his nine a.m. follow-up visit to go. A chill spread through his chest and sent a shiver down the middle of his back.

The gray-haired doctor sat across the table from Levi and nudged a box of tissues in his direction.

As if tissues could help anything.

"How can I possibly have cancer?" Levi's fingers dug tightly into the arms of the padded red leather chair as he leaned forward. "I'm only thirty, and I've lived a clean life. I don't drink alcohol or do drugs. Are you sure?" He realized it sounded like denial.

Dr. Cohen stood, walked around his large mahogany desk, and put a wrinkled hand on Levi's shoulder. "Son, I'm genuinely sorry." He sighed, his breath smelling of peppermint tea. "Unfortunately, the early stages of pancreatic cancer have almost no symptoms. I sent the biopsy samples to two different labs, and they both came back with the same results. The radiology scans we took last week also confirmed the level of metastasis. The cancer has spread into your lymphatic system."

Levi took a deep breath and let it out slowly. The tautness of his muscles dissipated as a feeling of resignation came over him.

"Stage 4? What does that mean? How do we treat this? What's the next step?"

Pulling a chair closer, the doctor sat across from Levi, their knees practically touching. "Stage 4 simply means the cancer has spread to other organs. In your case, we've detected the cancer in your pancreas as well as your lymph nodes. As to treatment, Sloane-Kettering and a few other research hospitals conducted clinical trials in 2005 that dealt with this type of cancer. Nowadays there are experimental radiation treatments that we could try, coupled with multiple rounds of chemotherapy, but at this stage of your disease, I'm afraid the odds aren't good." He leaned forward and with a solemn expression said, "My best estimate would be that without treatment, you might only have four to six months to get your things in order. And even with treatment, I'll be frank: only one percent have survived five years. Nonetheless, I've already made some calls and we've got world-class treatments that can hopefully improve those odds. I'll do everything in my power to help you get through this."

Levi's mind raced as he absorbed the doctor's words.

He'd always been known to those in his line of work as a fixer. He took care of sensitive issues when the mob bosses needed someone with a deft hand and not just pure muscle. He also fixed issues that the cops couldn't or wouldn't fix.

For this, he had no fixes.

However, he knew there were a few things he needed to take care of right away.

He stood and shook the doctor's hand. "Dr. Cohen, I know it must be hard to deliver this kind of news. Thank you for being honest with me. I'll be back in a couple weeks, after I've set my affairs in order, and we'll talk."

"But Mr. Yoder, you really should start the treatments right away. I called Sloane-Kettering and I've gotten you into one of their treatment programs—"

Levi waved dismissively and turned toward the exit. "I appreciate it, but I'll be back."

As Levi opened the door and left the doctor's private office, all he could think of was Mary.

When Levi walked into the bedroom, Mary, already in her nightclothes, shot him a brilliant smile while she placed a record on the turntable. "I just found this in an old record shop. You have to hear it."

The sound of Nat King Cole, one of Mary's favorites, came over the speakers.

"Love me as though there were no tomorrow…"

The haunting lyrics of the ballad brought a lump into his throat.

Mary danced toward him with a dreamy smile on her face,

enraptured by the music. Just as her gaze met his, she froze mid-step. Her smile faltered, and lines of worry formed on her forehead.

Levi had never been able to hide his feelings from her.

He stepped closer, cupped his wife's face in his hands, and stared into her beautiful dark-brown eyes. Her face was framed by a thick mass of jet-black hair and she looked as beautiful as the day he'd met her.

As he explained what the doctor had told him, his mind flashed back to when he'd first laid eyes on her. It was only five years ago when she'd arrived in America as Maryam Nassar, a twenty-two-year-old refugee from Iran. She spoke passable English and had responded to one of Levi's ads for a personal secretary. The moment he first saw her, it was like he'd been struck by lightning. His skin had tingled, and he'd barely managed to catch his breath.

They were married nine months later.

His chest tightened as a storm of emotions flashed across her face: disbelief, hurt, anger. Her dark eyes glistened with tears and her chin quivered as she exclaimed in her strong Persian accent, "B-but you prom—"

She pulled in a deep, shuddering breath, and Levi wrapped her in his arms.

"Honey, I know…"

He pressed her to his chest and rubbed her back as she sobbed. Mary was the only person in her family who'd chosen exile after the Iranian revolution. None of her family had any deep religious convictions, yet the moment she left Iran and married a non-Muslim, she'd sealed her fate. She couldn't go back. Mary had nobody else in this world, and that's what made telling her about his prognosis so difficult.

She also wasn't the type of person to let her emotions out freely—yet now she trembled in Levi's arms.

His throat thickened with regret. He could only imagine the fears she had going through her head. "I'll make sure that you never have to worry about anything for the rest of your life," he said. "This will always be your home, no matter what happens. Do you understand me?"

"I don't need *things*. I don't need Levi Yoder, the business-man. I *need* my *husband*." Mary fiercely grabbed both of Levi's wrists and stared at him with bloodshot eyes. "I love you."

He'd only heard her say that a handful of times. Each time had been a euphoric experience. Yet this time, it pained him to hear it.

He'd helped hundreds of people in the past. But this time, when it mattered most, when the person who needed help was the one person he cared more for than anyone in the world ... he couldn't help. He couldn't fix this.

"I'll stay with you as long as I possibly can—that much I promise you." He wiped the tears from Mary's cheeks with his thumbs. "I love you more than you'll ever know."

She grabbed Levi tightly around his chest and they held each other in silence, knowing that no words would fix what they were going through.

Yousef Nassar's skin prickled with anxiety as he watched the laborers empty the ancient burial chamber of an early-Egyptian priest. It had been only two days since Yousef had discovered the long-forgotten chamber, and already it was nearly empty.

Thieves! These men were all thieves, and knowing that he was in some way enabling this … the guilt gnawed at Yousef's stomach.

Trying to ignore the men who were stealing irreplaceable artifacts, he turned back to the wall with the faded hieroglyphs and continued transcribing them into his notebook. With his mind focused on the task, the world and its goings-on vanished.

"Dr. Nassar?"

Yousef flinched as he heard his name spoken in English, but with a heavy Russian accent. He turned to see one of Vladimir's men. Despite the heat in the underground chamber, the man was dressed from head to toe in a black suit. His chiseled face and stone-gray eyes showed no emotion.

"Yes?"

The large man stepped closer, and a small, precious, amber bead cracked under his foot. He pointed across the tomb toward the six-foot statue of Anubis with its arm extended. "Vladimir had instructions in case such a statue was found. Has the ankh been packed properly?"

Yousef's pulse quickened, and he struggled to keep his face neutral. "We didn't see anything near or on the statue."

The man's jaw muscles clenched and relaxed. "You're certain of this?"

"I am." Yousef hitched his thumb toward the wall. "When

you talk to Vladimir, let him know that some of what is written here needs to be preserved—"

"I'll inform Vladimir of what's been found."

The broad-shouldered man turned, and the workers scattered out of his way as he walked stiffly toward the tomb's entrance.

Yousef cleared his throat, and the sound echoed off the stone walls of the chamber.

Despite the oppressive heat, he felt a chill race through him as he began unraveling the meaning of a few of the images. The scenes depicted in the pictographic messages told of a time when southern and northern Egypt had yet to be unified.

"Yousef," a woman's voice whispered. "Have you gotten further in the translation?"

He glanced over his shoulder at Sara. In Farsi, he asked, "Did you…?"

She nodded.

Breathing a sigh of relief, he gave his wife a brief kiss and smiled. "I really think this might be one of the earliest tombs we've ever encountered. This is definitely from the early First Dynasty."

Sara peered at the notebook in his lap. "What do you have so far?"

He flipped to a prior page and scanned his notes. "Like you suspected, this is definitely a tomb of an early priest, but I don't see the markings of Atum, the sun god. It's something else. The messages are talking of a great war with the south. Here, listen to this."

"The land is aflame with disease and pestilence.
  "A piece of the sun came down and it was a man—"

Yousef put his finger on the next symbol and frowned as he wracked his mind on how to best translate it into something meaningful.

"Glowing like many stars in the night, his breath was like a crocodile."

"What does that even mean?" Sara asked.

He shook his head. "Your guess is as good as mine. It doesn't make sense. We'll need to research that when we get back to the university. In fact, the next several passages seem nonsensical."

Yousef shifted his gaze to the remaining symbols he'd yet to transcribe. He tensed as he recognized one of the hieroglyphs. "My God, what could *that* mean?"

Sara pointed at two of the symbols on the faded wall. "The catfish and chisel … doesn't that depict Narmer?"

Yousef nodded as he tried to glean meaning from the other nearby symbols. "It does, but it almost seems like the message is saying that this man who was a piece of the sun gave something to Narmer."

As he leaned in closer to the wall, the sound of something metallic clattered behind him. He whirled to see a grenade rolling over the sand-strewn floor, like a cluster of dark grapes.

Yousef's yell was trapped in his throat as the grenade exploded.

———————

"I guess today's a banking day for the Yoder family. Your wife was in a few hours ago."

Never having been one for small talk, Levi simply nodded and showed the man his key.

The well-dressed, gray-haired bank manager glanced at Levi's safe deposit box key and returned his nod. "Follow me, Mr. Yoder."

The manager turned, stiffly walked into the bank's vault, and panned his gaze across the metal wall. He moved toward the right-most section of the vault, and paused in front of the safe deposit box that held the number found on Levi's key.

Pulling a second key from his vest pocket, the manager inserted it into one of the keyholes on the front of Levi's box.

He held out his hand. "The key please, Mr. Yoder."

Levi handed the bank manager his key, and the manager inserted it into the remaining keyhole. As the manager turned both keys at once, Levi heard the snick of a lock disengaging. His box slid out half an inch from the wall.

The manager returned Levi's key to him. "Mr. Yoder, allow me to lead you to a room where you may go through your belongings in private."

Levi pulled on the handle of his safe deposit box. It slid smoothly out of its alcove.

Moments later, Levi found himself in a private room smelling faintly of wood polish and leather. The bank manager closed the door behind him as he left, leaving Levi alone.

Levi withdrew a thick envelope from his suit coat pocket and placed it in the metal container. Within the envelope were several legal documents regarding the house and his assets. Upon his death, everything would be placed in a trust, and Mary would never need to worry about anything from here on in. Their home had been paid for, and monthly expenses would automatically be debited from the trust.

Levi felt some small comfort that he'd done all that he could to arrange for Mary's needs.

Placing his hands on the safe deposit box, Levi bowed his head and sighed. The lump under his armpit, which he now knew was a tumor, had grown bigger over the last few months. It was the first of many that had spread through his body, but this one in particular was hot and throbbed angrily, keeping pace with his heartbeat.

He wasn't going to have much more time with Mary, and that was what he regretted the most.

His throat tightened for a brief moment, and he allowed himself to feel the sadness that he normally didn't dare show in public. He'd overcome so many things in life, yet this was going to be the end of him.

Levi wiped his eyes with the back of his hands and took a deep, shuddering breath. He gave one last glance at the contents of the box, and just as he was about to close it, he spied a package he didn't remember seeing before.

He pulled it out. It was a bit larger than his hand and about the same thickness, but heavy for its size. It was addressed to

Maryam Nassar—that was Mary's maiden name—yet the address on the package was their current place of residence. Heavily laden with postage markings, it had come from far away, yet it was still sealed.

"What in the world?"

Levi retrieved his folding knife from his pocket. With a press of a button, the blade sprang open. The box had been wrapped with many layers of adhesive tape, and it took some effort to hack through the seal.

When at last he lifted the cover, a hand-scrawled note lay inside the box, on top of something wrapped in cloth. It was written in the feathery script common to many Middle Eastern languages, which he couldn't read.

He set the note aside and flipped open the cloth wrapping.

His eyes widened.

Nestled in the bed of gray cloth was a gold object unlike anything Levi had ever seen. It was nearly the size of his fully extended hand, and looked very much like a cross, but instead of a vertical line running through the horizontal, the upper portion was an upside-down tear shape. Almost as if it was meant to hang from the overly large loop.

It seemed like a very strange thing for Mary to have received. After all, she was an atheist.

Levi furrowed his brow. "Why would anyone have sent you such a thing," he said aloud, "and why didn't you open it?"

He sat back and stared at the golden object. Somewhere in the back of his mind, he recalled seeing such a thing when he was in the city. It was in an Egyptian museum exhibit. What was it called? An ankh?

It was probably a trick of the light, but for a moment, the golden ankh shimmered as if it were alive.

Levi lifted the ankh out of its box, and almost dropped it. It had an unexpected greasy feel to it that made it hard to hold on to. He tightened his grip. It became oddly warm to the touch.

"What the hell's this thing made of?"

The world seemed to slow as Levi's neck and face flushed with heat. His heart began thudding loudly. A burning sensation crawled up his arm, and he felt a searing pain in his hand. It was as if the thing was attempting to burn through his palm.

It suddenly dawned on Levi: *drop the stupid the thing.*

His hand unclenched, and the heavy object dropped onto the wooden table with a loud thud.

Levi's chest was tight, and he struggled to pull in a deep breath. He winced at the throbbing pain climbing up his arm and spreading across his chest and the rest of his body. There was no blistering yet on the palm of his hand, but he knew that it would soon follow. The flesh there was red and angry with whatever it was that the ankh had slathered on it.

Levi began to sweat as he wiped his hand with a handkerchief, wondering aloud, "Mary, why did someone send this to you?"

He looked back at the object where he'd dropped it on the table. To his shock, it looked different now. No longer did it have a shimmering golden hue, but instead, it held a look of dull silver.

As the heat from the palm of his hand pulsed in time with his heartbeat, Levi wondered if the gold coloration had been some type of poison.

He snorted ruefully and shook his head. *What difference does it even make at this point?*

Bring it, he challenged the dull, lifeless object.

Using his handkerchief, Levi carefully placed the ankh back into its box and slid the cover back onto the container.

Driving home from the bank was torturous. His eyes felt sticky and began to burn, and his mouth was parched. He desperately needed a glass of water. His body ached; a high fever was taking hold.

Either he was getting a terrible case of the flu, or this was some unadvertised symptom of the cancer nobody had told him about. Could that ankh really have been coated with poison? Whatever it was, it seemed dead-set on making him as miserable as possible. By the time he'd driven into his neighborhood, Levi was sweating profusely and his eyes were drooping.

The flashing lights of a police car parked in front of his house brought him out of his stupor.

Levi pulled into the driveway and climbed painfully out of the car. An officer standing at his front door turned in his direction.

The policeman glanced at a photo in his hand and then at Levi. "Lazarus Yoder?"

"Yes, officer. That's me." Levi's heart thudded heavily in his chest as he wiped the sweat from his brow. Lazarus was his given name, but ever since he'd come to New York, he'd used Levi instead. "What's wrong?"

"Mr. Yoder, can we talk in private? I'm afraid there's been an incident."

Levi glanced toward the garage; it was empty. Levi couldn't fathom where Mary might have gone. She was a diabetic, and always came home at this time of the day to take her insulin shot. The muscles around Levi's chest tightened like iron bands, and he felt short of breath. The world began to spin.

The grim-faced officer placed a hand on Levi's shoulder. "Mr. Yoder, you're not looking well. I think you'll want to sit down for this."

Levi glanced at the photo in the officer's hand, and the blood in his veins turned to ice. The photo was blood-stained and torn, but he recognized it. It was his wedding photo.

The same one Mary carried in her purse.

It had been a week since Mary died in the car accident, and only a day since her funeral. Levi only remembered pieces of the ceremony; he'd passed out sometime in the middle, evidently due to dehydration from the flu he'd been struggling with.

Now he lay in his bed at home, a nurse hanging a bag of clear fluid on the IV pole.

"I've pushed an anti-emetic through the IV's access port, so the nausea should get under control soon," she said. She set a large plastic bottle of water on Levi's nightstand. "Please try drinking as much as you can. If you can't tolerate taking in fluids to maintain your hydration, Dr. Cohen says you'll have to be admitted."

Levi shook his head. "Alicia, you seem like a nice enough lady, and I know you mean well …"

His head fell back onto his pillow, his energy completely drained. His muscles ached as if he'd been working out nonstop for a week, and his joints seemed particularly affected. He felt like an arthritic old man. And that was nothing compared to the burning he felt in the tumors where his cancer had spread.

It reminded him that the flu was the least of his issues.

Alicia, the dowdy middle-aged nurse from Dr. Cohen's office, studied him with a sympathetic expression. "I *do* mean well, and I'll be back in the morning to check on how you're doing."

"Okay." It was the only response Levi could muster. He closed his eyes, trying to ignore the pain wracking his body.

He must have fallen asleep, because when he awoke, the sun had broken through the gap in the beige-colored bedroom curtains and blazed its early-morning welcome onto Levi's face.

His fever was gone.

The bed was wet from nighttime sweats, his eyes weren't burning anymore, and the aches had subsided. Yet he still felt … odd.

The sounds of the morning seemed somehow louder than ever before, as if he'd previously had cotton balls in his ears. Birds called to each other in the front yard, and somewhere in the distance a school bus's air brakes engaged. The old-fashioned wind-up clock on the nightstand ticked loudly with each movement of the second hand.

Suddenly, the sounds vanished, and for a moment it seemed like the world had paused … and then everything started right up again. The clock continued ticking, the birds chirped, and the bus disengaged its brakes.

As Levi yawned and stretched his arms over his head, he felt a tug on his arm, and the IV pole fell on top of him. He lurched into a sitting position and ripped the IV out of his arm. He flinched as the tape that held the clear tube in place tore from his skin. The odd slithering sensation of the plastic tube withdrawing from his vein sent a shiver of revulsion through him.

His skin tingled as he swung his legs out of bed. Blood had begun oozing down his arm, so he grabbed some gauze from the nightstand and pressed it against the site where the IV had been.

The bottle of water on the nightstand was empty.

"What the hell's wrong with me?" Levi shook his head to clear the cobwebs. He hadn't slept more than two hours at a time since Mary's death, and suddenly twelve hours had vanished in one go.

He stared suspiciously at the empty IV bag, now lying on the ground, and wondered what else the nurse had put in there.

He stood, feeling remarkably steady for a person who'd felt like death warmed over just the night before. Levi touched the burning lump under his armpit and winced.

Can't I ever catch a break?

For some godforsaken reason, his tumors now all felt like red-hot pokers.

Levi turned back to the nightstand, and the world seemed to pause yet again. This time, as the clock's second hand was frozen, Levi counted aloud. "One … two … three … four … five."

The hand began ticking again.

"I'm losing my mind."

Throbbing pain issued from more than a dozen points in his body. He grimaced and took a few deep breaths.

He knew what he needed to do.

Moments later, Levi was dressed and headed out the front door.

Dr. Cohen had some explaining to do.

As Levi raced along the Northern State Parkway toward Dr. Cohen's office, the frustration within him grew.

"After all I've been through, he should have leveled with me."

Something had happened to Levi last night, but he couldn't quite make out what it was. Dr. Cohen must have had Alicia put something more than anti-nausea drugs in that IV.

Everything around him seemed more intense. Colors were more vivid than ever before, and the sounds—birds flying overhead, the noise of the cars on the highway—were clearer, more distinct. His skin tingled annoyingly as the wind blew across the hair on his arm. It was as if he could feel each individual hair stirring.

Is this what it feels like to be high?

A car raced past him on the left, and he heard the whoosh of its six metal cylinders plunging in and out of its engine in near-perfect harmony.

Levi scratched at the burning spot near his armpit and frowned. It had been the place where he'd found the first tumor.

But the lump now felt … different. Smaller? And it was even hotter to the touch than ever, like a burning ember buried under his skin.

"Damn you, Doc. What's going on?"

As Levi walked into Dr. Cohen's office, the blonde receptionist looked up from the novel she'd been sneaking a peek at and smiled brightly. "Good morning, Mr. Yoder. I don't think you have an appointment today."

"Is Dr. Cohen in?"

"He's working on his charts, but—"

Levi strode past her and barged into the doctor's private office.

Dr. Cohen was busy scribbling in one of the many patient folders stacked on his desk. When Levi walked in, he looked up from his stack of work, and his eyes widened.

"Mr. Yoder. Alicia told me you were stuck in bed." The pen fell from his hand and rolled off the desk. "I was going to come over this afternoon to check on things. Are you okay?"

The heated tingling in Levi's body fueled his anger. "What the heck did you have her put in that IV? Everything feels strange, almost like I'm high or something."

The old man stood and leaned heavily against his desk. "What are you talking about? You were given a saline drip for your dehydration and a drug for your nausea."

At the old man's confused and earnest expression, Levi began feeling foolish for suspecting something nefarious. "I'm sorry, maybe it's just … I don't know." He rubbed at the burning sensation coming from the tumor on the side of his neck. "First things first. Why does it feel like I'm on fire?"

"I don't understand." Dr. Cohen walked around his desk and closed his office door. He put his hand on the side of Levi's face, and the furrow between his eyebrows deepened. Turning Levi's face to the side, he probed at the lump on his neck. "That's not right …"

The old man lifted Levi's left arm and probed with his fingertips along several spots, up to and including the armpit, which was throbbing painfully with heat.

"What's not right?" Levi said. "Don't tell me—let me guess. I'm dying."

The elderly doctor took a step back and donned a pair of rubber examination gloves. "Take off your shirt." The doctor's humorless expression brooked no argument.

Levi stripped to the waist. As the doctor prodded under his arms and the sides of his chest, Levi asked, "What do you see? What's wrong?"

"You haven't taken any radiation treatments or any chemical infusions since your diagnosis?"

"No. I didn't exactly see the point."

"I don't understand," the doctor muttered. "Levi, it seems as if the tumors infiltrating your lymphatic system have all shrunk since the last time I saw you. The few I'm detecting are very hard and warm to the touch, and the others … well, some I'm unable to find at all. I want to biopsy some of these to see what's going on."

Levi sighed. "Go ahead. Do what you think you have to."

Pacing back and forth in the wood-paneled waiting room of the Sloane-Kettering Institute, Levi couldn't figure out what could be taking so long.

His visit to Dr. Cohen several days ago had yielded nothing but full-body scans and needles. And at the doctor's insistence, Levi had spent this morning being prodded by still more doctors at Sloane-Kettering. It was now late afternoon, and he was still in the waiting room, already having read every magazine available.

From somewhere in the distance came the faint sound of raised voices—one of which sounded like the voice of Dr. Cohen. Curious, Levi left the waiting area and followed the sound through the hallways. He stopped outside a set of closed doors labeled "Radiology and Histology." Two voices argued on the other side. They were muffled by the doors, but Dr. Cohen's nasal tone was unmistakable.

"Frank, all I can tell you is this. Three days ago, that patient entered my office complaining about a burning sensation. I palpated some of his lymph nodes and confirmed the presence of abnormal growths, which I biopsied and brought here."

"Dr. Cohen, I'm telling you there's no way those biopsies you brought me and the ones I took this morning are from the same person. I don't mean to be rude—after all, you *were* my histology professor in med school. But are you sure you didn't mix something up? I couldn't feel any swelling or anything out of the ordinary in my exam. I felt bad putting that man through another biopsy, yet I did it anyway based solely on what you said."

Levi removed the bandage from his neck and touched the spot where the Sloan-Kettering cancer specialist had biopsied him. He couldn't find a hint of swelling where the biopsy had been taken.

As the doctors continued to argue, he leaned against the yellow cinder-block wall. The room wavered unsteadily. Levi shoved his hand into his shirt, accidentally popping off a button as he felt along the crook of his underarm. He couldn't feel the hard burning nodule there, either. It had been there only a couple of days before.

How is that possible?

The second doctor was speaking again. "Based on the biopsy and the PET scan results, all I can tell you is this: that man in the waiting room doesn't have a thing wrong with him."

Madison frowned as she suited up for her role as the mission's standby diver.

"Maddie, calm down," Jim whispered as he shrugged into his own diving gear. "It'll be okay."

It had been only fifteen minutes since they'd transferred onto a nameless ship off the coast of Turkey, but from the moment she'd set foot on the deck of the diving vessel, Madison hadn't liked anything about their mission.

There were five others on board. All of them seemed to be Americans, but it was pretty obvious that the ship was well shy of a standard Navy dive crew.

She clipped on her weight belt and leaned closer to Jim, who was adjusting his dive vest. "This is crap," she whispered. "They're expecting us to do a mixed-gas dive at four hundred feet and they don't even have a full crew. That's just a slap in the face."

With a slight shake of his head he tossed her a lopsided grin. "It'll be fine. This looks like a pretty typical commercial dive setup."

Did it? Madison was used to the standard twelve-man crew that the Navy employed, but she trusted Jim. He'd been an explosives specialist, diving everywhere in the world for over fifteen years. He'd seen it all.

She took a deep breath and released it slowly, trying to rid herself of her pre-dive jitters.

Jim snorted. "Sometimes the spooks take shortcuts."

Spooks?

All of the travel under the cloak of darkness, skirting the

spotlights in the Bosporus Strait, the lack of specifics regarding their mission … it all suddenly made sense.

Madison turned her gaze suspiciously to the others on the ship. Most of them were dressed like merchant marines, which meant they looked like a ragtag bunch of civilians. But they clearly knew their way around a boat, expertly scrambling from one station to another. They were taking care of business. Two of them were handling the platform while another operated the controls of the winch it was attached to. Another crewman operated the dive console.

But one man stood out from the rest of the crew. He was in his forties, blond hair, in khakis and a dark polo. He was no sailor. Madison wasn't sure about the rest, but if there was a spook on board, it was him. This guy screamed CIA.

The spook stepped forward and addressed them all with an authoritative tone. "Divers, we've got an old airplane wreck lying directly below us at about 380 feet. It's been down there a long time, and it has a pretty narrow cross-section. It looks like there was a landslide and part of the entrance is covered by the debris. If it weren't for that, we'd have used an ROV to survey the interior."

"What are we looking for?" Jim asked.

The spook pressed his lips together and hesitated. "I'm sorry, but the exact nature of the aircraft's payload is classified."

"Classified?" Madison scoffed, feeling a rising sense of indignation. "You're asking us to do a technical dive onto a wreck we know nothing about and you're not even telling us what we're looking for? How the hell—"

"Enough!" the agent barked. "I'll be asking you to be my

eyes down there and tell me what you see." He picked up a box-like device that resembled a metal detector and pressed a button on its handle. When a green LED on the box turned on, he handed the device to Jim. "Take that down with you."

Jim turned the box over in his hands. It looked like a sealed metal box with no markings, a telescoping handle with an already depressed button, and the now-glowing LED.

"What is it?" Jim asked.

"If it starts flashing, I'll want to know right away. It probably means you're near one of the items we're looking for."

Jim hooked the device onto his dive belt.

The agent addressed the full crew once more. "All right, let's move. We've only got five hours until dawn breaks."

Jim donned his dive helmet. One crewmember began reeling out the umbilical that would be Jim's lifeline and sole means of communicating up from the depths, while another man, at the console, yelled, "Comms check. Chief Uhlig, can you hear me?"

Jim's voice echoed through the dive console's speaker. *"Roger Topside, hear you loud and clear."* He gave a thumbs-up and stepped onto the metal stage. The stage swung over the side of the boat as the men called out instructions to each other.

Just as the winch operator began lowering the stage into the water, Madison made eye contact with Jim, and he shot her a thumbs-up.

She returned the gesture and recited the same prayer she did for every dive. "Guide us. Keep us safe. Let us live to dive another day."

Madison worried as she sat in her gear. As the standby diver, she'd only be getting wet if there was an issue.

Ten minutes passed.

Finally, Jim spoke. *"I'm at 375 feet. Panning the spotlight all around me and I'm not seeing anything yet. Just water in every direction."*

The man at the dive operator's console leaned in to a microphone. "Diver, the current has pushed you 75 feet away from the cliff's edge. If you turn to 255 degrees and move in that direction, you should see the ledge and the target."

"I need more slack on the umbilical."

"Roger that."

One of the crewmembers reeled out more of the thick cable containing air and communication lines.

Focusing on staying calm, Madison listened to the waves lapping against the side of the boat. The speaker crackled with the sound of Jim's breathing.

He must be swimming.

"Topside, I've spotted the wreck. It looks like the front half of an airframe got sheared off and fell to the ocean floor. The back half is barely visible with all the debris covering it."

The agent walked over to the console and pressed the microphone button. "Diver, I'll need you to clear a passage into it. The structure should be fairly wide open once you get in."

The sound of Jim's grunting echoed across the deck.

The console operator announced, "His heart rate has increased to 140 beats per minute."

"Topside, I've cleared a wide enough opening. This must have been a recent landslide—"

"Why do you say that?" the agent asked with a worried tone.

"The debris was only loosely stuck together. It just sort of pulled away as I picked at it. Topside, I need more slack. I'm standing at the edge of the drop-off."

The spool unreeling more of the umbilical made a loud clacking sound.

Madison licked the salt crystals off her lips. She closed her eyes and imagined herself down there with Jim.

Jim spoke again. *"Okay, this is obviously the remnants of an old bomber. I see the crumpled remains of the bomb-bay door lying on the floor ten-feet ahead.*

"There's lots of growth in the interior. Sponges and hints of coral. I see some rails attached to the floor, and we've got two large metal racks on either side of the doorway."

"What do you see on the racks?" the agent asked, his voice tense.

"Nothing. They're empty."

Madison opened her eyes and studied the agent. He seemed to deflate just a bit, his shoulders sagging.

"Topside, the box you gave me. Is there anything you want me to do with it?"

"Yes. What light is showing on it?"

"You mean the LED? It's still glowing green, if that's what you're asking."

"Wave it along the racks and the bottom of the cabin. See if the light changes at all."

"Roger that."

The agent paced back and forth with his head down. The frown on his face made him look as if he'd swallowed a lemon.

"No change in the LED," Jim said. *"But it looks like the lockdowns on the racks were sheared off, and not that long ago. The metal looks like it was pinched off by bolt cutters or something. There's no encrustations or remnants of paint, and it has no patina. Definitely way after this thing crashed."*

"Damn!" The agent turned away from the console and dug into his front pocket.

"Sir," said the sailor manning the console. "Is there anything else you want from the diver?"

"Just bring him back up." The agent retrieved a satellite phone from his pocket and walked toward the front of the boat.

The console operator flipped open the dive chart. "Diver, you've given us the data we were looking for. Start your scheduled ascent. First stop at 260 fsw for one and a half minutes."

"Copy that. Leaving the wreck and starting my ascent."

As Jim began the slow ascent with the scheduled decompression stops, Madison studied the agent, who stood twenty feet away with the sat phone pressed against his ear. He was still pacing and talking animatedly to whomever was on the other end of the line. When a light breeze blew in her direction, she caught fragments of his conversation.

"… B-47 …"

"… stolen cargo."

"… Russia … Turkey."

"… no detected radiation."

Madison's stomach did a somersault at the word *radiation*.

When the agent put the phone away and walked back toward the others, Madison waved him closer.

The blond man approached, his eyebrows furrowed in frustration. "What?" He didn't even look at her; it was as if his thoughts were a million miles away.

"Are you seriously telling me that you asked us here to dive on a missing nuke?"

The agent stiffened, and his gaze focused laser-like on hers, his expression turning to stone. "I don't know what you're talking about."

With a sudden surge of fury, Madison shoved the man, pointed at the ocean, and yelled, "You asked for Navy divers to go down onto a crash site that could easily have exposed us to radiation—and you didn't tell us!" Her heartbeat thundered in her head as she pulled in a deep breath and stared daggers at the agent.

He returned her gaze unblinkingly and said nothing.

"This is a Broken Arrow incident, isn't it? Does the Navy know?" *Broken Arrow* was the military term for an incident involving a nuclear weapon.

Glancing at the other men on the deck the spook shook his head ever so slightly. "I'm sorry, but this isn't something I can talk to you about."

Madison took a step back. She felt the rage drain from her, replaced by a cold chill that crept up the middle of her back.

Could the US have actually lost a nuke?

Worse yet, did we lose a nuke and someone else reclaimed it ahead of us?

"Diver," said the console operator, "you're now at 180 feet. Your heart rate is just a bit above normal. I'll be switching you from heliox to air at 170 feet and then to a fifty-fifty mix at 90 feet."

"Roger that, Topside. Pausing at 180 feet."

Jim was fine, and he'd be back up on the boat in another forty minutes or so. No harm done … this time.

Madison returned her attention to the agent. "I'm sorry I shoved you," she said. Her temper was one day going to get her in some serious trouble.

The agent's expression softened. He cracked a smile and rubbed his chest. "Hey, I understand. And I'm sorry, it's just…" He left the sentence unfinished and chuckled. "Join the agency someday, and … aww hell, even then I'll probably never be able to say anything. You know how it is."

Madison nodded. She'd been read in on more than a handful of highly classified matters before, and he was right. The list of people she could talk to about any of those things might as well have been zero.

She took a seat next to the dive platform and shivered.

A nuclear bomb is missing.

Levi had prepared himself for death; what he hadn't prepared for was having the rest of his life ahead of him.

Without Mary.

He'd received a copy of the final accident report, and its details haunted him. Mary had taken an off-ramp too quickly, her car had flipped, and she'd died at the scene.

It made no sense.

She'd always been a hesitant driver—in fact, Levi had been the one who'd pushed her into getting a driver's license in the first place. He'd never seen her speed. Mary had been frustratingly predictable, always driving five miles per hour under the speed limit.

Guilt weighed heavily on him as he considered an alternate explanation for the accident. She'd repeatedly told him that she wouldn't want to live without him. Did she commit suicide to ensure she wouldn't have to?

Perhaps the reason didn't matter. Either way, here he was—alone, with constant reminders of her everywhere he looked. His home, the city, even the clothes he wore reminded him of Mary. Her absence left him with a gaping wound that was too much for him to bear.

He found himself going on ever-lengthening walks. The smell of the spring air calmed his nerves. As he wandered farther from home, into residential areas he'd never seen before, the sense of unfamiliarity struck a chord deep within him.

He needed a change.

A dramatic one.

As he set foot onto the tarmac in Okinawa, Levi found himself surrounded by many unfamiliar sights and sounds. The roaring of aircraft engines thundered over the airfield as military transports took off to parts unknown; from somewhere in the distance came the chop-chop sound of a helicopter landing; and closer in, a hundred boots marched on the hot black asphalt in perfect lockstep. The drill sergeant's voice rang loudly for all to hear.

"Sound off, one two! Sound off, three four! Cadence count, one two three four, one two … three four!"

Someone placed their hand on Levi's shoulder and spoke loudly over the surrounding din. "Mr. Yoder, welcome to Kadena Air Base. I wasn't given any instructions on what else you might need; it's not often we get civilian visitors. I can arrange for a bunk in the officer's hall and—"

"No." Levi shook his head at the officer who'd come to meet him. "I'll be fine, Captain Lewis."

Levi had gotten here by calling in a few favors from people who owed him—although the New York senator who'd arranged the flight had tried to convince him to go somewhere more "civilized" than a backwater island. The senator had warned him, "Levi, the locals harbor resentment for us having a base there. They actually think that our being there is corrupting the island's culture. That and a few bad eggs with discipline issues have led to some serious tensions. Hell, it doesn't help that some of their elders have some awful memories of our occupation in World War II."

The senator's characterization of the island had only hardened Levi's resolve. The people of the island were scarred; that was exactly how Levi felt. The idea that Mary might have taken her own life because she refused to live without him was too much for Levi to accept, yet it was the only thing that made any sense—and he'd carry the scars of that survivor's guilt forever.

"Just point me to Okinawa City," he said to the captain. "I'll find what I'm looking for."

The captain pointed southeast. "It's about five miles in that direction. I'll get one of the men to drive you in."

"No need." Levi waved the captain away as he began walking toward the gated entrance to Kadena. He yelled over his shoulder, "Thank you for your help!"

Levi knew that the captain probably thought he was nuts. A lone man, walking into a foreign country with nothing more than a backpack of clothing hoisted over his shoulder.

Wiping a bead of sweat from his brow, the morning sun beating down on him, Levi felt a sense of satisfaction in finding a completely new environment. Ages ago, when he first heard the term "walkabout," he'd been intrigued by the idea that a person might just travel as a rite of passage. To break from one's past life, do something different—see other places, experience other cultures.

To not look back.

It was time for Levi to start over.

During his twelve years in New York City, Levi had experienced all manner of problems as he built his own connections—but he had proven himself repeatedly as someone who could take care of almost any bad situation. Sometimes, he'd found himself squaring off with people who were more than willing to use violence to stop him from getting what he needed, and many times he'd had to fight for his success.

The feeling he'd had after those fights was … extraordinary. Other than when he was with Mary, the sense of exhilaration he'd felt as he overcame physical obstacles was probably the most alive he'd ever felt. Being a fixer was a mental game. If you were prepared, you almost never had to pull your hands out of your pockets. But when he was forced into a confrontation, he never pulled a punch.

Sure, there was plenty of pain, and once even a broken arm. But Levi had never backed away from a challenge. There were entire shelves in his library devoted to the prowess of the Japanese fighting spirit. He needed to experience that sort of life-giving energy once again. Immerse himself in it.

Hence Okinawa.

His first challenge was learning the language. He spent the first three weeks trying to find a karateka who would take in an American as a live-in student. But even though he was more than willing to pay for lodging and lessons, he was repeatedly rejected. The senator's warning about the resentment of the islanders was proving to be well-founded.

So Levi decided to take a transport from Kadena to Tokyo. It was there that he was introduced to Mr. Saito, a local friend of the Yokota Air Base commander.

As Saito drove carefully through the busy streets of Tokyo, Levi explained what he was looking for.

Saito, a fifty-something Japanese man, frowned. "I know of such a place. It teaches something called Kyokushin, which is roughly translated to 'the ultimate truth.' But I worry for you."

"As long as you believe they would take me on and they are masters in their style, why worry?"

Saito slowed the car as he turned into a narrow street. "The dojo has a reputation for being severe with its students. I fear you may be injured if you aren't careful. It is very—"

"Perfect." Levi nodded grimly. "That's exactly what I'm looking for."

The car slowed to a stop in front of a building with a placard featuring images of girls in ballet tutus executing pirouettes, and the two men got out. Levi was about to ask about the sign when Saito motioned for him to follow, and scurried around the back of the building.

Moments later, Levi was in the presence of a stone-faced Japanese man wearing a karate gi. While Saito spoke to the man in Japanese, presumably explaining Levi's odd request, Levi looked around the dojo. Two dozen students sat in a wide circle while two others sparred brutally in the center. Punches were blocked, kicks were batted away, and students were tossed heavily to the dojo's floor.

Feeling a tap on his arm, Levi turned back to Saito. "Yes?"

Saito motioned to the man he'd been talking to and gave him a slight bow. "This is Sensei Yasuda, one of the dojo's senior instructors. He finds your request extremely unusual, but he believes your story might be compelling to his master. He is willing to take you on, but you must take your lessons seriously or you'll be immediately ejected from the school."

Levi nodded.

"And there is another thing. As a *gaijin*, you'll be required to pay twice what others would pay."

"*Gaijin*?" Levi asked.

Saito paused, with a pensive expression. "It means outside person. It is what non-Japanese are called."

Levi turned to the instructor and bowed. "Sensei, *doi suru*."

Levi thought he'd said "I agree," but Saito immediately

corrected his pronunciation and chuckled. "You have good pronunciation for a *gaijin*."

With a loud harrumph, the instructor, looking unimpressed, turned and yelled, "Tomiko!"

A woman jumped up from the sparring circle and raced to the instructor.

He spoke in Japanese to her while nodding toward Levi.

Saito bowed to Levi and said, "It was a pleasure meeting you, Yoder-san. Best of luck." He turned and walked out the door.

The short woman pointed at Levi's feet and barked in broken English, "Remove shoes now!"

As Levi began to unlace his shoes, the woman grabbed a white karate gi from a table and threw it at him. She pointed to a folding screen that separated a section of the dojo. "Dress there!" she yelled.

After yanking his shoes off, Levi grabbed the gi and jogged behind the screen. His heart hammered as the excitement of something new warred with the uncertainty he felt within.

At first, he was one of the many students watching the others grapple and fight, with the instructor occasionally yelling instructions, and Tomiko translating for him.

But then it was Levi's turn.

The moment he stood and walked into the ring, he knew he was going to get his ass handed to him. But for each hit he took, and for each time he was slammed to the floor, he learned just a bit more.

Levi remembered someone telling him that it was easier to learn through making mistakes than to be shown how something is done. If that was true, he learned a lot on that first day. He was tossed, kicked, punched, and otherwise taught lessons of humility from nearly half the class.

Tomiko was the last—and would soon prove to be the worst.

Licking the sweat from his lips, Levi stared at the pale-skinned woman. She had an ageless quality about her, and he couldn't tell whether she was twenty or maybe even twice that. She couldn't have been more than five feet tall, and he was twice her weight. Despite his lack of training, Levi felt a bit of confidence. He had done better than he'd expected against the others. On occasion, he'd managed to land a few blows, and as he was larger than most of the other students, he could absorb a lot of punishment without receiving any real injuries.

Tomiko stared defiantly at Levi and growled, "Attack."

She circled him, not making any sudden movements. It registered with him that she moved almost like a dancer. No … a cat. A cat that was probably toying with him.

Rolling his shoulders, Levi took on the ready stance he'd seen employed by the others, and leaped forward with the intent of landing a kick. But Tomiko sidestepped him, dropped to the ground, and swept his legs out from under him.

Levi landed heavily on his back, his breath whooshing from his lungs. He scrambled back to his feet, tiny sparks of light dancing in his vision as he struggled to catch his breath.

He moved much more cautiously around the ring now, searching for an opening.

With near-blinding speed, Tomiko leaped forward with what would surely have been a devastating kick to his groin.

But for a split second, it was as if the world slowed, and Levi ducked to the side and rolled out of the way—just barely.

Tomiko's eyes widened slightly.

Was that a look of surprise?

The tiny woman came at him again, and Levi managed to block her swift front kick—but before he could even appreciate his minor victory, she followed up with a spinning back fist that came out of nowhere.

The next thing Levi knew, he was on the bamboo mat spitting blood from a split lip and what felt like loosened teeth.

That was the end of the match.

After the sparring, Levi suffered through group exercises on the use of proper form. At the beginning of each form, he'd try to emulate what the others did—and inevitably, one of the instructors would race to him and shout a string of Japanese that needed no translation. They'd roughly correct Levi's form until they felt he was doing it properly.

Then came strength conditioning exercises that at times were beyond what Levi was capable of. As he was larger than the others, it took much more strength for him to maintain the stances that he was asked to perform. The muscles in his legs felt like they were on fire. But he gritted his teeth and pushed through the pain, even when the instructors walked by, pushing and pulling at the students, trying to knock them off balance.

By the time the sun had set, and Levi realized that he'd managed to survive his first day at the dojo, a great sense of relief flooded through him.

He'd survived.

The students ate their communal meal together. It consisted of rice, some kind of grilled fish or possibly eel, and a large bowl of pickled vegetables. As Levi ate, the others talked in Japanese. Tomiko wasn't among those who remained at the dojo, so Levi had no one to translate. He focused on his meal and listened to the foreign sounds of Japanese being spoken all around him.

When he and the other students had finished clearing away the meal, Levi walked slowly to the back of the dojo, trying not to make it obvious he was in a lot of pain. Following the lead of the others, he stripped out of his uniform, splashed water on his face and body from the faucet, and grabbed a change of clothes that had been provided for him. In a back room, some of the other students rolled out their tatami mats to sleep, and with a barely suppressed groan, Levi lay on the wooden mat he'd been assigned.

As he stared up at the ceiling, the throbbing aches he felt reminded him that he'd pushed himself far beyond anything he was used to.

He wasn't sure if the pain was an affirmation of life or a punishment for having lived when Mary didn't.

His first day at the infamous dojo had been a lesson in pain. So when Levi woke early the next morning, he fully expected to feel his entire body bruised, battered, and non-functional.

Yet as he sat up and stretched, he felt only the slightest bit of stiffness. Even lying on a wooden mat for the first time hadn't stopped him from getting a good night's sleep. He licked his lips, and barely felt the cut that he'd received from Tomiko.

He hopped up onto his feet, rolled up his mat, and set it in its place. He walked out of the sleeping quarters, weaving past a half dozen of the other students, who were still asleep. As he entered the main area of the dojo, he saw Tomiko stretching with some of the senior instructors, along with another man he hadn't seen before.

Levi bowed and began stretching like the others. Sensei Yasuda looked up, stone-faced, and said something to him in Japanese.

Tomiko translated. "Sensei Yasuda wants know why you not resting with the others."

Levi stretched his legs and reached for his toes. "I feel rested, and didn't want to risk missing any lessons."

Tomiko translated for Yasuda. The instructor's face registered no change in expression, but he gave a slight nod.

The new man said something in Japanese while giving Levi an amused smile.

Again Tomiko translated. "Master Oyama hopes that you continue to show excellent attitude. He says that only intense focus will purge that which haunts you, and he will ensure that you're pushed harder from now on."

Levi was unsure how to respond to that. He bowed his head to the master, and silently wondered what he'd gotten himself into.

ADDENDUM

The type of novels I write almost always tend to weave elements of science into their fabric. It may seem to some that there are components of my stories that seem fantastic, or impossible, yet it's my goal to always base things on current science or scientific theory.

I've often said that I tend to write two type of novels, one that lands squarely in the technothriller genre, and the other being more a mainstream thriller (e.g. like the Connor Sloane series or my Levi Yoder series.)

It would be reasonable to ask, given what I've already written above, "If you always weave science or technology into your stories, why make a distinction between technothriller and mainstream thriller?"

The answer is simple:

To me, the key thing that differentiates a technothriller from a mainstream thriller is that in the former, science is not just an ingredient of the story, but a key part of it. For instance, *Darwin's Cipher* is a technothriller about a scientist who believes he's found a cure for cancer through unlocking some mysteries of DNA, but when his discovery is abused, very bad things end up happening. You wouldn't have much of a story without the cipher (the science behind the DNA modification).

I should note, that even though a mainstream thriller doesn't have traditional science as its key element, various technologies abound throughout our daily lives and we don't think of it as science per se.

Flipping on a light switch and a light goes on: there's plenty of science behind that. How a gun works, the expansion of gases as an explosive pushes a bullet down a barrel and how the grooves in the barrel impart spin, making the bullet more stable and thus lending it more accuracy. These are all scientific advances that we often overlook. They're a given.

In this addendum, I wanted to note some things that I've used in this story, and give you, the reader, an insight into how some elements of science might relate to them or serve as inspiration. For example, I've put poor Annie through the wringer and had her disarm a nuclear bomb. What if I told you that the description I gave is very much accurate? I'll talk a bit more about that.

Like any sufficiently complicated technology, there are often misconceptions and debate around a topic, which is completely fair. Anyone who ever claims that the science for something is settled is often leading you astray.

Always question. Always doubt. Always verify.

In this addendum, I'll give very brief explanations of what may be very complex concepts. My intent is to only leave you with sufficient information to give a remedial understanding of the subject. Although I might have inadvertently taught you in this book how to break into a home. I'll cover that too.

For those who want to know more, it's also my intent to leave you with enough keywords that would allow you to initiate your own research and gain a more complete background understanding of any of these topics.

This should also give you a peek into some of the things that have influenced my writing of this story, and maybe have you start asking what all authors inevitably ask themselves when they set pen to paper, "What if?"

Breaking and entering:

I normally stick to science, technology, and history in the addendums, mostly to explain some of the elements I talk about within the book. Well, I did talk about something that many people might think is made up, but as a Public Service Announcement, I think it's worth talking about the scene I wrote where Connor breaks into a house by simply lifting a door and sliding it open.

Can that actually work?

Sadly, the answer is yes. And this is why I strongly advocate for anyone who has a sliding glass door to at the very least place a stick in the bottom track to prevent unwanted people from opening your door. It's the simplest possible solution, but too many people don't do it.

The reason lifting on the handle with force and sliding the door tends to work is because the "locking" mechanism in a sliding glass door isn't actually a lock. It's a simple latch mechanism.

And a latch can often be overcome by doing on simple thing: lifting the door.

Most sliding glass doors have enough play in them in the upper track that if you do exactly what Connor did, you'll be able to open your door.

Nuclear weapons:

Nuclear weapons! They are the most destructive weapons ever created by man.

The president's brother talks about a very simple type of nuclear weapon and describes it in this way:

"This particular nuke is a really simple gun-style design. Basically a glorified gun barrel. You're familiar with how a bullet is lined up at the back end of a barrel and there's some target you aim at with the business end. This is basically the same thing, but instead of a bullet with a shell casing, you have a doughnut-shaped chunk of highly enriched uranium on one end and your target is a cylinder of the same stuff on the far end of the barrel.

"You're trying to put the doughnut hole back together with the doughnut. When it's go time, cordite or some other type of high-explosive acts like the equivalent of a blasting cap and shoots the doughnut down the barrel. The doughnut is going well past supersonic speeds, and if you actually saw it in slow motion, you'd see it starting to sparkle and get angry as it gets closer to the doughnut hole made of uranium. At about a foot apart it goes critical, and if designed properly it only goes supercritical when the angry doughnut impales itself on the doughnut hole at the end of the barrel. At that moment, you better hope nobody is nearby, because everyone within a two-mile radius will witness a very big boom."

Is he right?

He actually is. Let me explain by first focusing on what a nuclear explosion even entails:

We've all heard about uranium. It's one of those scary elements that people talk about in nuclear weapons science, but why?

A nuclear explosion is simply put a runaway reaction. I'll explain in simple terms:

Imagine you light a single match. That's a lot of energy. And theoretically that one match can light other things, but more than likely it'll eventually just blow out.

Now imagine you had an entire warehouse filled with match heads. You light one of the match heads at the entrance to the warehouse, it's easy to imagine what kind of fiery maelstrom will occur because that one lit match head will like three others and they'll light twenty more and so on and so forth.

Well, a nuclear explosion is sort of like that, but on some serious steroids.

Let's take that example, and now step up in complexity a bit and talk about uranium.

Uranium is like cheesecake. (Bear with me, I'll explain)

Some cheesecake is light and fluffy.

Other cheesecake is thick and dense.

Yet they're both cheesecake, right?

Well, that's kind of how I like to explain isotopes. You have heavier versions and lighter versions of the same thing.

Now it just so happens to be that Uranium isotopes have some different behaviors associated with them.

U-238 is the heavy and most common variant of Uranium. Think of it as being sluggish and happy the way it is.

It's still radioactive, but it won't spontaneously cause a runaway reaction.

U-235 on the other hand is the lighter version of Uranium. It's the more volatile of the uranium brothers. If jostled, it's much more likely to react in an unhappy way. But that's really an over-simplification.

Imagine we have a microscopic pool table that had one atom of U-238. If I strike it with my microscopic cue ball, it's not very likely to have anything happen, and even if we manage to cause the atom to react (split) it's going to react by spitting out cue balls, but not nearly as many as its U-235 brother.

Is it likely that one of the cue balls hits another U-238 and with enough energy to make it also split and continue the chain reaction? No.

However, do the same to U-235, and it sends out a lot more of those cue balls. And statistically, it could send out enough to likely hit another U-235 atom. If it does, the chain continues. Sometimes, it might hit two, and each of those would send out cue balls. And you can imagine at that point you have the beginning of a very nasty chain reaction occurring.

HOWEVER: what if those cue balls run into those sluggish U-238 atoms again. It's more likely that the chain reaction will stop.

This is why you hear in the news that people are worried when certain countries are able to create "highly-enriched uranium." For a bomb, you don't want your cue balls hitting U-238 atoms, you want them to hit U-235 ones. Because then for each U-235 you hit, you'll hit greater than 1.0 more U-235 atoms and continue the process.

Ultimately, this is what causes the massive explosion.

What if you have a very large amount of U-235? This is the highly reactive version. It's very pure. Now, remember - uranium is radioactive. That means cue balls are somewhat spontaneously being created because of instability in the atom itself.

In the book I talk about a magic amount being roughly fifty kilograms.

So, if you can imagine that each of the atoms are unstable

and you might stare at one atom and in your lifetime it doesn't do anything. It looks stable to you, but under the covers, we know better. Now if you have a handful, is it more likely you'll see one of those atoms do something? Yes.

Obviously, there's been a lot of testing in this area, but when you start collecting millions and billions and (WAY MORE) atoms than that - it's guaranteed that some of the atoms in that chunk of highly-enriched uranium are going to have a reaction. Not every reaction causes another reaction. There's not enough reactions typically going on for it to have a runaway reaction, but it could. When you collect over fifty kilograms of the highly-enrich uranium into one space, guess what happens?

Enough reactions are occurring in that mass that suddenly it goes critical, meaning there's sustained chain reactions occurring. That's exactly what happens in a nuclear power plant. And when various factors such as heat increase the rate of fission, you go into a supercritical mode that triggers a runaway chain reaction resulting in an explosion.

The gun-type fission bomb is basically forcing this situation by smashing two sub-critical amounts of uranium together and by the sheer force of having large amounts of fissile material (U-235) being slammed together, it passes critical and goes into supercritical. The energy released goes from minuscule to unimaginable in a millionth of a second. And that's where you get the devastating atomic explosion.

The gun-type bomb is literally the simplest version of the nuclear bomb, but it requires the most amount of fissile material.

There are other types that are more efficient such as an implosion bomb. This takes a smaller amount of U-235, surrounds it with high explosives and when those explosives are perfectly timed, it's in effect squeezing the ball of U-235 really really hard. Sufficiently hard that it kick it from sub-critical into supercritical in less than a blink of an eye.

There's lots more that I can say, but if you're really interested, there certainly enough key words in my explanation to probably send you to google for quite a while. My apologies.

Brice's Smart-lenses:

Both Connor and Annie used a special set of glasses that almost seem magical. It's almost literally a Swiss Army knife of features. Let me go ahead and break down the different things it does and talk about what's real versus what isn't.

Communications: I think we often take for granted how many things in our lives are "wireless" nowadays. One of the first things that became wireless was the remote for the TV. I'm old enough to remember when a "remote" didn't transmit information via pulses of infrared light, which actually how many of our remotes work. Old-school remotes actually had a wire that allowed you to change channels, or maybe hit record on a VCR with a box in your hand that had a long cable that connected to whatever device it was that you were controlling. Nowadays, we have all variety of remotes, including our cell phone. That's the ultimate remote. Without going to crazy into the details, wireless communication boils down to a few key technologies.

There's infrared, which is how many TV remotes work. It's like shining a flashlight, for it to work you have to aim it in the correct direction and it should work fine.

There's WIFI, which is almost like a sort of radio signal, just at a much higher frequency, and it's able to go through walls and various other obstacles. You don't need to aim it generally speaking.

There's bluetooth, which is a very common communication protocol for things that are close to each other. It uses very little power and is often what people use when they pair a set of headphones to a cell phone.

I can go on and on, because I am who I am, but I'll stop now and note why I bring it up. Because the glasses can communicate with the phone that both Connor and Annie had, it doesn't require the glasses themselves to have certain features like satellite communication, or even GPS. By having the glasses talk to the phone and the phone talking back, it allows the glasses to not have to carry more electronics than it needs to. This makes having an intelligent set of glasses feasible, because if you're limited what they have to do themselves and leaning on the phone for some other stuff, you can make normal-looking frames. They can theoretically look like normal glasses.

For example, GPS. Could you put GPS in the glasses? Sure - but why bother? Just have the glasses ask the phone for the current location.

Same goes with satellite. Allow the phone to carry burden of a satellite communication link.

And let's not forget that with internet access our phones are gateways to all the world's knowledge. So if we wanted to have the glasses look something up, it could: by talking to the phone.

But for some of the cool stuff we can't lean purely on the phone, the glasses have to do some stuff themselves. Like in the book, we wanted to be able to see someone with the glasses and automatically identify them.

Well, that requires a video camera of sorts. Hidden in the hinge, it would be reasonably easy to hide a very small camera. And if the camera is always running, we don't need film or storage really, we need the ability to capture an image, send it to a program on the phone, and then let the phone interact with the internet and "search" for that person. If the person is found, it can then communicate that back to the glasses with whatever it discovered.

But that leads us to how do Connor or Annie see what was discovered. Well, there's various technology today that allow us to see things on one of a piece of "glass" and not the other. Sort of like one-way mirrors. Some cars have heads-up displays which only the driver can see, but the passenger who is just two feet away can't see the image.

I suppose in summary, all of the things I described are known technology. Some of the limits that exist are really having to do with the speed of the connection to the internet from the phone and how fast some things take to look up. In time, all of these things will improve dramatically.

ABOUT THE AUTHOR

I am an Army brat, a polyglot, and the first person in my family born in the United States. This heavily influenced my youth by instilling in me a love of reading and a burning curiosity about the world and all of the things within it. As an adult, my love of travel and adventure has driven me to explore many exotic locations, and these places sometimes creep into the stories I write.

I hope you've found this story entertaining.

- Mike Rothman

For occasional news on my latest work, join my mailing list at: https://mailinglist.michaelarothman.com/new-reader

You can find my blog at: www.michaelarothman.com
Facebook at: www.facebook.com/MichaelARothman
And on Twitter: @MichaelARothman

Made in the USA
Monee, IL
07 August 2022

eae188cc-3267-43b1-97d2-62e8de1dbf8aR01